Manipulated Lives

H.A. Leuschel

Manipulated Lives

ISBN:101534708979
ISBN-13:9781534708976

Manipulated Lives

For my sister

Manipulated Lives

CONTENTS

Manipulated Lives

Acknowledgements

I could not have written *Manipulated Lives* without the advice and often courageous contributions from my sister Caroline nor the insightful comments from my mother Doris. Both understood the collection of stories for what it is – the story of five people who, at different stages of their lives have to come to terms with the damage caused by someone's manipulative perversion.

Thank you also Kathleen, Suzy, Lisa, Michael, Sharon, Christina, Susan, Alex and Suzanne for reading various manuscripts of the stories and especially for encouraging me so generously to plod on. Special thanks also go to my daughter Shona who helped me improve Holly's way of speaking in *Runaway Girl*. Without her, I wouldn't have been able to convey how my teenage character needed to speak and think. A special thank you goes to Suzy Turner, my patient and generous author friend whose own success story has not only inspired me but her professional help in formatting my first book spared me from making mistakes during my first steps into self-publishing.

Many thanks also to my wonderful editor and proof-reader, Elaine Dunning, who is everything an editor should be – honest, sensitive and indispensable in the final stages of fiction writing, turning my book into what I wanted it to be.

Lastly, love and special thanks to my tireless husband Michael, for being my generous partner and friend, merciless critic as well as wise and pernickety first editor. All along my writing, he reminded me of what empathy and kindness mean.

H.A. Leuschel

TESS AND TATTOOS

From a distance it looked like any ordinary big house, the roof tiled dark grey and casting the odd blinding shimmer when the sun shone brightly. The immaculate garden surrounding the property was made up of mature oak and birch trees, interspersed with thick rhododendron and rose bushes and generous expanses of green lawn, all of which kept a team of two gardeners busy all year round. Most trees sheltered noisy groups of sparrows, black birds, and the odd woodpecker or robin. For the gardeners, it was a place where there was always something to snip, a path to clear or leaves and branches to pick up. Whenever they stood up for a few minutes to stretch their aching backs or wipe their moist foreheads, they'd gaze up to the building, an attractive three-storied, red-brick structure, offset by white wooden panels and shutters that gave it a modern appearance.

Most days, the gardeners could sense that eyes were looking down on them. No matter how much they'd hunch over a scraggly bush or concentrate on raking up the cut grass in tricky corners, the intense gaze could reach them from the second floor sunroom where, if the wind wasn't howling as it often did in this part of the world, you could often hear the sounds of a piano drifting faintly in the air. On the odd occasion, like today, when they would need to talk to the director of the establishment, they'd leave their familiar, green work place and, after wiping their hands on their clothes and their boots on the doormat, they'd enter a sanctum of tranquillity.

Brightly coloured paintings adorned the entrance hall and the receptionist would simply nod to them with a smile before ushering them towards a back room on the first floor. Their feet would traipse over thick carpets and, in the midst of the tunes of the piano, they would hear muffled conversations and the odd shriek, laugh or cough. The staff employed in the building would often be seen walking down hallways, holding the frail hands of the inhabitants - elderly people whose lives were made as comfortable and fulfilling as possible. When they would eventually leave again, it was sometimes with the smell of apple pie in their nostrils or the scent of lavender, emanating from incense sticks placed in thin glass jugs standing on elegant sideboards. The gardeners would leave behind a haven that they knew was only destined for those who had the means to pay the hefty bill.

Today, if they had had the opportunity to watch on for longer, they would have noticed one of the carers knocking on a door, then entering one of the serviced apartments. Their imagination went no further though, as they were led into the director's office and offered a cup of strong tea and a biscuit before discussing their next month's duties.

oOo

The nurse entered the room - as she did every day of the week - to open the blinds and check that Tess was okay. Accompanying her was the smell of early morning coffee and the noise of a house coming to life after a long night. The old lady would sometimes chuckle to herself and then

2

say, 'Yes, I'm still alive,' under her breath. Most of the time she was already awake before the carer addressed her with a usual, 'Good morning, Tess,' followed by, 'How are you this morning?'

Tess did not need to open her eyes in order to know which nurse was making her rounds that day. The greeting, the way the nurse would knock on and open the front door, or the way she walked about, were sufficient indicators to identify who was on duty. The nurse's tone also conveyed the kind of mood she was in. Tess felt that she had led such a lonely and reclusive life over the last two decades that she'd become acutely sensitive to the most minute differences in their voices. Despite often being up long before anyone knocked on her door, hearing someone calling out for her was still a life saver. No matter how hard it was for her to relate to people now, there was no denying the fact that she relished the moment a nurse came in for a visit.

Tess decided to delay answering the nurse's cheerful call. It had proven to be the best strategy so far to keep a nurse's attention, once they'd entered her small and comfortable apartment in the care home. This was just one of many times Tess marvelled at how manipulatively people could think and plan their actions in order to achieve a specific goal, even though she thought this description was too harsh. If a toddler lost her temper in the middle of a supermarket, there might be a degree of calculation involved in knowing that screaming might achieve her wish, but a frail pensioner pretending to be asleep so that a carer's attention was extended, was surely just a basic mechanism to receive human attention. It was harmless manipulation to say the least. The nurse would always find her quite quickly anyway and then, after opening the curtains, turn for a smile and gently encourage her to get up before efficiently concluding her duties and rushing off to the next elderly resident in need of care. It was so simple yet so nice, just like the endless hugs she'd had with her baby boy. She smiled at the thought of her boisterous son, always swaying between extremes as a child, one minute professing his complete independence, the other looking for shelter in her arms.

She sighed and looked around the room, still drowned in half-darkness that indicated yet another grey and rain-filled sky. Turning onto her side, she tucked her legs closer to her body, enjoying the warmth her feet encountered. She knew that pretending still to be asleep was futile and yet she enjoyed the little ritual, the idea of a person searching her out.

Even the most elaborate ploy didn't change the fact that all of the nurses knew Tess was mentally alert and still capable of doing her chores by herself, even if it took her anything between ten minutes and an hour to get up and dressed. After all, a long, yawning day was ahead of her and she had to find a way to fill it. The nurse would have left long before she had procrastinated, examined her old sore joints and tense muscles, and wriggled herself out from under the duvet. All the nurse did really was check on her, open or draw the curtains, clear the small kitchenette area, or pass on information about the activities available that day.

Tess had reached the age of eighty-two and had been living in the serviced apartment for the elderly for three years now. She was proud of her achievement and the fact that her independence had not diminished too much. Contrary to the majority of her neighbours, she had been determined to focus on a set routine that would force her to do most of the daily tasks herself. No matter what day it was, how she felt, or whether a virus of some sort was keeping her from leaving the confines of her small apartment, she would centre her attention on sitting up at the edge of the bed, her feet searching for their slippers, and finding her bathrobe to throw over her shoulders. Getting up day after day was hard, but it had to be done.

Then she'd shuffle over to the kitchen, determined to initially walk without her stick and then, leaning onto the sink, she'd fill the kettle with tap water, pick a fresh tea bag to throw into a mug and wait for the kettle to boil its contents. Pouring the steaming water over the tea bag and shuffling again, this time to the fridge for some milk, would conclude her morning ritual, essential prior to contemplating any further projects. She chuckled each time she used the word 'project' because, really, was there any point calling a stroll through the lush green park that surrounded the old folks' home a project? However, it was one of her main morning tasks, considering that she did not have any visitors. She had lost contact with her friends a long time ago and her only son lived far away in Australia with a beautiful wife and four children.

She was heartbroken each time she looked around her four walls. In the not too distant future, her relatives would all board a plane and travel thousands of kilometres, however, not in order to chat and spend time with her, but so that they could lower her urn into the hard Scottish ground. For now, her son's weekly calls - oozing with guilt and regret - kept her going, and she knew there was no point pitying herself. She gave a customary, lingering glance towards her mantelpiece where a framed photograph of her son and his family was displayed, neatly centred so that she was always able to see it, whether she was nestled under a warm blanket on the sofa or sitting at the small dining table.

There is so much I would like to tell you, my love, but I fear there is not enough time left, nor is there the opportunity to let you know during our weekly phone calls what is really on my mind. It is a matter that would need to be discussed when we are alone together, ideally far away in a cosy little chalet in the Alps, surrounded by snow and blue icy skies, so that we can talk away the years that have sadly separated us for too long. I fear there is very little chance of us finding the time and energy to travel to such an idyllic place. Still, I will try to talk to you in my mind because, you see, no matter how much I've tried to convey the powerlessness that engulfed my life decades ago, and also the reasons for leaving your father and causing you grief in the first place, I foolishly dismissed the warning signs and just kept telling myself that no one could understand.

I hope that you do, one day, accept that I never intended to hurt you. It feels so good to be put onto a pedestal by one's partner. I was loved, passionately adored, cajoled, cuddled, cared for, and there was no wish that I was denied. When things changed though, love and tenderness withheld, I would try and literally feed on these 'special first moments' because I believed that things could go back to that perfect encounter when I had been made to feel special. Believe me, it is hard to admit to myself, worse even than admitting it to someone else, that I have made a grave mistake. I'd met your dad when I was too young for a family, too immature to know what a relationship entailed and yet, I was young enough to dream about a person that would appear and make me feel like Cinderella. Had I been that naïve? I must have been, because I believed that the reason I was less and less attractive and that I made so many mistakes in the other's eyes was that I clearly had not deserved the attention I had initially received. And now I cannot even voice the person's name ...

It was so easy to be talking to her son through her thoughts, so simple to form the words and let them flow. The reality was that during their weekly talks, they'd retreated into a superficial chit-chat that carried no further than the kind of talk she used to exchange with a friendly neighbour.

She was half-listening to one of the 24-hour news channels when the customary second knock startled her out of her day dreaming. She turned away from the TV screen so that she could greet her next visitor. The daily schedule was always the same. This second visit was to check that she had taken her pills, ask whether she wanted to participate in the day's activities, and to deliver any post that had arrived.

'Good morning, Tess.' She knew instantly on hearing the voice that it did not sound familiar. She was probably about to meet a new member of staff, she thought. The woman entering the living room was in her mid-thirties with an energetic step and friendly smile and eyes that conveyed sympathy. *Oh well,* Tess told herself, *that is a good start.* The nurse's uniform was light blue and her shoes squeaked slightly as she walked over to Tess, holding a clipboard. There was something different and fresh about this particular nurse and Tess didn't think it was due to the brand-new shoes or what looked like an only recently unwrapped and perfectly ironed uniform. It was hard at the best of times to explain why one was drawn to certain people and not at all to others. Was it the smell? The sound of their voice or … Before she could finish her thoughts, the nurse's hand reached out to take hers.

'Hello, my name is Sandra.' They shook hands, Sandra's warm and Tess's cool and dry, while both smiled. 'I'm a new member of staff and I'm here to introduce myself.' Sandra cupped her other hand over Tess's, now holding it like a pearl in an oyster. Tess was startled by how comforting it felt and a blush rose up her cheeks before she smiled coyly at the nurse. She quickly cleared her throat before managing to answer.

'Oh hello – nice to meet you! Would you like a cup of tea?' She was genuinely pleased to meet Sandra who had somehow, within seconds, managed to light up the room and spread a soft perfume of heathers – her favourite flowery smell. *There we go, maybe it is the smell.* She smiled inwardly at the awkwardness of some of her thoughts. *Thank goodness mindreading only goes so far. People can only guess your thoughts, never really read them.*

'Most definitely! I'd love a cup of tea and while you're doing that, I'll check over my list. Would that be okay?'

'Yes, that sounds good.'

Tess reached for her walking stick and after wriggling herself towards the edge of the seat, heaved her slight and aching body up. While she was walking slowly over to the small sink, she stole a glance towards Sandra who had taken a seat and was poring over what looked like a thick wad of paper attached to a clip board. She must be doing her rounds and getting acquainted with each person living in the home, Tess thought. She was anxious to prepare the two cups of tea as fast as she could so that she wasn't losing any of the precious time Sandra was able to allocate to her. She realised with amusement that she was curious to know more about her.

'May I take the tray for you?' She hadn't noticed that the nurse had gotten up, walked over to the kitchenette, and was now standing right by her side. She was giving her a dazzling, gentle smile again which rooted Tess to the spot. She felt a tingling in her right hand, announcing the return of a tremor, a scary remnant from her past. She was surprised to feel it now, causing unease deep into the roots of her hair. It was a tingling that only a medical device would be able to detect, a machine but not a fellow human being, unless it got worse. She took a deep breath and gave out a little laugh, stretching her hands and smoothing down the sides of her cardigan to keep them busy and in order to compose herself. Some basic tricks often helped to keep a tremor at bay and, with relief, she noticed that this time also, she managed to conquer it.

'Oh, thank you very much. That's a good idea. I've become awfully clumsy.' She smiled back at Sandra and reached for the tin of biscuits, willing her right hand to keep steady and was pleased that it did. 'Why don't you take this as well? I know it's a bit early for a chocolate biscuit, but who would care?'

'Mmm, I agree, even though I shouldn't. I've been trying to lose some weight, but my good intentions are clearly not good enough,' Sandra answered with a hearty laugh, patting her tummy. They sat down on the two spare sofa seats that were piled high with comfortable and brightly coloured cushions.

'By the way, I hear that you're actually not clumsy *at all*. The work you're producing during the arts and crafts sessions is stunning! I saw those beautiful paintings hanging in the entrance hall and was told you were the artist. I must congratulate you.' Sandra's eyes watched Tess over the rim of her cup, then she looked around the room and spotted further evidence that Tess was a prolific painter.

Tess was startled by how quickly Sandra had been able to notice her art. It was the one activity, organised twice a week, that she never missed, whether she had a cold or was feeling shaky that day or not. Her favourite place for sketching had become the sunroom on the second floor, where she could observe the gardeners at work most days, and trace her pencil until she found the shape she was looking for, concentrating on the right proportions. Art was such a release for Tess; the wonderful experience of putting a brush or pencil to paper and making something come to life. The hours would fly by as quickly as birds disturbed by footsteps on a path. For many years she'd had to push her passion aside due to her partner's comments that her work was mediocre or, that in any case, she was wasting her time over something that didn't make money. The world had to be measured in numbers and if those numbers weren't long enough, they were not worth considering. She swallowed the bitter thought that arose like stomach acid from thinking about the past. She shrugged, as if a fly had sat on her shoulder, and looked up at Sandra's bright face.

'Well, it keeps me going really. There is not much else I can do these days.' She ended her comment with a wink.

'As much as I'd love to stay a bit longer, I need to continue my rounds, Tess. It was a pleasure to meet you and thank you very much for the tea and biscuits. Just what the doctor ordered.' She giggled and, for a short instant, she looked like a young girl as her hand reached up to her hair, swept an escaping curl out of her face and tucked it behind her ear, before she brushed her uniform into shape.

'The pleasure is all mine,' Tess said. A good observer would have noticed that upon Sandra's last words, Tess's shoulders dropped slightly and a small sigh escaped her pale lips. Within seconds she was going to be alone again, thinking about how to fill the next hours of the day.

When the door clicked shut and there was only Sandra's perfume left to remind her of their pleasant first encounter, Tess reached for the remote control so that the sound would help her forget the solitude that had settled back into her home. There was nothing more refreshing in her view than spending time with a nice person, someone who was generous with her smiles and genuinely interested in what remained of her – an old lady with a past that was fading fast and that would not be filled with many more exciting memories. She did not crave excitement, come to think of it, and despite being on her own she did count herself lucky. *I did get away and I do get to do, now, what I most like to do – paint.*

She turned on the reading lamp next to the sofa seat and picked up her sketch book. This had been her favourite game of all time - trying to remember someone or something she had just seen and jotting the contours down on a piece of paper. She had never been good at maths or English, nor any good at figuring out which rivers ran through which country. She had managed to impress with her special ability to draw three-dimensional pictures accurately and swiftly, on the back of a glass mat in a café, on scraps of paper, or with chalk on the school blackboard. Her artistic skills landed her a well-paid job in advertising as a young adult and she fondly remembered the years creating original brochure covers, overseeing the production of glossy magazines and then landing the much coveted business deal with a major auction house that would dramatically change her life. There had been so much gossiping behind her back thereafter. And she had to admit that it had partly been justified. The director at the auction house had not only chosen their agency because of her clever pitch but because Tess had been the one presenting it. What her colleagues didn't know was that something had gone terribly wrong in her life and to extricate herself from it would come at a great cost. But jealous they remained for many years, clouding their vision from noticing what was truly happening behind closed doors.

Here we go again, I'm talking to you, my love. I think that jealousy is the worst of all human character traits. It kills so much potential, destroys so many friendships and relationships in general. If there is one thing I would like to be able to eliminate from the human race it is the capability to feel jealous and act on that negative feeling. It would be best to find the bit of DNA that is responsible for making us act in jealous and envious ways and simply snip it out of the helix. It sounds so good to say this, and I admit I'm getting rather childish in my old age. Of course, there is a reason for feeling jealous. It will have been a feeling that spurred on our ancestors in securing land, maybe, building a family and community, acquiring skills that outdid the neighbour, colleague or brother. But would we really be worse off without jealousy?

What if we all got up tomorrow morning and decided that we'd always be genuinely pleased for those who did better than us, who may have been given more talents, more endowments, and better life conditions at birth than us? Would we never aspire to do as well as them, pick ourselves up to show the world that we were equally worthy of a lion's share? Who knows? I think being able to say, 'Well done' to someone else and say, 'I'd like to try and achieve what you have achieved' is being confident and contented. Exclaiming, 'This is not fair' and 'I want what you have' are comments driven by different motives. Ultimately, you are not choosing what you really want to do, but only aiming to outdo someone else, including yourself. If you do this all your life you'll never be happy, because there is always someone better, prettier, cleverer and faster than you. Argh, enough said.

She shook her head, then rested it onto the soft pillow tucked behind her neck, scolding herself for her silly monologue. Before closing her eyes briefly, she thought back to the tremor she had managed to conceal earlier. It had become a rare event but remained a curse, waiting to strike at unexpected moments, ones she could not shrug off completely no matter how hard she tried. She remembered the day when it had first crept into her hand.

She'd just moved into her own one-bedroom flat, a major step towards regaining her independence. She'd been lying in her freshly made bed, the new linen sprayed with lavender to soothe her nerves after a long day emptying boxes, when she'd heard a scraping noise coming from the corner of her room. It had been late and the room was set in half darkness. The sound caused the small hairs at the back of her neck to rise with fear and she had felt the blood drain from her face. Something or someone was nearby. She knew it wasn't a cat but, worse, she was afraid it could just have been her imagination gone wild. She had become acutely aware of her surroundings over the years. Rather than get up and verify where the noise was coming from or check that the locks were still meticulously in place, her whole body remained frozen, her heart thumping in her chest. When she next heard the noise, it had been even closer. That had started the tremor, a burst of energy that had found a strange place to settle. Her right hand had started to shake as she dove further under her duvet covers, taking with her a heart that raced like a small animal writhing against her chest. She'd been terrified and knew all too well who her tormentor was.

oOo

She had been anxious about her new job. One part of her was unsure she could fit it into her busy life as a single parent, another part of her knew that she had to in order to feel complete. Getting her three children ready for school that morning had been a nightmare and her heart had pounded as she'd driven to the residential home, pushing excessively onto the accelerator whenever possible. She would have been mortified to have been late on her first day.

Her car had initially refused to start up and, after the umpteenth turn of the key, the panic caused her to speak to the dashboard as if the car were a person in need of cajoling and encouragement. Meanwhile, her two youngest children sat in the back seats squabbling as usual, pinching each other, and her eldest hovered too closely over her shoulder, trying to fix her eye make-up in the rear-view mirror. It culminated into an outburst of impatience, which was interspersed with soothing words that made her look like a mix between a warrior and an over-worked peace maker. She took a deep breath, closed her eyes, and rubbed her face with both hands before trying to start the car anew.

'Come on, come on - don't do this to me on the first day of work. I *need* this job,' she implored, while the children looked up and stared, wondering whether the car was going to respond to their mother's mounting frustration. They looked frozen in space, as if someone had pressed a pause button on their movements while the main protagonist – their lovely and ever optimistic mother – carried on begging the car to start.

'Right, I'm going to let it rest for a few minutes, then try again. Please, all of you, could you be quiet just for once? I need to concentrate.' She didn't notice their calm composure, but spoke as if they were still squabbling. Looking into the rear-view mirror, she was reassured that her patient but firm voice mixed with a slightly threatening undertone in its pitch had had its effect. Her children remained still, sat in their seats, waiting.

'The guy in the garage said everything had been fixed, so there should be no reason for this.' She closed her eyes momentarily as if in deep meditation and shook her head with the unfairness of it all, before directing her hand to the ignition again where her car key was dangling amongst all her other keys and, with them, a small replica of the Eiffel Tower. Just seeing it gave her a pinch in the stomach, a reminder of happier days. Her husband had taken her to Paris a few months before his liver had finally given up. He'd been a hands-on, caring big kid, a jolly, optimistic and handsome partner; one who'd put up a brave fight, even when no bravery could prevent the cancer cells from invading his organs and finally making him draw his last breath. She gasped every time she thought about him lying in his bed, gaunt and pale, and with a courageous smile etched on his generous lips. She had loved his carefree demeanour, his tireless patience with the children, and his clumsy attempts at cooking meals. No matter how many recipes or cooking programmes he'd watched, he just didn't see the point of weighing, measuring, or following each step when it came to replicating the dish in the kitchen. Why this thought had come up right then, she did not know. Many of our thoughts seem to be triggered at the oddest moments, she thought.

They'd been far from a picture of the perfect family with their socks lying around, old magazines strewn on sofas, and report cards that reflected three healthy children but who, apparently, lacked specific ambitions. They had not minded that they were not a family who took expensive annual holidays. While others were gliding down snowy mountain slopes in winter, rolling around sandy Spanish beaches in summer or jetting off for fashionable city breaks, they were more than happy staying local. Yet, when Keith had started waking up sweating with pain at night and had to increase his sick days, things had changed their insouciant viewpoint for ever. Cancer had started to threaten their laid back attitude and forced them to re-evaluate their lifestyle.

Keep going, he had said repeatedly. And then he'd suggested a trip to Paris, to focus on something fun and exotic. They hadn't managed to get all the way up the steep cobbled roads leading to Montmartre because he'd been too tired to continue, but it hadn't mattered in the slightest. They'd stopped for hot chocolate and fresh croissants in a café instead, laughing about the impatient waitress who had tapped her pen on the notepad as they squeezed out their basic French. They had just held hands like a young couple freshly in love and watched the world go by, listening to, 'Oui, Monsieur' and 'Bonjour Madame', over and again. Being together was what mattered.

She lifted her chin at the thoughts, pushed them aside, took a deep breath and, with renewed determination, attempted to start the car. By some miracle it decided to respond to her pleas at last and the agitations and ensuing discussions of her children resumed. There were no further challenges thrown at her, though. She dropped the children outside the school gates and, with butterflies fluttering in her tummy, drove into the indicated staff car park at the nearby care home. She took another deep breath, checked her reflection in the mirror and, despite the aching tiredness of yet another fitful sleep-depraved night, summoned up all her energy to help make this first day a success. She was a person who readily said 'darling', 'dear', 'honey', and 'sweetheart', and no one was going to stop her from applying the vocabulary to the weathered faces and aching bodies in the building, who were expecting her. She wondered what their lives had been like so far and why now, of all times, they did not have family close enough or loving enough to include them in their midst. Then again, she wondered if she'd be able to bear being a burden to her own children and stand in their way of living out agendas they had chosen for themselves. She did not know, and after a few glances to the surrounding gardens with its well kept lawns that were dotted with generous amounts of flowers and bushes, and even a small pond with ducks gliding over the surface, she concluded that there could be worse places to live. She'd have to wait and see though, before she could allow herself to judge.

Her feet crunched on the gravel as she walked towards the front door, energetically, and with purpose. She was ready. 'Here we go,' she muttered under her breath, giving herself a mental thumbs-up. By the time she sat down in Tess's sofa chair, she was genuinely pleased to get off her feet for a few minutes. Sipping a hot cup of black tea and dipping a delicious biscuit into the brew was the boost she needed in order to get through the rest of her first work day.

She'd been so nervous for weeks, her sleep broken and erratic, and anxious about whether the children could cope with their new routine. She'd procrastinated for months before deciding to pick up her former job. When she'd received the acceptance letter from the home, she had danced around the living room with such excitement that the children had thought she'd been invited to the Queen's tea party. Meeting the mysterious Tess, seeing her colourful paintings, and watching the elderly lady's happiness for

16

sharing a cup of tea with her, had confirmed her intuition that going back to caring for the elderly had been the right decision. People dissolved so quietly out of life, and she was determined to make those lives as meaningful as she could.

oOo

After Sandra had left and taken her bubbly self with her, Tess resumed her chores: washing the tea cups and putting the biscuit tin back in the cupboard. She found that if she didn't make sure each item had its place and was returned exactly where it had come from, she would start going downhill.

She walked over to the window, Sandra's infectious laugh still lingering in the room, and saw that a few of her neighbours had assembled outside for a group walk. She watched on and suddenly spotted Sandra strolling over the lawn with the head nurse, attentively nodding during what looked like explanations and instructions being given to her all at once. She decided that she would take a stroll herself, book in hand, and make up her mind, once she was down on the path, whether she'd join the group or not. After all, the day had turned into a pleasant and dry one, the clouds having blown westwards towards Glasgow. Once one was dressed for the occasion, there was no reason not to enjoy the rare warmth of the autumn sun.

The thought of feeling somehow useless then stopped her in her tracks. Most days she felt that getting up in the morning meant facing the same inevitable truth - that all she was really waiting for was death to make its appearance and that, when it did eventually happen, she'd not even know. Dead was dead. So, come to think of it, she thought, as long as her feet could hold her, she may as well get out for a walk into the village or simply enjoy the stunning garden that wrapped like a thick, green blanket around the building. No one was getting out of this place unless they ran out of money or had breathed their last lungful of air. She might as well pretend that she still had an active schedule to follow and things to get and do. But all that pretence for what? For whom? It was, she concluded, in order for her to avoid the brutal truth that the best she could hope for was for someone like Sandra to hold her hand when she did sigh for the very last time. The thought of that lovely bright face leaning over her during her last moments brought comfort and warmth to her heart, not that she was ready to depart the world just yet. She was surprised to notice that although all the other carers were very kind and considerate, she had actually felt like hugging a complete stranger today, simply because she was able to reach her emotionally, in such an uncomplicated fashion. She told herself that there was not much more to hope for, now that she lacked a group of friends or any close family to step into the nurse's place. She would have relished the idea of moving out to Australia to assist her son with the children and help cook and clean, to do whatever it took so that she was not alone and useless and, of course, so that she could watch her grandchildren grow. She could have taught them to draw, to mix colours, and to discover the peace that painting can provide, but she knew her son had never truly forgiven her and this was the reason why the invitation had never come and now probably never would.

I have made great progress. I can tell when someone is pretending to be nice and when someone is genuinely kind. If you are observant, you can see it all in their eyes. If you can interpret what goes on through the eyes of another, you are okay, you'll not fall into the trap of the cunning. I know all too well. Stepping into their trap is like being sucked into a dark, narrow hole.

She'd once walked passed a home for the mentally disturbed, those that no love nor care could bring back to normal daily life. She'd stopped momentarily and, from the road, had looked into an adjacent garden, then into the living room where she spotted them – their backs permanently bent through the sheer weight of their mental burden, talking to themselves. One of the patient's hands had erratically flapped out as if there was a fly to catch and it appeared inconceivable for the person to ever look someone else in the eyes again. The gaze had been shut tightly, not letting anyone back in. Others had either stared into space, as if looking at something far away, or lowered their eyes to the floor, wringing their hands and stumbling through the day. All that separated her from the mentally ill was a thin, transparent sheet of glass. That was it. But that difference – being the one standing out behind the mesh securing the premises, while they were locked in safely in a bare, near-empty room lest they injure themselves – meant everything for her own recovery. She had witnessed in a few minutes what could happen to people who'd been driven to the brink of losing their minds. The tremor, the fear, and the heavy weight of her past would be part of the price she'd pay for not having to be a part of this group, stuck behind that window. She knew how precious that fact was and how content one could be for simply being allowed to remain rooted in the world of the sane.

oOo

Six months into her new job, Sandra had finally found the routine and stability that she had hoped for. She used to take it for granted because, with Keith in tow and three fun children to bring up, she'd had what she always wanted. The parents who ran right, left and centre in order to secure their off-springs' first prizes in flute exams and karate sessions, and paid for extra tutoring so that they would always end up above average in school exams, had baffled her. Watching from afar with the kind of relaxed, chubby-cheeked glow of a mother everyone liked yet would not consider as a role model, she'd even managed to accept the

19

odd recommendation from a self-important parent. One woman had suggested her children would benefit from joining the after school activity centre, that children nowadays needed to be pushed lest they be left cleaning corridors or dependent on benefits. The truth though, was that their children actually enjoyed being with them, and the very fact that they made time for them to bake, cycle and paint filled their primary school years, without them having to fall into their beds exhausted from endless rehearsals or training. They were, however, allowed to while away their time with friends, dance in the living room or tap away on some electronic gadget. Would they have chosen otherwise had they noticed an unusual talent in one of the children? Possibly yes, but probably not. You don't turn a donkey into a race horse. They had been excited about discovering Amy's maths skills, Theo's fantasy in writing and Emily's bright singing voice. There was enough talent to push and prod without instilling the need for being anything other than a normal child, whatever that meant. It was not so much that she knew it was the right way to bring them up but rather that it just felt right to them. She'd once worked in a home with severely mentally ill people, so had a fairly good idea of what constituted healthy behaviour. She remembered her first week there, getting used to the building's inhabitants, the big empty rooms, and vast windows looking out onto a small garden and, from the dining room, she had even been able to watch people walk past on a small country road, ideal for people with dogs or children taking in the air. Many of them peered in – she would have – curious to see what a world of lunatics looked like. Could they tell by the way she was holding her coffee cup or the way she would walk about the room, checking on her patients, that she was not one of them? She was convinced that they could. People learned this capacity early in life. It was essential for survival, to be able to interpret a fellow human being's actions, to discern their intentions and goals.

Why think about this now? she asked herself. The past was the past and there was nothing you could do about that and, considering Keith's short life, he certainly spent it enjoying the company of his family to the fullest. The fact that she was the only parent left to love the children and guide them to adult life had left little room for grand plans anyway. As ever, Keith had put his family first, before he lay down and said that he could do no more. He'd left a comfortable sum from selling his electrician's business and, along with her position as nurse and carer in the home, it meant there was enough to see them through the next few years without having to count every penny.

The only person she had found most puzzling to care for was Tess. She was so independent that very little had to be done, once she'd checked on the contents of her small fridge, the state of her clothes, and whether she needed help for running a bath or a reminder to take her medication. Yet, she had to admit that Tess managed to keep her lingering in her apartment longer than any of the other residents. She'd been told that Tess was in good health considering that, for some mysterious reason, she had a frail heart. There seemed to be no history of any major illness or infection that could have caused the weakness. Unless, of course, Tess had not told them the whole story. Over the last months she had seen her behaviour change. She was more willing to ask for help for simple tasks such as folding clothes or filling the dish washer, or even to look for a lost earring. Sandra knew that this was most likely just a ploy to stretch out her visits. Tess was an independent octogenarian but she was also lonely, very lonely. She had noticed that Tess was a well-read woman who must have led a cultured life, but where and with whom she still did not know. She had seen novels by Virginia Woolf, Doris Lessing, and Milan Kundera set next to her reading lamp. Here was a person who shunned the company of others, yet brightened when Sandra came through the door. She once read that every person has a different way of interpreting the truth and that shaping it somehow – making a past memory your own by adding or taking away certain details - was a way of finding the truth you'd be able to live with. But as much as she was determined to make Tess feel less lonely, there were only so many hours in a day. When she was sitting in her little house at night, overlooking the children's homework and sipping a glass of wine with her aching feet up on a stool, her thoughts often wandered back to the many lives, who just a few minutes' drive from her house, were now getting ready for bed or falling asleep in front of a loud TV set. What was Tess doing now? What kept her going? She did wonder, and only her eldest calling out loud demands for help with French verb conjugation managed to pull her out of her reverie. What else could you do in life than try and live it as best you could?

oOo

She knew that she should have asked for help, considering she'd had an unusual urge to have a hot soak late at night. She had felt an overwhelming exhaustion and her bones had ached due to the persistent cold and damp weather. And why not? She was free to do what she wanted, and who cared whether she would get up later the next morning? It was not like she had to go to school or be on time for a job or had any other pressing commitment. Yet, she'd been lying in the bathtub for an hour now, the bubbles long gone and her skin more shrivelled than ever. She was starting to get the feeling that the chilling water was going to give her an infection, when she finally gave in and called a nurse via the emergency button, set at an easy reach from the bath. It was flashing red as she waited. All she had to do was listen for the hurried footsteps down the hall, the key in the door and the exclamation of the nurse on call, looking for the elderly in need.

Tess had been so determined to prove that no matter what she encountered, and regardless of the sadness she felt about losing her son to his life in Australia, she could fight the inevitable and face her destiny bravely and independently. You just had to put your mind to it and it would work. Yet tonight, it was her body which had resisted the instructions and obstinately stuck her in a spasm of pain that went from her lower spine right into the heel of her right foot.

She pictured herself - like she had so many times before – with her two feet positioned one behind the other on a tightrope. Her arms were stretched to either side at shoulder level and she was concentrating intently on gliding the centre of her back foot in front of the other. She was breathing carefully but thoughtfully, all the while keeping her eyes focused on the task at hand. There was just her and the balancing act, the feeling of the air all around her, and she could vaguely perceive the people underneath, some of whom were holding their breath. It was so quiet. They would be scared that any noise could put her off, make her falter and fall to her certain death. She felt that she was constantly standing on that tightrope high up in the air, balancing her unique life over troubled waters, distractions, and emotions that guided her from one encounter with the world to another. She was suddenly feeling happy and content because she realised she was still breathing, her only failing being that her back had seized so badly that she could not sit up in the bath any more, and it was okay. Her pride had evaporated to nothing.

When the nurse answered her calls from the bathroom, she was prepared for the strange looks she would inevitably get but didn't care for anymore. She could smell coffee on the nurse's breath as she was gently heaved out of the cold water, softly scolded, and wrapped in a big, thick bath towel as if she were a small child. But other than that she could not detect any awkward looks; the nurse's eyes had not widened as they should have with shock, unless her poor eyesight had failed to pick up the signs. What did it matter now? It had been a nice feeling, she did concede – only to herself though – being tucked up into bed, a warm beverage by her side and the nurse holding her hand for a while. She had been at peace and fallen into a dreamless slumber, one she had not known for a very long time.

oOo

It dawned on Sandra, when she'd heard the news from the night nurse, that Tess had more hidden secrets than she had initially believed. Why was it that young children and, for that matter, senile adults were often put into a category of innocence and naiveté? This could not be further from the truth. What unified their needs was a craving for attention, love and care. Young children and the frail elderly often struggled with the same problems: standing on their own two feet, keeping a balance, holding a fork the right way and navigating themselves through life. Just as a young toddler would need an encouraging nod and a smile, so would an elderly person, too. Where they differed was that the young still had the difficult task ahead of building their identity, finding their purpose, whereas the elderly in a home were intent to hold on to it, despite being in an environment that had changed. If somebody's identity was constructed around a role or rather several roles, then losing one or more of them inevitably meant they'd feel useless or, worse, discarded. Personal identity became just a ghostly reminder of the years when one was an active part of society.

'I know you will have heard about my misadventure last night, Sandra,' Tess said, after just a few minutes together. Sandra walked over to her and said nothing. Instead, she wrapped her soft arms around her and held her for what seemed an eternity, sensing Tess did not want to let go. The signs of past abuse: cigarette burns and bruises left from broken bones did not need explaining, but rather the hidden mental scars that must have made it so hard to live ever since.

'The incident has brought back in a flash all those years that I kept my head up high, too busy running after *one person* with endless, senseless, mind numbing requirements,' Tess added, while the tears started to flow. She didn't even use the name when mentioning the one person who seemed to have meant the world to her at the start and for whom she had subsequently done everything, sacrificed everything, and in the end, had robbed her of her core self.

When Sandra noticed that Tess had arrived at a point where she could cry no more, they sat down on the sofa side by side.

'What would you like me to tell the others? You know how it is in life. People talk and nurses are only people – hence, they talk and rightly so. We need to make sure you are as well and happy as you can be,' Sandra said.

'I know, I know. Never mind, love. It really is not important any longer.' Sandra guessed that the injuries were the reason for Tess wearing long sleeved, turtle-necked pullovers, even when the weather was too warm for it. Equally, her legs were always either stockinged or she wore long trousers. It answered a few of her questions, Sandra thought.

'But Tess, how did you manage to conceal your medical file? Surely, the staff here would have received a report stating all the facts,' Sandra said slowly and gently, her baffled eyes fixated on Tess. She was genuinely puzzled.

'There is a file stating injuries, yes, but if you read the list, there is never any statement relating them to abuse of any sort.'

'Oh, I get it. You actually …'

'Yes, I protected my tormentor … at the time and …only to some extent.' Tess's voice was calm. 'It doesn't hurt any more. What is unbearable is the fact that when I eventually came out of the nightmare, my therapist told me that I had possibly suffered with what experts call *Stockholm Syndrome.* I did ask that this would not be revealed to any third party.'

'Oh, I've vaguely heard about this condition. I think it refers to a famous incident in Sweden, where hostages had actually bonded with the hostage taker, no?' Tess nodded whilst wiping a tear away from her cheek. 'Correct me if I'm wrong, but I also seem to remember that it's a survival strategy. We can all fall into this trap.'

'Yes, well, I guess there is some truth in that, but I think some people have more of a tendency to develop attitudes and feelings towards a clever manipulator than others. It tends to be because one has very little self-confidence. This is what I didn't want to accept at the time. Actually, I felt quite offended, confused, and even angry. Because this implied, well no, it actually blatantly told me that I had willingly collaborated with my abuser. But, with time and some distance, I came to understand that it was a blessing to know there was an explanation for the painful fact that I had indeed defended that horrible person. I felt such disgust …'

'It's bad luck, Tess, really bad luck. We meet people and little do we know how deceiving they may be, how untrustworthy.'

'Yes, but you know, deep down I knew that it was all wrong. I knew, really, but I was trapped, a hostage in a true sense.' She shuddered intensely at the thought and Sandra was about to subtly change the topic when she was surprised about Tess's turn of conversation.

'I tried to get some tattoos painted over the scars one day. Seriously, after …. after … well, all I wanted was to erase what had happened to me. You see, I still wonder time and again what really has happened to me. How could I have done what I have done, year after year after year? How can you look after someone, be there for another person who does not at all deserve it? Worse, who enjoys humiliating and watching you hurt? It takes a certain type of person to be able to torment another like this.' Tess looked up as if trying to get her bearings, looking like someone lost in a deep dark wood, unable to find the path home. Then she locked eyes with Sandra, suddenly cool and collected.

'When I woke from the nightmare, I just kept thinking how much precious time I'd lost and wasted. I cannot believe to this day *why* I did it. Why did I not simply run off?'

'Is that why your son left?'

'Well, it's not surprising at all, is it? He'd tried to make me see that the occasional niceties thrown at me by the one I blindly loved, the odd gift that made me falter – they were all a charade set up by an abuser. Think of a donkey walking in front of a carrot, there really is not much of a difference. As long as between the lashes there is the odd pat on the back, you keep hoping that around the bend you'll find that it was worth it. But you see, back then I had also decided that I had to accept my fate. Still, if I had another chance and I could tell my younger self what to do, I'd say, Run, run as fast as you can.' She was shaking her head now, her heart surely aching and her hands wringing, restless.

'He must have taken all your closest family and friends from you, too.' Sandra's voice was low but she knew by the widening of Tess's eyes that she must have hit a nerve. Tess shook her head.

27

'It wasn't really …' She had begun but her throat closed up, strangling the words that wanted to escape.

Sandra knew better than anyone that there had so far been no one to visit and, apart from the customary weekly phone call with her son, she could have been a hermit secluded in a small apartment with no contact at all with the outside world. She noticed Tess taking a deep breath, lowering her eyes with some kind of shame or sudden embarrassment. It was difficult for Sandra to interpret the silence that ensued. They could faintly hear the sound of footsteps coming from the adjacent apartment and an ambulance siren in the distance. Tess's breathing was laboured when she eventually continued.

'Well, yes, no …argh, it wasn't like that you see …'

Her eyes misted over and Sandra knew that it might be because of a past memory haunting her friend and - by the retreat she could make out through her drooped shoulders, her eyes set on her hands now interlocked and resting on her lap - it was not a nice memory.

'Okay, you know what I think we should do this weekend?'

Tess looked up at her with renewed interest and a relief etched all over her face for the change of topic, while Sandra explained her plan with a sparkle in her eyes.

oOo

'Do you like it?'

Tess nodded in silence as she stepped out of the backroom, where a tall lady with long, thick hair and lavishly coloured ink laced around her neck had placed a tattoo at the top of Tess's arm. Tess had not wanted to tell her about the picture she'd chosen yet, even though Sandra could tell that she was literally burning with impatience when she walked over to her with a cheeky smile.

Later that night she would think back to the scene – her elderly friend standing in a tattoo parlour, surrounded by photos of people exhibiting every possible body part adorned with colours, patterns and motifs of multiple kinds. She had looked out of place with her classic pair of trousers, comfortable flat shoes, and an elegant silk shirt with a long golden necklace trailing at the front. Her grey-white hair had been beautifully swept up into a bun and her small oval-shaped face had not hidden the years etched into it, but she had still looked beautiful and alert.

This lady has real strength, Sandra had thought.

'Do I like it? Well, I guess it's exactly right. Who'd have thought that at my age you could still find a fleck of skin good enough to tattoo?' She gave out a giggle and a wink while fishing out her purse from her handbag. She looked frail all of a sudden and her eyes took on a tired sheen, her shoulders slightly drooping forward with the effort of staying upright for so long. Sandra's observant eyes detected what others may not have easily noticed and she could tell it was time to take Tess somewhere she could rest.

'Let's go to my place now and celebrate.'

Sandra had been worried that she'd possibly gone too far in suggesting a dinner at her house. She'd grown so fond of the old lady, who was seemingly wrecked with a sadness that was almost unbearable to witness. She felt like trying to fill the void yet, at the same time, she could sense that some wounds could not be mended because the scars just run too deeply. She'd had a husband she desperately missed whereas Tess seemed to have lived a long married life until there had been a drastic change, throwing her off course. She had to ask her more about her past in an attempt to somehow share the burden with her. How was it possible for Tess to stay with someone when even her son had learnt to work out the abuse and deceit perpetrated by his mother's partner? Tess must have fallen into the trap without seeing any way out. But how and why?

oOo

The next day, Tess was sitting in her sofa seat, smiling at Sandra who was busying herself with sorting out the pills for the week and taking notes on her clipboard. She knew her friend was confused about her reluctance to show off the tattoo. Sandra being Sandra, she'd kept her impatience at bay during last night's dinner, happily chatting to Tessa who was watching her prepare a big pot of fish stew. It had been delightful to see Sandra's nimble hands gradually produce a heap of cubed potatoes, slices of carrot, leak, fresh herbs, spinach and courgette. They had finished off their dinner with Profiteroles and mint tea. She'd visibly been proud of her efforts to produce a tasty, fresh and well-rounded selection of dishes. There was something oddly reassuring when she'd watched Sandra in her apron in front of the cooker, preparing vegetables while breathing in the scent of thyme and basil. She was no master chef, but she'd displayed confidence that she was enjoying the preparations and cooking with fresh ingredients. The children had asked question after question and Tess had been happy to answer them all, realising that it had been a long time since she'd felt such joy at being the centre of attention.

'Why have we not done this earlier?' Sandra had exclaimed later in the evening, shaking her head, and Tess had nodded in agreement. The weariness she'd felt upon leaving the tattoo parlour had become a distant memory thanks to Sandra's three boisterous children and her infectious, cheerful mood.

Once the children were all in bed, teeth brushed, and showered with cuddles and kisses, Tess had told Sandra that looking back at her past, she could not believe that she had done what she had done. After all, only she knew how ferociously she had sided with her partner, discrediting her friends and family by telling them they did not understand just how hard someone's childhood could be. She had always tried to cover up any of her companion's failings, had made excuses for them, and in the process she had lost all credibility. More than one friend had expressed concern over her unwavering protection of her partner's obvious arrogance. Still, her companion had been clever, had known how to confuse, expose people's faults in order to always look like the stronger, cleverer one. When you rehearsed something long enough, you became an expert at it, whether it was practicing the violin or, for that matter, practicing pretence and deception. She'd been worn down over the years by a person who'd revealed a lack of inhibition and a constant air of deserved entitlement. Yes, she had believed the tears and the distress professed, believing that she was needed and appreciated and that, surely, no one was capable of pretending such feelings. She had never been able to keep other people's pain from entering her emotional sphere. But over time her personality had become blurred. She had really wanted it to work out, especially when she'd spent hour after hour talking and smiling - despite the sadness. Yet, with each subsequent incident, hoping that things would settle at last, she'd simply numbed herself from accepting the truth. By the time she was admitted into hospital for multiple fractures and burns – claimed to have been caused by a fall from the garden ladder – it had been too late.

oOo

The next day, Sandra found Tess sitting in her armchair, her eyes wide and her face pale and gaunt. She rushed over in order to reassure herself that all was well with her friend. Her many errands and a few newcomers into the home had meant that she'd made it to Tess's apartment later than usual.

'Are you felling okay, Tess?'

'Oh yes, thank you. Thank you so much for yesterday. It was very special. I guess I'm still a bit tired from the late night.' She gave Sandra a wink, who in turn patted her shoulder and offered to prepare her a cup of tea.

'Not yet, Sandra. Come and sit with me for a few minutes if you can, please.'

'Of course,' she answered, carrying one of the dining chairs over to where Tess was sitting.

'I have been thinking so much lately. I want you to know that despite what has happened to me, I also had many happy moments. You see, there was much laughter and excitement, too. And somehow I was simply too stubborn to admit that I had been wrong from the start.' She gave her a weak smile, her clear-blue, gentle eyes offset by the white strand of hair escaping her bun.

'You must know what I mean if I say that when you are with someone, in some sense you merge with the other person, at times consciously, at others subconsciously – I can't tell now. All I know today is that my age is taking its toll and memories themselves are starting to blur and they seem to be taking on different shapes. Maybe that has been the key to my behaviour all along. I'd looked back at events, attempted to confront my partner with evidence, only to be rebuked and submitted into doubting my own recollections. The only witness left in the end had been my son and he'd decided he needed to travel all the way to Australia in order to stop the pain from invading his mind.' Her eyes were drifting off to a place that Sandra could not reach. Tess woke from her day dreaming and looked over to Sandra.

'I'm amazed that I was able to build a friendship with a normal person, with a normal life and normal problems. I should have been the one losing my companion early, not you, Sandra. This injustice says it all. You're the first person I have befriended since ...oh, there is no point reminiscing! I often wondered what good it was to be alive when, for so long, I have felt so utterly powerless and trapped, especially when I found out that I aided the other person in setting the trap and all the other traps thereafter.'

'Oh Tess, I am truly sorry.' They locked eyes for a moment before Tess took a deep breath to continue.

'Just be watchful if you ever notice that one of your children has difficulties with distancing themselves from someone else's emotions, because some people might use it to their advantage. In itself that is a lovely trait and people turn to these sensitive individuals for comfort and support. But they need to learn to protect themselves. It's like a doctor who is unable to distance herself from her patients' suffering, moods, and emotional outbursts. Actually, I read somewhere that it does make them worse doctors rather than better ones. When the last patient leaves the room and the next enters, the doctor needs to be ready to literally close the door on the past, in order to deal with the present and look into the future with independence and confidence. All sounds easy, doesn't it?' She laughed out loud and Sandra told herself that things were improving and that, hopefully, it was never too late to heal past wounds, be they physical or mental.

'You never managed to close the door though, let

the past be the past?' Sandra said.

'No, it was too windy and the thunder and lightning ripped that door into shreds. I was helpless in a room full of confusing life events and lies that seemed to get bigger and bigger over time. And then there was my son. He kept me going, and still...' Her voice trailed off.

'I had been so much in love by the time I realised that everything I ever said, any insecurities I ever admitted, or any weak moments I ever showed, had been used against me in order to further someone else's desires and needs. There had never been enough room for me because I was never seen as a person but just an object that could be thrown about and discarded when not required.'

She shrugged to herself, reached for the remote and switched the TV on. They watched in silence as the news presenter announced the devastation caused by a recent earthquake in Nepal. Sandra glanced sideways and saw that Tess was crying and, without a word, she reached over to change channels. A repeat of 'Strictly Come Dancing' was in full swing on another TV station and she observed as Tess smiled with delight at the shiny costumes, the energy of the moving bodies, and the light conversation that followed each act. She got up after another few minutes and walked over to kneel in front of Tess, taking her hand, and then told her that she would first clear the dishes before continuing her rounds but would be back later, prior to heading home. Tess's cheeks had a strange glow and her eyes were still shining from watching an energetic tango performed by a glamorous pair of dancers now waiting for their score, out of breath and smiling with relief.

'Oh, I've always loved seeing people dance. It's so much fun to watch, don't you think?'

'Yes, definitely!' She smiled contentedly and

nodded. 'I'll remind you of the day the programme is on, so you won't miss it.'

'Oh … thank you, sweetheart.'

It's never too late! she thought to herself again, whistling to the tune of the music. In the kitchen, she placed the used cups and saucers into the dishwasher, making up dance steps as she went along, and on her last little twirl she looked over her shoulder to check if Tess had noticed her attempt of a performance. To her dismay, Tess seemed to have nodded off, her face looking pale and slightly ashen. That was when she could not bear it any longer and silently crept over to where Tess was sitting and already emitting small snoring sounds, while the music was still accompanying the next enthusiastic dancing couple on screen. She whispered Tess's name a few times and then, without any further thought, raised her friend's sleeve to the top of her arm.

She was speechless at what she discovered. Tess's arm was surrounded by a row of interlocked shackles. They were thick and black and she was taken aback by the courage of this old lady for choosing such a strong design. At the front of the arm though, the link was broken and instead of the metal chain, small detached pieces were progressively floating up her upper arm where they took on the shape of a group of birds flying off towards the top of her shoulder.

Sandra sat back with a great sigh, pulled the sleeve back down and reached for the cover that laid by her side. While she covered Tess's legs and ever so gently placed another cushion behind her head, she could sense her friend's hand, the skin dry and cool, reaching for hers. She was startled by the unexpected gesture, her thoughts racing with a mixture of guilt and embarrassment. She knelt close to her, holding her hand for a while, when she heard a small whisper coming from Tess's mouth and she lowered her ear, asking her to repeat what she had just said.

'Thank you so much... I'm sorry for leaving you so soon, my love.' Sandra's eyes widened in disbelief. What on earth was Tess talking about? Before she could set her forehead into a deep frown, she sensed her heart drop into the centre of the stomach. *It is too late,* she told herself.

The room suddenly felt oppressive and stuffy and the air was still with foreboding. Sandra got up and frantically opened one of the dining room windows, knowing the feeling all too well, even though it had been a while since she last experienced it. The fresh gust of air blowing into her face was rejuvenating and refreshing but she was frightened to turn round. In the nearby trees she could hear the birds singing and twittering as if it were just another normal autumn afternoon. She took another deep breath, her eyes streaming now with tears of frustration, and resolutely walked back to where Tess was now slumped awkwardly in her chair. The meaning of the tattoo was staring her straight in the face. Tess had lost her imaginary wings before she had ever learned to fly.

And she had not seen it coming.

oOo

When she met Tess's son, Daniel for the first time, Sandra could not but wonder about how much children sometimes resembled one of their parents. He was as tall, lean, and blue-eyed as she had experienced her friend. His hair was salt and pepper coloured around his temples and there were a few wrinkles around the eyes, betraying his otherwise youthful looks. Other than that, he looked like a healthy, sun-tanned man in his early fifties.

'Thank you for looking after my mum. She

mentioned you so often, when we spoke on the phone,' he said, after they exchanged a few pleasantries. She hadn't been able to stop herself from occasionally resting her hand on his forearm, just so she could experience a connection with someone so closely resembling her friend. She hoped it might bring her back into the room breathing, talking, and smiling.

'I loved your mum. We had such a great time together, even if only for a short time.' Her throat choked up with emotion as she folded her hands in front of her, fighting back the tears.

'I'm sorry.'

'Sorry? For what?'

'After all these years I still couldn't forgive her. It was too much.'

'When was the last time you saw your mum?' Sandra's warm eyes were set on Daniel's face.

'Did she not say?'

'Oh, don't get me wrong. She spoke about you and your family every week, since I met her. She missed you terribly but also seemed to genuinely understand that you were too upset to see her. You see, I was always happy to listen but I never pried.'

'I haven't seen her since my early thirties.'

'I don't understand. I thought you left after your dad died.'

'My dad isn't dead.'

Sandra was increasingly feeling ill at ease. Had she completely misunderstood Tess? Her hands started to sweat and her heart was beating in her chest like a wild animal, an unfamiliar feeling for her.

'My mum left my dad when I was sixteen … she left us for ... her lover. Well, to be exact – I don't know if she told you this but, she came out as a lesbian. Well, she'd not admitted it to anyone until she met a woman through work. She'd been preparing a pitch for a major auction house and that's how they met.'

'Oh.' Sandra's eyes widened; not because of this new revelation but because she realised that all these months she had wrongly presumed that Tess's husband had abused her. Why had Tess hidden the truth from her? Before she could continue rattling off a list of questions coming into her head, Daniel continued.

'My mum found out - or should I say, admitted to herself - very late in life that she was gay. She left us for a woman who was a venomous, deceiving snake. Initially, it had been really hard to stomach, not so much the fact that she was gay actually, but the fact that she'd so quickly cut the ties with many of her old friends and then gradually with me. Even Dad, who had been willing to continue on friendly terms, had given up trying to stay in touch, and I was the one left to call her and persuade her to meet up. I really loved my mum, we had previously been so close. But I reached a point where nothing I said or did was any good.' The pain in his voice was palpable.

'That must have been so hard on you,' Sandra said, giving him an encouraging nod and placing her hand on his forearm. She tried to hide the fact that she was shaken by what she had just heard. How easily we could misunderstand people.

'Don't get me wrong, it took me a long time, too long I suppose, in order to understand that it was not my mum but her partner who had made her turn her back on those, who until then, she had loved having around her. That was so hurtful that I sometimes let months go by without calling her. Then when I did, I would always have *her* to talk to first, all chirpy and *what have you been up to, stranger?* That kind of nonsense talk. I eventually did see someone myself, a therapist, just so I could get it off my chest. My dad had refused to talk to me about any of this, understandably so. He'd given up and whenever I tried to broach the topic, he'd just shrug.'

'You don't have to tell me this if you don't want to. I can tell that it's very painful.'

'Oh no, it feels good, actually. You're like a bridge for me because you met her after all this … and when she was really alone. I regret that I had already created that physical distance between us by moving to Australia. At least I made sure she had everything she needed.' He looked up at her and in that instant he appeared like a little vulnerable boy again, confused and insecure about whether he had done the right thing.

'I'm amazed she survived at all,' she said gently, before asking, 'Did you make up?'

'Oh yes, whenever we spoke it was great. The distance allowed us to feel safe from mentioning the pain and anger that had been part of our relationship for so long.'

'What anger?'

'Oh, I was so angry with her. How could she have stayed with someone abusive and manipulative for so long and not tell anyone? She'd even defended that monster year after year by claiming that her partner had had a tough time because of an alcoholic father and absent mother. Who knows which bits of the tales she told my mum were actually true? My therapist told me that this person was a narcissistic pervert. I couldn't bear to see what she did to my mum and in turn I despised her as well. I'm sorry that you didn't seem to know. The psychologist I was seeing helped me, though. She was able to piece together all the elements into a coherent picture and, when I understood what my mother was suffering from, the penny dropped at last. I could also see that, after all the upheaval – coming out, leaving me and Dad - she was reluctant to admit defeat.'

'What do you mean?' Sandra's gentle gaze was set on the tall man's misty eyes.

'By keeping me away from that witch, she was instinctively keeping me safe as well. That she was the victim of mental and physical abuse, I only found out much later, though.'

'But where is that person now? What happened to her? How did your mum manage to afford this place?' She gasped at her own intrusive questioning. 'I'm so sorry, it was wrong of me to ask. It's none of my business, of course. Please forgive me.'

'Don't fret. It's quite alright really. It all came out because my mum eventually ended up in emergency services. A nurse did voice her concern to a doctor and once word got around there was no stopping it. I think my mum was lucky that when she got back to the apartment, the locks had been changed and her few possessions discarded at the bottom of the staircase. She perfectly understood the message. It had been the final blow though, despicable, and she had no strength left to even make a deposition at the police station. But she had a chance then and took it.'

'So …'

'That had been the moment Dad and I had been

waiting for. We picked her up, we spoon-fed her as best we could, suppressing our own grief and all the while watching a lady come back to life, a person we once cherished and loved. Nothing was ever the same again of course, but she got back onto her two feet, found a small apartment and enrolled on an arts course, which led her to a low-paid but fulfilling job in adult education. Of course, the wicked witch did try to suck her back in, stalking her with phone calls. She was probably afraid, somehow, that she'd get into trouble after all. By continuing the threat, she tried to make sure the fear would prevent my mum from speaking. There was no way I could have come back with my family and I thought long and hard about inviting her into our lives in Australia… but I just couldn't.'

'Your dad is a saint.'

'Yes, he *is*. He gave her enough money to live comfortably …' His voice trailed off before he could take another breath to continue.

'Oh, and one more thing. You know that I spoke to mum every week or so?'

'Yes, I think that really kept her going, Daniel.' She nodded and gave him a comforting smile.

'Well, she did tell me about a month ago that if she'd ever understood something about life, it's that she should have fallen in love with someone like you.' He blushed slightly, lowering his eyes.

She reached out and hugged the stranger who, she had been able to sense, was grateful that his mum hadn't died completely alone. His tears were wetting her shoulder and she felt as if his grief and sadness was like a dam breaking its walls.

'She did get revenge of some sort, though. Her ex-partner haunted her for years after the separation, despite the fact that she'd also been busy abusing her next victim. She'd jump over the fence and climb onto her terrace and make awkward noises to scare her. She'd call her and hang up after breathing down the line, or worse, turn up at her work place.' He took a deep breath.

'Anyway, you probably don't know this, but the woman was an art dealer. She was well known in the arts circle and particularly the jewellery departments of the main auction houses. I don't want to know how many lies she'd told people, but I know that she fell out with many. My mum managed to take one piece with her, from the apartment they'd shared. She'd pretended to want to talk, then used the bathroom, where she knew the precious item was hidden in the medicine cabinet. She knew that her ex-partner would turn the place upside down to find it. She managed to divert the blame and eventually convinced her that she had to fire the cleaner. It must have been a very hard time for my mum, but one she never regretted. She was a woman who was always intent on never causing any pain to anyone. But here, I think she must have felt an odd sense of satisfaction in taking something that meant so much to her tormenter.'

He cocked his head now, his eyes gleaming mischievously.

'After some thorough reflection, she went to one of the auction houses and put it up for sale.'

'That's amazing. Wasn't she terrified of the reaction? Surely her ex would have gotten wind of it?'

'Yes, she actually made sure of that. We were involved in it, by the way. My dad believes that possession is nine tenth's of the law. There was no documentation stating that the item wasn't my mum's to keep. We agreed that she would claim that it had been a gift between partners.'

'I'm impressed.'

'You should be, because the initial explosion of anger was impressive but very quickly squashed by my dad telling her that they had watertight evidence to take her to court for abuse and domestic violence, and if she lay as much as a little finger on my mum, he would not hesitate to take action. And you know what?'

Sandra's eyes widened with expectation.

'She was never seen again. It's as if she'd vanished from the surface of the earth.'

'So, what was the item that she sold?'

'A beautiful ruby and diamond ring. That witch had boasted about stealing it from her cancer-ridden mum, claiming that at the time it wasn't going to be of any use to her soon anyway. People like that tend to be excessively materialistic. I found out that statistically 75% of abusive manipulators tend to be men, who are fixated on money and power, whereas the women mainly seek to prove their superiority. So, they are often obsessed with their appearance. They know how to use those first impressions – driving in an expensive car or wearing clearly branded clothing and sparkly jewellery. Anyway, the sale was a good move and allowed my mum a nice little start into her new independence.' He sighed at the thought, smiling weakly at Sandra, who nodded with approval.

oOo

She was stretched out on her bed in a fresh gown, the crisp bed linen covering the slim outline of her body; her long, brittle hair was brushed and smoothed out around her oval face. She looked peaceful and her skin was soft and cool to the touch. Sandra lowered her lips to give her a last farewell kiss, whispering, 'Sometimes your wings fall before you fly, but now you are free my sweet Tess – fly wherever you like.' She remembered what Tess had said not so long ago, when during one of their short tea sessions she had sighed and exclaimed, 'We are like candle flames, so fragile, so easily blown out by a gust of wind. Yet here I am, even if only by a small glimmer.'

Meanwhile, the gardeners were sheltering under one of the big oak trees outside, hoping for a reprieve from the heavy showers that had interrupted their snipping and their attempts to clear the leaves on the footpath that wound through the now water-logged grass. They looked up to the massive shape of the house, cast in semi-darkness against the grey sky. Lights could be seen glowing in the windows and their thoughts turned away from the people inside, whose stories had been shaped by time and past memories. They sighed and, as they agreed on calling it a day, assembled their tools and watched a squirrel hurry over the lawn and swiftly ascend a tree. As the gardeners' feet crunched over the gravel path towards their van, their attention was caught by the soft and throaty cooing of a pigeon, and the sound of a hearse entering the estate.

THE SPELL

He had a small, delicate body, thin legs and arms, and a torso that was short and fragile. He almost looked supernatural, like a beautiful version of an elf, with his startling light blue eyes and hair as dark as charcoal. Later on, when we were as familiar with each other as a mother and son would be, he wrapped himself warmly around me like a shawl or a small monkey anchored to his mother's body for the day. His lightness added to my initial impression that he looked like a beautiful, fantastical character who'd walked straight out of a children's picture book, yet I quickly found out that my female instincts to protect him were undeniably linked to a human child whose cheeks reddened with exertion and whose occasional stroppiness could only be found in the very young. And I need to tell you right from the start that he is not my son, because I am not his biological mother. Yet, we would have both liked to have been each other's family and, for a short while, we actually were. I know that because of the way he looked at me, the way he snuggled up whenever he saw me, and the way he always saw goodness in me. He had the capacity to make me melt there and then and I would forgive him instantly for small tantrums or cheeky retorts. He seemed to endear himself to my laughs and smiles and I loved his thin, fine fingers reaching out to claim a hug, one of so many he desperately needed.

You will wonder whose son he was and why he is

no longer with me; and I will tell you why, so that I don't go crazy with grief and so that our story, and the stories of those who were involved in it, may come to convey how life can deal you a difficult card.

I met Leo's father shortly after meeting *my little guy*. That was a nickname I'd frequently use for my new and very special friend. Leo was a grand name for a small person with fluffy, wispy dark hair and a voice that never carried far, yet if you took the time to lower your ear towards his words, you would be enthralled by their wisdom. This child was unusual in so many ways. Leo loved to sing and that was exactly how I noticed him, sitting by himself in the kids' play area which was part of the private sports club I frequented. He was singing a little song to himself and seemed very happy with his own company. I had just turned thirty and was already well acquainted with young children, thanks to my sister's and my brother's growing families. I just loved being their hands-on, and fun-loving auntie, and therefore making eye contact with strangers' children came naturally to me.

However, when I turned my head towards the sound, the owner of the voice was nowhere to be seen. I was relaxing in the club's café, adjacent to the play area, and had just ordered my usual cup of matcha green tea latte with a slice of fresh cake, well-earned, I thought, after a very demanding and dynamic yoga session. I looked at the green mix of tea and foamed almond milk and took a sip, enjoying the bitter-sweet taste. I was half-way through the thick raspberry-filled cheesecake when I heard the singing again. My fork stopped in mid-air as I listened more carefully. It was the funniest melody I had ever heard. He was copying the lyrics of a popular song, frequently aired on the radio at the time, so I caught on to it very quickly. However, it was unusually out of tune. Not only was the voice squeaky and mouse-like but the intonations were all wrong. I stifled a laugh, telling myself that this was incredibly cute, and I looked up once more to try and find the unusual singer. I couldn't see him fully at first, but a few of his black wisps of hair were sticking out above a large, soft cushion which gave him away to my probing eyes. Convinced now that he was the singer I was looking for, I lowered my gaze further and widened my eyes with surprise. I had locked onto a big set of blue eyes, peeking round the corner of the cushion, looking straight at me. It was as if he'd deliberately sung again, to see whether I'd notice him. Questions were forming in my mind. Did he notice that I had been listening? Worse, did he know that I had been amused? I was taken aback, to say the least, and made sure he wasn't actually looking at his own parent, by checking the people sitting beside and behind me. No one seemed to take any interest in the little fellow. So, I just smiled and he smiled back and our first meeting was sealed.

We had somehow found a secret understanding which was the base for a series of encounters that led me to talk to him, ask his name, and find out why he was on his own and query who was looking after him. He told me not to worry because his dad had left him to play while he was doing a 'round'. That's how he had put it anyway. I know now what he meant by *rounds* but, initially, I had been appalled. To leave a small child to his own devices was bad enough, but to do it for a few hours was criminal in my view. Why I had not reported it then, I don't know. My excuse was that I'd built up a special relationship with a little chap, who became my friend before his dad did. Had he not been there, I don't think I would ever have spoken to David. I imagined him as a small person himself, maybe even a Woody Allen type of a man, pale and skinny with big glasses, but my imagination was proven wrong when I finally did set eyes on him.

It had been a dark and rainy day when I eventually ran into David. I had decided to not only linger a bit longer at the sports club in the hope that the torrential rain would ease off, but also because I was wondering who the mysterious dad was. When I finally laid eyes on him I was pleasantly surprised. The man was tall and broad, his eyes blue, and his face was surrounded by wavy black hair. I could tell that he'd only just left the shower because his hair smelled clean and moist. His cheeks were still flushed from doing exercise and a big smile revealed a set of straight white teeth. He was a good-looking man, but with a strange insecurity. I would notice later that he did like to keep his T-shirt on to hide his waist, only slightly pudgy, when sitting by a pool or walking down a beach. Despite being ten years my senior, he had kept well-toned arms and legs and his voice carried far. The fact that I had met his son before I'd met him was the reason why we struck up a conversation.

'Oh, so you're the amazing Sophie who my son's in love with!' Of course, my cheeks burnt upon hearing this, as if I had been found out doing something illegal. He hitched his sports bag over his shoulder and we exchanged a few pleasantries, heading to the warmth of the café with a beaming Leo in tow. After some small talk, we ended up in front of two glasses of wine and an apple juice for Leo, who was chatting happily over a plate of pasta bolognaise. To this day, I cannot tell why being fond of a little boy had meant that I trusted his dad more quickly than any other stranger.

'I must admit that I wouldn't have picked you among a group of potential dads,' I said eventually, with a cheeky grin. Alcohol had that effect on me that even half a glass of wine could easily loosen my tongue.

'Yes, I know you probably wonder how this little fellow could be my son.'

I reassured him that I had met a family with three children as a child and had seriously wondered for years how they could even be remotely related to their parents. They each looked so different; had features that could not be connected to the others.

'He must take after his mother,' I said casually. David instantly seemed to change. My words must have struck like lightning because, as soon as they were out of my mouth, they took a life of their own and caused him to hunch up, lower his eyes, and twist his fingers. I also noticed a nervous tapping of his foot, which added to the overall unease. I had said the wrong thing or, at least, I must have said it in the wrong way, I thought. David's friendly, jokey mood had changed to a clammed-up posture and the atmosphere turned awkward. What if Leo's mother had died? Or maybe he was his step-dad? Many scenarios were plausible. How insensitive of me.

'I'm very sorry for saying that.' David raised his hand and waved it dismissively, reassuring me that no harm was done. No further word was mentioned about the mother and I decided to leave it at that until he would maybe be ready to explain himself. Looking from David to Leo, I concluded that at least their hair colour and the lightness of their eyes were strikingly similar, two features that could connect them clearly as father and son. But what I was really thinking about at that very moment was, *Is there something wrong with the little fellow? He's so small.* I was curious to know why Leo was the way he was. I knew I had spoken too quickly, but sensed that talking about Leo's mother was completely taboo.

'Really, I'm so sorry. I realise this is awkward and it's none of my business.' I smiled uncomfortably, trying desperately to re-establish the ease of our initial meeting.

'It's OK, Sophie. I understand you have lots of questions and … I wish it was simple but it isn't.' He indicated to me with a glance to Leo that it was not a good moment to talk about it.

'Sure. I understand.' I didn't really, but sensed that

I had no choice but to accept for now.

Despite a difficult parting, David and I did click and the fact that, during an hour long conversation, Leo was edging closer to my side until we felt stuck at the hips, was a sign that he trusted and liked me. I must have been exuding the confidence of whom I was – a person who had been raised in a loving, caring family, where there had always been someone to fall back on if things had got a bit rough.

Initially, I had been a bit startled and uncomfortable with David, but not for long, because anyone who had met his son, seen his big blue eyes and felt his trusting nature lock onto theirs, would have faltered, too, I'm sure of that. He made me believe that I could trust David. He was reserved at first, his eyes shifted and darted this way and that way, but I had put that down to him being a bit nervous, embarrassed probably. After all, he had to admit to leaving his son unattended at the busiest time of day because it *was* the busiest time of day. No one had questioned him because people would have thought that, surely, one of the many adults lingering in the café must have been Leo's parent. In the meantime, I presumed that he was lifting weights or attempting to outrun a friend at squash.

At some point he had hinted on Leo's mother being a bit unreliable but hadn't said why. His sigh had made me feel sorry for him again. Maybe it was only curiosity, maybe the attraction to the unknown, but I became hooked on meeting David, initially at the café, handing over Leo as if I had been a professional childminder all along, then later at the park on weekends or a local playground where we would watch Leo play, sipping on our take-away lattes.

'Thank you so much for being Leo's friend. You're all he ever talks about these days,' he said one day, while I was in the middle of tying Leo's shoelaces.

I simply shrugged my shoulders, smiling, not knowing how to respond. I realised then that my unease was due to the fact that I wanted to be more than just his friend.

Sitting in my jogging bottoms and a T-Shirt at my small kitchen table later that night, I pondered my feelings again. I was upset for failing to broach the topic of Leo's mum for the umpteenth time. I had been determined to find out what was going on. And then he'd said that I was Leo's friend - *only* a friend, I added in my head. *What else did I think I was?* I scolded myself then, but it was a question that was to be answered soon.

It was without any warning that one day he reached his arms around my waist, placing his hands on the small of my back, and pulled me close to him, his chin pressing lightly into my forehead. When he let go again it was in order to cup my face between his hands and kiss me. Goose bumps travelled down my spine, making my heart beat faster, and I closed my eyes and drifted off, letting myself forget the world around us, floating, until we were interrupted by a small person embracing our legs and pressing his head between our hips. Leo's upturned face said it all: he was happy to watch our growing intimacy. A strand of curls blew into my face and, before I could tuck it back behind my ear, David had reached for it and lifted it aside to give me another kiss on my cheek. His eyes were watching me intently, almost amused. For the first time in a while I felt able to share my deepest feelings with a person, other than members of my family and my closest friend.

The first evening that I was officially invited to their two-bedroom flat, I was surprised by the lack of light in the windows that were visible from the road. David had explained in detail how to find his apartment, where to park, and which buzzer to press. I had done just that and sure enough, after ringing the bell, the door opened remotely at the entrance.

I had stepped into a typical modern staircase, cold light-coloured tiles greeting my high heels and echoing the sound off the walls as I climbed up. When I arrived at the top flat I saw the door slightly ajar and as soon as I opened it further I was greeted by a warm, soft kiss. I was in darkness, being kissed by whom I was hoping was Leo's father. It was disconcerting as much as it was an experience that made my stomach flutter, and my fingers pressed into his shirt to stop them from shaking with nerves. To be greeted so secretively with one of my senses unavailable to me, I understood then what it was truly like to be swept off my feet. For hours thereafter I would remain in a bit of a daze.

David had managed to surprise me and create a feeling of adventure. I was equally torn between ease and unease. He was clearly a man who didn't like routine. A few candles had been placed and lit around the room, creating a gentle glow that I found strangely reassuring. I felt the small hairs on my neck tingle and my arms were covered in goose bumps. Had he done this before, I wondered. Next, I found myself entangled by his arms and legs. What would have happened if I had resisted? All I did manage to whisper into his ear, in between our passionate endeavours, was the question of whether Leo could hear us.

'No, he's not with me tonight,' he answered swiftly.

'Oh. I thought …'

'Shhh, I wanted to surprise you. Don't spoil it.'

He did surprise me indeed, and I left the next morning having been spoiled with an intensely sensual night and an elaborate breakfast – fresh coffee with croissants and a variety of jams, freshly squeezed orange juice and to round it all off nicely, a few slices of smoked salmon with dill. I left well fed and deliciously sore. I didn't notice then the odd marks on the wall, the slightly musty smell of the sofa in the living room, or mind having had to share one big towel with David. These details entered my subconscious but were brushed over by looking through rose tinted glasses. I saw adventure then, where later I would see something very different.

'I'm a consultant for a big marketing firm,' he had told me. 'It pays the bills.' He had winked at me and, before I could ask him any further details, he was firing questions at me instead. David wanted to know more details about my job, my family and friends, my hobbies, exactly where I had gone to school and university. I don't remember anyone ever showing as much interest in me as he had that morning. It was like opening all of the doors, curtains, and wardrobes of my house, then leaving my diary out for a person with an insatiable interest in every small detail of my life - past and present - to read. I put it down to his fear of being hurt ... again. He'd hinted on that much himself, with downcast eyes and a warm hand resting on the top of my thigh.

Subsequently, we would meet either at a restaurant he had 'specially' chosen for us, or at the cinema to watch a movie he'd heard 'amazing reviews' about, or at a cocktail party organised by one of his longest standing clients. He'd make sure that I dressed appropriately for the occasion, having previously made a comment about my wardrobe being a bit frumpy and in need of a lift. He had a way of taking control and convincing me that I had to improve on my various flaws, without making me suspect that he was just making me do what he wanted. I rarely ever got to stay at his apartment again, but I did become Leo's childminder every time I stepped into the gym in the late afternoon, playing and reading with him, looking after him as if I was his mother. My part-time job at a PR firm meant that I could dedicate the rest of my time to writing literary reviews for women's magazines, as a freelancer. Rather than work at home, I'd take my laptop to the café in order to spend as much time as possible with Leo, yet not for long.

It had begun with one of David's text messages, telling me that Leo had begged for me to pick him up and be taken to my place. Would I mind? I felt like I should have thought he was being cheeky but I actually relished the idea of meeting Leo at the gym's play area, his arms wrapping around me for dear life as soon as we spotted each other, and that David trusted me enough to ask me this favour. I was so proud holding his hand and taking him with me as if he was my own son. The thought alone had been exhilarating and hence I'd agreed on the spot. Only ten minutes later, my hasty agreement to look after him became the cause of an embarrassing telephone conversation with my best friend Anjali. She asked me where we would meet that night, prior to the movie we had planned to watch. I had completely forgotten about our agreed rendezvous, something completely out of character for me. My feelings of elation about walking home with Leo to *my* place had taken precedent over everything else. I quickly made up a lame excuse about not feeling right and asked if she would mind if we met another day. The idea of having to explain my involvement with a single dad and his little boy seemed too complicated. *Why?* I ask myself now.

I also started buying toys to entertain Leo at my place - children's books, various basic card games such as 'Old Maid', and Lego. I gradually learnt what made Leo smile and laugh.

As we walked down the street towards my flat that day, I noticed a woman sitting on the front steps outside one of the houses across the road, facing our direction. Despite straining my eyes, I couldn't make out whether she was known to me or not. I hadn't yet become accustomed to wearing my new glasses all day but decided there and then to brush my vanity aside and I picked them out of my purse to set them on my nose. I had also instinctively tightened my grip on Leo's hand and it was enough to startle him and stop his current flow of chatter, as he looked up at me. I smiled at him reassuringly and told him that we should hurry as it did look like it was going to rain at any minute. The sky was dark and menacing, as if preparing for a heavy downpour, and the air had grown chilly with the fading light. As we reached the entrance to my apartment, just in time to shelter from the first raindrops, I quickly threw another glance over my shoulder to check that I had seen correctly. The woman on the steps had vanished.

'Oh, thank goodness we made it in time.'

'I don't mind getting wet,' Leo said, looking at me as if he knew I was relieved about more than just avoiding the rain. He'd been right. I had to get used to the fact that our friendship was well and truly becoming the centre of my life. Cancelling dates with friends was going to be one of the many things I'd do in order to make room for my little guy and his father.

I told Leo to make himself at home and have a look around but he decided to sit down on the sofa first, waiting patiently for my attention. He smiled each time I poked my head around the doorframe to check that he was still there. I had put the kettle on, taken some chocolate biscuits from the cupboard, some fresh grapes from the fridge, and opened a carton of apple juice. I prepared our improvised afternoon tea on a tray and walked through to the living room, where I found Leo standing in front of a picture frame, intently staring at my family members all lined up and smiling at the camera.

'That's a picture of my family.'

'I know.' He looked up at me cheekily.

'Oh sorry, I sometimes forget just how clever you are. How did you work that out?' He just shrugged in response. I ruffled his fluffy hair, giggling, and asked him if he'd like to join me for a snack. His eyes lit up at the sight of chocolate biscuits, grapes and apple juice. Then followed an avalanche of questions about my family, interrupted by flying crumbs, crunching and gulping, with big blue eyes looking at me intently as he listened to my answers. Leo wanted to know everything and anything. His attention span was impressive for a six-year-old.

'Do you have any homework to do?'

'Yes, I've got to do a bit of reading and I've got spellings to learn.'

'So, should we get going with that?'

'Will you help me?' He jumped up to fetch his schoolbag and I nodded and gestured for him to sit at the table in the kitchen. When I opened his spelling book I was greeted by neat, regular handwriting. I looked at him with wide eyes and exclaimed, 'I don't think I wrote that nicely when I was your age. Well done, sweetheart.'

After showing off his reading skills, followed by a round of games on the living room floor, I told him that we should start preparing dinner. We both poked our noses into the fridge and the adjoining cupboard and decided on soup for starters, a salmon main course and ice cream for dessert.

'Can I help?' he asked eagerly.

'Of course, you must actually. I need an assistant.' I put my mobile on radio mode and we started setting the table and pulling out all of the necessary ingredients onto the kitchen counter. I took a picture of the two of us and posted it to my Facebook account with the caption, 'Cooking with a special friend today'.

David joined us after work, drenched to the bone. He told me that he often had to meet clients and frequently would have to organise a babysitter or, in the worst case scenario – here he looked sadly at me with a 'you know' - which I knew meant leaving Leo at the gym in order to meet his employer's expectations. He'd arrived with a big bunch of flowers, his smile bigger than ever, thanking me profusely for taking Leo home with me.

'I can do this any time, David. I'd much rather be the one looking after Leo than him being alone at the health club. You know you could lose custody for doing things like that.' My reproach hovered in the air for a short time and, upon hearing my words, David's broad smile disappeared, his shoulders drooped, and he sat down heavily on one of the dining room chairs.

'I know but I …well, we don't really know each other that well yet. Can I really ask you to do me such a big favour?'

'Yes, you can, and please switch that smile back on. That broody face doesn't become you. Leo and I have planned a three-course menu extraordinaire and we expect a bit of enthusiasm. This is Masterchef in the making.'

From then on it was a verbally sealed agreement that I would look after Leo on the days that David was tied up with meetings and we'd round off the day with dinner at my apartment.

'Come on Daddy, I'll show you to your seat.' Leo's little voice sounded squeaky and gentle but he was capable of adding an undertone that implied that refusals were not permitted.

Later that night, when I was already nestled under my duvet and blissfully about to drift off, I received a text from David.

Honey, thank you so much for an amazing evening, the dinner, and everything really. I'm so sorry to have to ask you this awkward request. Please don't ever post a picture on Facebook again with Leo. I will explain tomorrow. Big hugs and sleep well. xxx

My brain was racing with confusion. What had I done wrong? After that message I wrestled with my thoughts along with the urge to just call him and ask him outright, but I knew he had an early meeting the next day and that he had to be up at the crack of dawn to prepare some notes before waking Leo and setting off to work. What made the text even more uncomfortable was the fact that Anjali had left a comment on Facebook as well and reminded me that I should stick to the truth when it came to changing plans with my best friend. As for David's message, I concluded that it must be hard to be a single parent, and difficult to decide whether posting a picture of a young child on social media was safe. I couldn't help but be annoyed though, that it was OK in his eyes to leave a child in a busy café on his own, yet unacceptable for Leo to be seen cooking with … well, was I his girlfriend? It took me a cup of hot milk with honey and half an hour's reading to settle back to my initial slumbering self.

When I woke the next day I texted him back.

I'm sorry, I should have checked with you whether you'd be okay with me posting a picture of Leo. He's so young, after all. See you later and good luck for the meeting. xxx

That's how Leo and I started a habit of locking hands at the gym and walking to the underground station together, chatting until we reached my front door. He would not stop asking questions, babbling away about his day in school and telling me who did what to whom, why, and when. He was an astute observer and I could tell he was starving for a dedicated listener. My living room changed from slick and tidy to being invaded by toys and boys' jumpers. I often ended up finishing my articles late at night or getting up earlier to finish an assignment. When David managed to join us in the evenings, an outsider looking in would have seen a picture of the ideal, happy family. Only this was not going to last. David's moods started to bother me. He was either open, warm and smiley, or edgy, withdrawn and serious. His work schedule had pushed me to set up a bed for Leo, which of course meant getting him up in the morning, making him breakfast and then driving him to school. Unfortunately, this did not tie in well with my job and I would frequently arrive at work late, tired, and irritable. When I did scold David, his eyes would either be downcast, looking for sympathy, or he'd reach out for an amorous embrace, making it impossible for me to shrug him off. What really held our relationship together, I knew, was Leo. Brave little Leo.

The only rule that David asked me to respect – apart from never posting pictures on social media depicting my many activities with him and Leo, changing my wardrobe, and accepting that his work was tough and demanding – was never to ask any questions about Leo's mum.

'It's been very difficult – the separation and all – I just can't talk to you about this yet, but all I can say is that Leo is better off without his mum.'

Those last words struck me as significant. People often say things and forget that you can interpret more into them than they believe they are giving away. If someone tells you only part of a story, you will wonder, and not always in their favour. I somehow gathered then that Leo's mum had no access to her own son and that even if I didn't know why this was the case, I was hoping that it was for a good reason. I could not deny that suspicion had crept into my mind. *Was David being honest with me? What if the injured party was Leo's mother?* I do feel ambivalence when two people fight. *Can there be only one truth? What if we are all creating our own truth, as we often need to, on a daily basis?* After all, we cannot be honest and straight all of the time, lest we hurt people's feelings. When people fall in love they all too frequently merge their beliefs and desires into one common plan. That is problematic at the best of times. If one is a more dominating character, the other is inclined to fight back or surrender. I wasn't sure which, if any of these situations, was applicable to David and his ex-partner, or David and me for that matter.

When I asked David, months into our relationship, why Leo was so small, he answered gruffly that some people were born tall, others small. *Why does it matter?* he asked. I know I was not a mother in the strictest sense of the term and I could only empathise with any parent who had to accept that their off-spring was somehow not quite the average height for their age, not quite as resilient, or was unusually mature. Leo was all of these things and I found it disconcerting.

'Look Sophie, Leo is small because he probably doesn't eat enough fruit and vegetables. Maybe you can try and convince him.' He'd taken me into his arms apologetically, diverting the attention. I nodded, not so much because I agreed with his idea, but because of my conviction that Leo needed a normal routine, regular meals, and friends his own age. When I asked Leo whether he wanted a playmate to come round one day, I was surprised that he didn't answer straight away. He had been in the middle of doing a puzzle when I prompted him. His frown clearly indicated to me that I should give him space to ponder. I was by then well aware that he seemed entirely content with his own company, but it was the intense hugs and long reading sessions, stuck together on the sofa, that brought back his need for love and affection. It seemed only right to organise a play date for him. He finally answered with a shrug and a non-committal pout of his mouth.

'Have you ever invited a friend over for play?' I insisted.

'No, never. Daddy has no time.'

'Of course, silly me. Your daddy is working very hard. Tell me if there is ever a friend that you'd like to bring home, will you?' He simply nodded and continued building a Lego spaceship.

Eventually, curiosity got the upper hand of me. I did ask him outright about where his mother was. He went quiet, when just moments earlier he'd filled my attentive ears with laughter and chitchat. The way his eyes moved made me guess that he'd gone to and come back from a place I could not see.

'She's in another place, somewhere safe,' he answered calmly, yet I could just make out that he was clenching his teeth when he spoke. Initially, his words startled me, then their effect caused a nagging feeling that this sentence had been repeated with care more than once. So, his mother was somewhere and she was safe. I decided to go no further, for fear that it could upset Leo.

Had she actually died? Was she mentally ill? Had she done a runner? I had always had a vivid imagination and this meant that my list of possible scenarios was long.

Spring made way for summer and David suggested we spend a few days by the sea in a little town near Brighton. It had been unusually hot and clammy in London, so taking a break from our busy schedules and getting some colour into Leo's white cheeks was a welcome project. He'd been nursing a sore throat and high fever, which made me discover the tough side of parenting. Looking back at the sleepless nights and hearing David begging for my help, mostly at the other end of a phone line, I learnt what it was like to live on caffeine. I didn't notice the moment of transition either, when my settled routine – a great job, my freelance projects, and family and friends – was sidelined so that I could look after a young child and his exhausted father. I relished the idea of a break, away from the chaos and the constant juggling of my timetable, and I was especially looking forward to us all being together under one roof for longer than the customary few hours.

As we settled into our compartment on the train, Leo and I pulled out activity books and colouring pens. David had relaxed into his seat, amused with our abundant amount of energy. The strain he'd been under in recent months was visible by the dark circles under his eyes but, despite the fact he had not elaborated any further about 'his past', we had created something that resembled a normal family life. David had kept his flat for convenience but most nights he joined Leo and me in my apartment. There was talk of us moving in together somewhere bigger, but accommodation was expensive in a metropolis so, for the time being, we decided to keep to a routine that suited us all.

We were half way through our journey to the coast when I noticed a lady sitting diagonally opposite from us. She wore a dirty rain coat, her hair was filthy, and as my eyes subtly travelled down her silhouette they settled on a pair of muddy Wellington boots. *How strange, to wear boots in summer*, I thought, and before I could avert my gaze from the stranger's piercing set of eyes, she looked at me. I flinched for a second then she smiled with a grimace before I turned away. As London commuters, we are used to encounters with 'odd' people - those who carry a glazed look in their eyes, wear clothes that are in dire need of a wash, and have demeanour that strongly suggests serious psychological issues. David had dozed off, so I quickly lowered my eyes down towards Leo, who'd nearly finished one of his join-the-dots puzzles. The exchange of looks had made me shudder, even more so when I became aware, from the corner of my eye, of a shadow passing through the aisle. I knew that it was her because of the stale, musty smell left behind. I sighed with relief, noticing that Leo was watching me over his colouring pens.

'Did you see that odd lady?'

His innocent eyes travelled from one passenger to another, searching for a lady that could pass as 'odd'. He shook his head.

'Never mind. Luckily she didn't stay long,' I answered, beaming a reassuring smile at him and commenting on his current choice of colouring pen to divert his attention.

It took me a considerable amount of time to relax again. I kept looking up to check whether David's twitching was an indication that he was waking up. Noticing the circles under his eyes made me soften with empathy. No wonder he sometimes switched moods abruptly. It couldn't be easy to work full-time for a demanding boss and raise a small child at the same time.

When he woke up eventually, he looked at me with bleary eyes and a soft smile, and I envied his oblivion of not knowing what had gone on so far. Shortly after, an announcement was made, telling us that we would soon be arriving at the train's final destination. As we started gathering our belongings I quickly told David about the creepy encounter, consciously choosing my words so that they would not worry Leo. He asked me what the woman had looked like and when I gave him a sketchy description, his shoulders seemed to relax and he said, 'Just a weirdo. But let me know if she bothers you again, okay?'

A jolly taxi driver took us to our holiday accommodation in Peacehaven, a little town on the outskirts of Brighton. It had seemed far enough away from civilisation, but close enough to allow us to dip our toes into shopping and leisure activities if we felt like it. The weather was set to remain unusually hot and, despite a heavy haze covering the sky, we could make out the chalk cliffs and the nearby sea from our rented cottage. Within minutes we made the acquaintance of the elderly couple next door, who assured us that the owner renting out our place would arrive within minutes to talk us through the property. And true enough, a cheerful lady arrived in her blue car shortly after, enquiring about our travels and insisting that we must be exhausted and that we should come in quickly as it was too hot to stay outdoors. Seemingly without as much as a breath, she continued commenting on what a cute little fellow Leo was, impressed that he was nearly six, and asked whether we needed any information about the area. Then she went on and on until we knew about every single hob and door handle in the house and she had finally offloaded her rich repertoire of small talk. Phew! was all we could say to each other and burst out laughing as soon as the lady had pulled the front door closed with a click, her eau de cologne still lingering in the air. I instinctively reached for the window handle and opened it out wide, inviting in the smell of the sea, the sound of the crashing waves, and the shrieks of seagulls nearby.

'Let's have a little snack and a cup of tea and then head out. I read online there are steps leading down to the beach. We must explore, what do you think?' David picked me up with a spontaneous outburst of happiness, kissed me, and agreed, giving his son a high five. Leo was beaming and I decided there and then that I'd never been happier before. I pushed aside my siblings' concern regarding the age difference between David and me, my parents' reluctance to call our relationship serious, and my disappointment of not meeting David's family yet. What was it with everyone that they couldn't accept that I was happy with an older guy who happened to have a son, who I incidentally loved from the first moment I had set eyes on him?

We nestled onto the sofa after I'd brought out a tray with steaming hot tea, a glass of lemonade, and a plate of biscuits. The view of the sea suddenly brought the quiet and calmness to our attention. After hours of travelling, listening to people's chatter, moving bags and dozing, we'd arrived in a neat place where we could give our busy heads a rest.

When an hour later we all slipped through the front door, our feet free at last to breathe in flip flops and sandals, we could make out a figure walking on the path facing the sea.

'Look Leo, we're not alone. That's where we're heading as well.' I pointed to the person ambling down towards the open sea and took deep breaths of fresh air, motioning to Leo to do likewise, who decided to skip off instead, pick up the small stones strewn in our way and drop them into his bucket. David wrapped an arm around my waist and we made plans for dinner that night, deciding that it had to be fish and chips.

'Wouldn't it be nice to live by the sea?' I mused.

'Yes, it'd be bliss,' David answered, with a faraway look in his eyes.

He unhooked his arm and sneaked up behind Leo, picking him up with a roar, and said that he'd have to throw him into the sea for a swim with the fish. Leo giggled and laughed, writhing under his dad's hands. It was so easy to pick the boy up, what with his feather-light body and delicate bone structure. I never seized to be amazed by the contrast between David and Leo. As much as their appearance was like chalk and cheese, their temperaments were more similar. They were equally serious and sensitive, yet able to switch and laugh about the silliest of jokes.

David ran back, gathering me up as well, swinging me round and stopping to kiss me longingly on the lips. As we walked on downhill, I gave him a side-ways glance and thought if ever there was a man that I'd wanted a child with, it was David. As we reached the lowest set of steps, directly leading onto the pebble beach, the cloud that had created a hazy, humid mist suddenly lifted and the sun broke through. I had conscientiously set a cap onto Leo's head but had forgotten about myself.

'I forgot to bring my sunglasses, David. I'll quickly nip back to the house and fetch them. I won't be able to stand this glare otherwise.'

'Okay, we'll just stay close by. I'll start making a stone castle with Leo.' He smiled at me and gave me another quick peck on the cheek.

'Come back quick,' Leo bellowed.

The walk back uphill reminded me of the sudden tiredness that had earlier come over me. It had been a long day. As I turned back into our road, I could somehow sense someone's eyes on me. I was well aware that local residents in the street probably wouldn't want to miss observing tourists like us. We were a welcome distraction from boredom, I imagined. And sure enough, as I searched the windows, I saw a curtain fall as soon as I was about to lock eyes with the spectator. I stifled a laugh and wondered how I would handle being watched daily, was I ever to live in a small village. It made me shudder at the thought, everyone knowing me and all of my little idiosyncrasies. Come to think of it, I would possibly start prying and meddling myself.

I swiftly entered the silent cottage and picked up

my glasses in the hall, just where I remembered leaving them. I took a quick mouthful of water from the bottle that was cooling in the fridge and looked out onto the tiny garden that adjoined the kitchen. It was lined with small yellow flowers and a hedge that was about as tall as Leo. I could make out footprints on the lawn that looked like it had recently been watered. The place was in perfect condition and when I had checked the bedrooms earlier on, every fold of bedding had been meticulously ironed and the pillows piled up symmetrically. I was almost afraid to sit down anywhere in case it was like a house of cards that would come crushing down with the slightest change.

As I hurried back to the entrance, keys jangling in my hand and lightly humming to myself, my heart suddenly stopped beating as I came face to face with a woman standing in the doorway. I gasped, recognising her instantly - it was the woman I'd seen on the train. I swallowed, telling myself to stay calm, but I felt my heart race. I was shocked and panicked and my voice rose an octave too high when I finally drew another breath to confront her.

'What on earth are you doing here?' I managed to squeak, trying to look behind the lady in case I would see someone who could help me. I was unable to decide what the best course of action was, when the woman answered.

'It's such a funny coincidence that you're staying here. I saw you arrive earlier on and remembered you from the train.' Her voice was eerily calm and she seemed to weigh up each word.

'Yeees,' I added, trying to calm my nerves by stepping outside and closing the door behind me. 'You gave me such a fright just standing there.'

'Oh, I'm so sorry. I was just going to ring the door bell.'

'Really?' The word came out sarcastically, yet the woman did not seem to catch on to my undertone, as she continued to talk and followed me down the small path leading to the sea.

'Yes, just to say hello - as we're neighbours now.'

This was getting creepier by the second and I decided to cut her off there and then. All I wanted was to get back to David and Leo and escape from this strange encounter.

'If you don't mind, we're here to have a quiet holiday and we aren't looking for any company. So, if you'll excuse me, I'd like to get on. Have a nice day.'

I tried to walk as confidently and calmly as I could, but by the time I'd reached the place where I had parted from Leo and David, I was hyperventilating and running. This meeting had put a damper on my initial happiness and I was determined not to let it spoil our holiday any further. What had made it all the worse was the smirk that the woman had thrown me when I'd told her about our wish for a quiet holiday. I thought, *what a psycho*.

As soon as I saw the silhouettes of a stocky man and a child in the distance I started to slow down my pace and, by the time I reached them, my bare feet were enjoying the feeling of the warm stones, a slight breeze was cooling my cheeks, and my pulse had calmed. David and Leo greeted me warmly, so I managed to bottle up my anxiety until the moment that Leo decided to wander down to the water's edge to fill his bucket. David's face turned a grade paler when I quickly told him about the strange woman. He asked me a long list of questions, such as how the lady had spoken and exactly what she'd looked like.

'Why are you asking me all this?'

'Well, if she does start to seriously annoy us – stalk us – then we'd have to be able to describe her to the police.'

'Yes, I guess you're right. Who knows, maybe she's a druggie? If I had to imagine a person with a drug addiction, she'd be the perfect fit, I tell you.'

David took me in his arms and hugged me reassuringly.

That evening and the next day I kept looking over my shoulder, scanning the various curtained windows in the street, and observed our neighbours whenever we happened to see any. Most of them turned out to be elderly couples and I also noticed two young families and a lady dressed in a business suit. Apart from these people, there was no sign of the scruffy stranger who had so startled me on our first day. I started breathing more freely again and had almost forgotten about her until later on the third evening, as I was cooking a meal for the three of us. I'd thrown spaghetti into a big pot of boiling water and cut up fresh herbs. mushrooms, aubergine and tomatoes for a veggie sauce. I was taking plates and cutlery through to the dining room table when I froze in horror. From the corner of my eye I was able to sense that something or someone had appeared outside of the front window. My heart started thumping and at first I was scared to raise my head. I smoothed down one of the napkins, pretending I hadn't noticed, then managed to pull myself together and look up. A face was staring straight into the front of the living room, where Leo was focusing on his latest Lego creation on the carpet. He was completely unaware of the person observing him, only occasionally looking up at the television that was set on the cartoon channel. I heard David whistling under the shower upstairs. I clearly experienced then why there was a saying that an upsetting incident could make one's blood run cold. It was literally what I felt when I saw that ghostly face staring at our little boy. I reassured myself that

Leo was still too absorbed to notice anything and quietly sneaked through the kitchen to reach the front door. At that moment, David walked out of the bathroom and must have seen me approach the entrance in a strange manner, treading quietly along the corridor.

'Where are you heading, beautiful person?' he called from the top of the stairs, frowning slightly.

As I turned to look at him, his smile froze as he saw my ashen face and understood that something was amiss. I motioned to him and whispered that I had seen the weird lady again, this time staring into the living room from outside.

'I've had enough of this person spoiling our holiday.' he said, rushing towards the door, oblivious of the fact that he only had a small towel wrapped around his waist and wet hair sticking up every which way. There was no one in sight as he stepped outside, marched barefoot to the small front gate, and checked whether anyone was hiding behind the hedge or standing anywhere near the property.

'She's gone, that witch.'

I remember telling Leo - who'd heard the commotion and jumped up from the carpet and joined us wide-eyed at the entrance - that we thought we'd heard someone knocking at the door but that we must have been wrong. David and I exchanged a conspiratorial look and, to distract Leo from asking any further questions, I told everyone to gather for dinner. I'd grilled fresh prawns with herbs and had mixed them in with the spaghetti and sauce. We were all famished and although we did not mention the strange incident again, both David and I wondered about the intentions of our unwanted visitor. What if the woman was very lonely, had lost her husband, was childless? Many questions raced through my head as I tried to convince myself that maybe I should have been a bit kinder. Yet, she had given me a weird stare on the train, accosted me when I'd headed back to fetch my sunglasses, and now she'd looked through the living room window, staring at Leo – all of which was way too creepy. But it did not make her a person with criminal intent.

That night, I tossed and turned in bed long after Leo and David had slipped into blissful sleep. The full moon was stuck onto the starlit sky like a giant, bright sticker. I decided to get up and warm up some milk in the kitchen, and stirred in a spot of honey, which I'd found in one of the cupboards. With my drink made, I switched on a lamp next to the sofa in the living room and set the steaming cup down on the side table, noticing a slither of light coming from the opposite side of the road. So, I wasn't the only insomniac that night, I thought, lifting a magazine onto my lap and sipping at the sweet drink while leafing through the pages.

About half way through the magazine, I heard Leo murmur in his sleep and went to check if he might have actually woken, like he sometimes did during the night. As I reached his bedroom door, I heard him murmur again. This time I could make out a few of the words he was saying, and as I looked down on his small frame lying sprawled over his crumpled bedsheet, I watched as he continued to speak in his sleep.

'My Mum's helper …crazy …'

I gently lowered my face towards his ear and asked, 'Are you OK, Leo? Who is Mum's helper?' His face twitched before another flow of words came out of his mouth.

'A special secret … don't tell.'

I was not only very confused but starting to feel a

71

growing suspicion about David's reluctance to reveal details about his past. Leo was having a strange dream and, despite my whispering and soothing, his mumbling only let up later in the night. David's sleep was as deep as a hibernating bear's, so I decided to finish my lukewarm drink and after rinsing my mouth with tap water, slipped back under the duvet.

What Leo had said stuck with me long into the next day, but I felt it would possibly embarrass him to ask him whether he knew the significance of his words. If I had said something to him then, maybe events would have unfolded differently. What led me to ignore this opportunity was more than just self-delusion. I knew that I was deliberately pushing it out of my mind and avoiding a confrontation because I feared that my own role as an adopted Mum would be put in jeopardy.

We decided to spend an afternoon in Brighton and, despite my repeated yawns and aching muscles, I relished the stroll through the city's main shopping centre. I was looking for a new pair of sandals and hoping to pick up a few new activity books for Leo. We all entered the bookshop together, picking up a magazine here and a book there, strolling through the aisles, when Leo spotted a puzzle and sticker book with a set of pens stuck on the front as a special offer. I agreed to get it for him and he hugged it to his chest, smiling. David called Leo over to another aisle filled with games and toys. I told them I'd have a little wander by myself and was soon engrossed in reading the blurbs of various cheap paperbacks on offer.

The next thing I remember was David rushing towards me in a panic. *Have you seen Leo?* He told me that he'd been chatting to him and when he turned round just a minute ago, he'd vanished. He added, as I knew myself, that Leo would never walk off by himself. At the very least he would ask if he was allowed to wander along an aisle. My heart instantly beat faster, my hands shaking with anxiety as I caught onto David's panicked explanations. I ran to the nearby cashier first, telling her that we were looking for our son, six years old, black-haired, wearing shorts and a bright red T-Shirt. I said son and really, at that moment, I felt like my child was gone, my flesh and blood violently ripped away from me. We ran through every aisle, asking people if they'd seen a boy in a red T-shirt. They all shook their heads and then started looking for Leo as well. I ran outside looking up and down the alley of shops but all I could see was a sea of bodies and shopping bags. There was no sign of Leo anywhere. I knew that he would never have walked off with a stranger and if someone had as much as dared set a finger on him, his high-pitched voice would have carried far enough to alert either David or me. I started hyperventilating, joining David in his frantic search, tears brimming in my eyes then flowing down my cheeks. He held me briefly, reassuring me that the shop manager had already alerted the shopping centre's main desk and that security had been informed, who were on their way to the main entrances. CCTV cameras were being scanned for any adult with a young, slight child in tow. All the horror stories of lost children - the Madeleine McCann's and Jamie Bulger's and all the others whose names I couldn't remember - came flooding back into my mind. My hands were still shaking and I couldn't help feeling like a trapped animal who was forever repeating the same movements again and again but to no avail. We had lost Leo. He seemed to have slipped away from right under our watchful eyes. Yet, not watchful enough, I kept cursing myself.

That's when it hit me, and without having the time to tell David I ran off, shouting to him to keep looking and that I was heading back to the bookshop. I rushed into the aisle where we had last seen Leo and looked around, then spotted what I subconsciously had noticed before but had not paid full attention to. The sticker book Leo had insisted on carrying himself was lying on the floor. Further ahead, I noticed a door with the word 'private' on it, and turned as pale as a hospital wall when I noticed it had been left slightly ajar. I ran towards it and pulled it open, despite a member of staff behind me calling out that this was not an area accessible to customers. I was thinking that if there was anywhere in the shop where Leo could still be, it was behind that door. So I carried on regardless, ignoring a member of staff who was eating a sandwich and obviously unaware of the missing child. After rushing past his cubicle and being told, again, that 'sorry madam, this is for staff only,' I heard the noise that alerted me to another adjacent room. What I saw gave me a feeling I had never ever felt in my life – the exhilaration and relief of a mother finding a lost child. Leo was sitting on the floor, whimpering and talking to himself. As soon as he saw me he ran into my outstretched arms, his tiny frame slumping against my tummy, his wet cheeks streaking the bottom of my T-shirt. I didn't care what anyone would say and I picked him up right there, holding him tight as he wrapped his legs around my hips and rested his head on my shoulder. My tears started to flow again as I breathed soothing words into his ear. The questions would be asked soon enough, but at that moment all that mattered was holding Leo close. He wriggled free when he spotted David in the shop, and when we stepped back into the non-restricted area, we stood for what seemed an age, just huddled together like a group of penguins. We were a family again. *Safe and sound, safe and sound, safe and sound*, I muttered into Leo's ear.

Then came the questions from the shop manager and the shopping centre's security staff. But bizarrely, whatever information anyone tried to squeeze out of Leo, nothing came. He just shook his head, gazing up at me and David. He was close to tears again because the pressure was getting to him.

'Sweetheart, at the very least, we need to know whether you walked into the staff room by yourself or if someone made you. If someone did take you, please tell us. No one is allowed to do that to you without asking your parents, you know.'

Leo answered with a great sniff and then, with a barely audible whisper, said, 'A lady asked me to follow her. She said she had a message from my mum.'

'What do you mean?' At these words, David came alive again, brushing his hand through his hair and looking very agitated. Meanwhile, I was carrying the deepest frown on my face and I suddenly noticed that I was drenched with the exertion of frantically running and searching for Leo. This was all so confusing. It struck me as more than odd to be on holiday with two people, I had to admit, whom I knew very little about. We had been shopping and, within seconds, one of them had vanished from the surface of the earth, only to reappear in tears and in pieces half an hour later in an adjacent staff room. It did not make sense and that was exactly what the other adults present at the scene were saying, too. It was suspicious to say the least. *How did they notice me entering the staff-only room and not her?* I wondered, and then said, 'So where did the lady go, Leo? When I found you, you were alone and in tears. Did she hurt you?'

'No, she was really nice to me. She said she'd just go and talk to you and ask whether you'd have a picnic on the beach with us.'

'A picnic?' Both David and I repeated the words with wide-eyed incredulity.

Only later that evening did it dawn on me. When I uttered my suspicions to David, he agreed, sitting up in bed with a start. We decided to get up again and poured ourselves a small glass of sherry from the cabinet in the living room. The bottle did look a bit dusty but a small shot wouldn't hurt, we thought.

'He must have met her before, David. He would

never walk off just like that, would he?' I suggested.

'Oh, I hope it's not all my fault for leaving him all those times at the gym. How does that make me look?'

'Well, I do agree it was foolish, but then there was this amazing woman who came and scooped him up.'

'Hahaha.' We both laughed out loud, then clasped our hands over our mouths to stifle the noise.

'No, honestly, you can't ever do that again. I really thought it was strange to do that. Now we have to wonder whether there's another person Leo has befriended who he's not telling us about. For all we know, it could be that weird woman who's been hanging around,' I said.

'You're so right, Sophie. Children disappear every day and … oh I feel I've been such a bad father.' He cupped his face into his hands. 'My life has been so complicated …' he added, rubbing his eyes as if they were itchy but I assumed that he was wiping away tears.

That's when my curiosity and impatience got the better of me. Above all, an explanation was more than overdue because I was caring for Leo like a mother. I had the right to know.

'Where is Leo's real mother, David?'

'If you think the lady Leo walked off with is his mother, you're mistaken.'

'I wasn't implying that, but please, carry on. Whatever it is, I think you owe me an explanation,' I said, as firmly as I could muster. He'd been an expert at avoiding the topic, but I was no longer going to let him get away with a diversion.

'She's being treated in a psychiatric clinic in the

North of England. She's not the woman who took Leo, because I would have been informed, I'm sure, if she'd been released.'

I was stunned to say the least. So, Leo's mother was mentally unstable. That had been the secret all along.

'And anyway,' he went on, 'Leo doesn't know what his mum looks like.'

'How is that possible?' I exclaimed, astounded. 'Have you never shown him a picture?' I was flabbergasted.

'She was sectioned when he was born.' He pressed his lips together, visibly struggling to continue. 'Her mental state meant she needed therapy and - initially anyway - in isolation. There was one incident when she started screaming at me during one of our many fights and said that she'd kill our baby if I ever told anyone about her losing her job. She'd lost so many so-called friends, the bank was after her, and she'd run up bills with the dentist, shops … the list is long, Sophie. It was awful to live with a deluded lunatic … who wanted to kill my beautiful son.' His right hand was clenched in a fist and his eyes had turned cold. I shivered briefly, hugging myself.

'You need to tell me a bit more please, because this is seriously freaking me out.'

'I thought it would. My ex was a very charming, pretty woman when I first met her. There was nothing I sensed then, that gave away her devious character. Well, I had a suspicion here and there but she was an expert at diverting the attention away from any doubts. In clinical terms, she's been diagnosed as a narcissistic pervert with psychopathic tendencies,' David said, raising his eyebrows knowingly. 'You see, people like her literally feed on others, crush them into submission so that they come out looking good. But by the time I'd finally worked out her strategy, and she was pregnant with my son, her image was gone. She'd created her own world in which she was the most admirable, beautiful, and irresistible creature. But people around her either turned away from her or they were after her because she owed them money. She was lazy as pig shit.'

I cringed upon hearing the swear words, rolling my eyes. It was a bone of contention between us that I disliked bad language, whereas David thought that I was overly sensitive.

'Sorry – anyway, I was the one holding her hand at every move, encouraging her, drying her tears, talking others into believing in her, talking myself into believing in her come to think of it, which is really embarrassing. The problem was though, that she never physically abused me. It was years of mental humiliation. She'd charmed my parents, my friends and family, then made sure I'd become estranged from them. Behind their backs she'd treat me like an imbecile or talk me into believing her fabricated stories about them. Don't get me wrong, it wasn't black and white. These things never are. I did back her up big style. I admit that … but I was frightened.'

'What were you frightened of?' My words came out in a low whisper and I swallowed hard, bracing myself for what I would hear next.

'I was frightened of losing my sanity. It's like backing a villain because if you don't, he'll strike you with a knife at night when you're sleeping, oblivious and defenceless. So, I just went along believing that it was me who was at fault. I lost all my willpower to fight back until the day she threatened to kill my baby.' Tears were welling up in his eyes and it was painful for me to watch.

'Oh, David, this is so awful.'

78

'I believed that she could change. I thought that when she was sorry and tried to make up for whatever stupid thing she'd done or said, she wasn't that bad after all. I did hope that she'd turn for the better with my support. But that never happened.' He sighed heavily. 'I, the stupid slave, thankful for the smallest sorry she'd utter, went along with it until...'

'Until what?'

'Until she threatened to harm MY baby. She knew how desperately I wished to be a father. What she didn't know though, was that one of my friends had overheard her, standing in the room next door. I'd not had the time to tell her that Frank had come home with me that day. We'd been trying to sell a cumbersome barbecue unit for months because we never really used it. He'd decided to move to a bigger place with a garden and it made him think that maybe he'd enjoy having it there. Well, it never came to that because the moment I crossed the threshold she attacked me, starting her endless tirade of reproaches. I let off steam, too, but it only made things worse. It was so embarrassing but it allowed my friend to witness what it was like for me. He admitted to me that he'd been scared of the deranged look on my wife's face. She'd become so pale and skinny, despite being pregnant.'

'So, what happened next?'

'I believe that she tried to seduce him – I remember her saying repeatedly just what a nice guy he was – and that suspicion left a painful thorn in my memory. You're probably thinking how ridiculous this all sounds. Don't say no, please. It *is* ridiculous and had I been capable of accepting that I was never going to change her, ever, it would have ended much earlier.' He was avoiding my gaze, nervously rubbing his eyes.

'But there was Leo.'

'Yes, there was and there is. He's fantastic and thank goodness he made it through in one piece. He's so clever, too.' His eyes were shining with pride then, and I was blinking back tears. I could not help but lean over and give him a long warm hug. However, deep down, somewhere from my stomach down into my guts, I felt awkward. Could someone be that bad? Was I listening to the truth, the whole truth? Was there even such a thing? I was the one who decided to change the topic this time. Instead of sharing my doubts, I concentrated on what we had been through together. I'd seen a glimpse of David's past, but now I wondered what to think about Leo's strange abduction and reappearance.

'I think it's really dodgy what happened today,' I said.

'Well, it reminds me of the feeling I had for all those years that I lived with my ex.'

'What feelings?'

'The fear of losing control, losing everything that was important to me – family, friends, security. I tried to leave her twice and no matter how hard I tried to stay away, she would either shower me with pretend love and affection or reproach and induce feelings of guilt. I didn't see that all she was after was to continue using me so that she could carry on living in her illusory castle. People like her are strangely dependent on people like me. She literally could not even write a CV without my assistance, or respect deadlines, or just be punctual. I've come to learn how some people are good at making things up, worst of all to themselves. It's utterly incredible but you can believe me because I've lived with the champion extraordinaire of illusion and self-deception.'

'She must have been trapped in her own world and unable to connect properly with other people,' I said.

'Yes, you've got it. You're so clever, Sophie. I'm very lucky to have met you. At the time you befriended Leo at the gym, I was only just coming out of the stupor of anger and frustration. So many years I sacrificed for a lunatic.' He patted my head, conveying some kind of pride.

'Don't be too hard on yourself. You need to forgive yourself for believing that you could actually turn things into normality. How did she get sectioned, actually? That's pretty heavy, by modern standards anyway.'

David shook his head, seemingly unable to find the words to answer. I had that feeling of unease again, wondering how a strong man could allow himself to get into such a mess. I swallowed hard this time before asking again, formulating my question differently.

'Why is she not allowed to see Leo?'

'After the major scene that erupted in front of my friend, she packed her bags and left. She knew that I'd try to find her, not so much to bring her back, but for my baby's sake. I wouldn't let her take my child.' I noted with irritation that David was always talking about *his* child or *his* son. I didn't think that was fair. 'That's when I found out that she'd been having an affair for years.'

'How did you find out?'

'I received an email from him.'

'What? He sent you an email?' I stared at him in surprise.

'Yes, he'd seen us together.'

'So, hang on a minute, when did you get this email?'

David looked at me sadly, his shoulders looking

strangely defeated. 'I found out around the time that my ex announced she was pregnant.'

'Oh. So, did you not suspect that Leo …'

'Leo is my son. I asked for a DNA paternity test to make sure.' He said firmly. 'My ex was very petite and I guess that's why Leo is a bit smaller than average, too. There you have it – no mystery in that.'

For a few minutes we just sat and stared at the light cream carpet in the living room and the Lego castle that Leo had been busy building since we arrived.

'David, would you like a cup of tea? I'm off to make one.' I knew it was so typically English to prepare a cup of tea when confronted by an emotional hurdle, feelings you thought you could not control anymore but would most certainly be kept under a bubbling lid if you sipped away at a hot cup. I needed some time to think about what I had just heard and, especially, I needed to try and make sense of the possibility that Leo's mum was on our heels. How else could we explain Leo's strange abduction?

It was starting to get light outside and I was yawning every few minutes. However, I was determined to hear the whole truth, or at least what David would reveal of it.

'The guy also implied that she wanted a divorce and that I had to let her go.'

'How weird,' I whispered.

'Oh Sophie, you have no idea. I was flabbergasted, angry, shocked, whatever you want to call it. We'd been through two break-ups, endless painful rows, but never had there been talk of a divorce. She'd never leave me because I was the one with a proper job and a small inheritance. It was ludicrous. Why would she leave me when I gave her everything?' My eyes widened and he noticed my raised eyebrows.

'Yes, I know. Why did I not realise that all she ever wanted was my money? She believed that she was entitled to it. From poverty-stricken Cinderella to the rightly-earned status of Princess,' he added in a sarcastic tone.

'I'm so sorry, David. It really sounds awful; well worse. There are no words to describe an ordeal like that. But, I can't help feeling, it would have been the best for you – a divorce, I mean.' I felt a lump forming in my throat and it was difficult to swallow. I was feeling stressed. It was as if David's story was mine and that the sadness and anger he felt were being passed on to me.

'No, I wasn't going to let her have my son.'

I didn't know what to answer but thought that David must have been the victim of a manipulator. I remembered a bully at school – a loud, self-important, attention-seeking individual who had never taken responsibility for his mistakes and made sure what he said was never clear, just so that later he could claim never to have said what someone had indicated to have heard him say. He had twisted people's words, laughed at their weaknesses or idiosyncrasies. I shivered and David wrapped one of his arms around me. I wondered whether he was comforting me or whether it was him seeking my proximity. Possibly both. As we sat silently, sipping at the hot tea, we were lost in our own thoughts. I felt unexpectedly weighed down by the amount of information David had revealed to me. I knew he would have told me one day, when he felt the time was right.

Eventually, we went back to bed and lay side by side in the early morning light. A gentle sea breeze was ruffling the curtains and we listened to the sound of the waves crashing nearby. I must have fallen asleep at some point because when I next opened my eyes again David had gone, and I heard his voice chatting to Leo downstairs, the smell of fresh coffee filling my nostrils and gently coaxing me to get up. I rolled onto my side, taking a few moments to wake up, wondering for the first time whether I had taken on too big a task – just as my parents had suspected all along. I pulled a light sweater on and walked down to the kitchen in bare feet. David was standing at the sink rinsing his coffee cup when he saw me walk in. We embraced, looking into each other's eyes without words.

That day we walked about in a stupor, Leo on our heels and oblivious to it all, skipping happily in his small sandaled feet. We decided to spend the whole day at the nearby sandy beach with sun lotion, towels, buckets, toys and a picnic in tow. I'd picked up a cheap magazine before leaving for our trip and what my fatigue-leaden eyes could only manage doing that day was glancing through the glossy pictures, dozing on the warm sand, and watching the castles, walls and hills emerge under Leo's agile hands. Not a word was spoken about the incident, mainly because we were too tired for any further discussion. I was busy digesting all of the information that had been relayed to me and was trying to make sense of the memories and experiences that had shaped David's life. It created a whole new picture for me.

I grew up in as normal a family as you could find, if there really was such a thing. There had never been complications of this kind. My parents had been fun to be with, had annoyed us when we were teenagers, like all parents do to some extent, and we'd all found our way to study for a degree we enjoyed prior to finding stimulating jobs. If there was a problem, we'd come together and talk about it, help each other and move on from there. Our approach was down to earth and we spoke about life and death in a way that didn't involve godly intervention.

84

Nevertheless, we still felt like we were leading meaningful lives with a purpose. Listening to David's story had opened my eyes to the fact that my family had possibly been right. I had stubbornly dismissed their concern about my relationship and involvement with a young child and older partner. I'd defended David and Leo but had to admit that I was slipping into a situation that I might regret later or, worse, that would somehow change me.

It was interesting to think about the idea of changing. What transformation would David have gone through over the years? He had sympathised with a person whose moods had been unpredictable, whose ability to blame circumstances and other people would have been very convincing, and whose self-importance could swallow up anyone empathetic enough to believe her stories.

Sometime during the afternoon, I sensed David glancing in my direction several times. I'd raise my hand and nod at him reassuringly. By the time we assembled our sandy towels and cleaned the buckets and toys, I knew that the day I'd spotted Leo for the first time in the health club café had completely changed the course of my life. If I had decided to carry on as usual, without making eye contact, minding my own business, I would still be dreaming about being a mother. I made a mental note to contact my friends and family upon my return to London, to share the events with them and to make sure to listen to their advice. That's when a cold shudder descended down my spine as David walked over and hugged me and then, looking into my eyes, whispered, 'Please, under no circumstances, tell anyone about what I told you last night. I've put the past behind me and I need your help for that. For Leo's sake,' he added.

I nodded, lowering my gaze, and mumbled 'of course.' A slight breeze ruffled my cotton dress and strands of my long hair blew into my face, tickling my nose.

'Oh, I can tell from the look on your face that I should never have told you.'

'No, don't be silly. You had to tell me. I'm pleased that you trusted me enough to share it with me,' I replied. 'I think I just need time to digest it all.'

'Yes, but I don't want you to share it with others. I trust *you* and …' His eyes trailed over to where Leo was digging a hole in the sand, '*We* need you.' He pressed his index finger into my chest and smiled seductively. In the meantime, Leo had stood up, buckets in hand and his eyes rolling with impatience.

'Can we go now?' he bellowed, startling us with his unusually strong voice.

'Yes, sir.' I laughed, trying to make light of the situation.

'You always do that, Daddy,' Leo said suddenly.

'Do what?' I asked, alarmed by his stern tone. He then pursed his lips and imitated our smooching.

'Come on, let's go. And you, Leo, behave!' David said, cutting the conversation short and looking coldly at his son.

Before deciding on what to make for dinner that night, I stepped into the shower and imagined that the water would wash away all the contradictory thoughts that had accumulated in my head during the previous twenty-four hours. I imagined how they would run down my shoulders, tickle the inside of my elbows and send little signals through my thighs and calves before getting washed away through the small holes at the bottom of the shower basin. They would shortly mingle with the foam and make a gurgling noise, then literally be taken down the drain. I smelled the sweet coconut perfume of the shampoo and enjoyed the warmth of the water massaging my aching neck. It had been an eventful holiday so far and I did look forward to getting back to my own place in London. I imagined myself closing the front door, the quiet of the living room calming my agitated nerves. In my mind's eye I watched myself unpacking, filling the washing machine with the soiled clothes, putting the kettle on and gazing out onto my tiny back garden, a small square fleck of grass but grass nevertheless. It was where I could unfold a towel and lay on my back, look up at the open sky, and imagine myself being anywhere. That simple moment of freedom could calm me and bring me back to my senses.

I stepped out of the shower, refreshed. One look into the steamed up mirror made me shrug and think that it was for the best I could not see my tired eyes then.

In the evening, after David and I had managed to produce a delicious but simple dish of risotto with peas and chunks of tinned tuna, we sat out in the garden, a bottle of Chardonnay open, and played cards until we had tears of laughter coming from the corners of our eyes. It turned out to be the best fun we'd had during the whole holiday, and it made us almost forget and swipe clean from our minds the traumatic events of the last few days.

As I tucked Leo into bed that night, I sat with him and we chatted until, as usual, his eyelids fluttered and his little hand, held in mine, gradually went limp as he dozed off. There was no sweeter, more endearing sight than that of a young child's slumber. His tiny murmurs and innocent expressions, the pursing of his soft lips or the twitch of one of his cheeks, had always caused me to melt and watch on in awe.

Two days after the incident at the shopping centre a police officer came to our cottage and, during an awkward interview session in the living room, we confirmed that nothing untoward had happened since: no strange phone calls, no obnoxious neighbours or strange sightings of any sort.

'Well, you know where we are. If there's anything you need to tell me or you observe something strange, please make sure to report it.' We then took his details and I saved his number in my mobile phone. We shuffled towards the main door and exchanged pleasantries before closing the door behind him.

The police officer's visit brought back the weirdness of our situation.

David walked into the kitchen later that evening as I was waiting for the water in the kettle to boil and, sensing my deep thoughts, he wrapped his arms around me. I felt irritation about his proximity and gently freed myself from his embrace.

'Sophie? What's up?' he asked. 'Is there something wrong?'

'No, nothing's wrong, David. I'm just trying to come to terms with what you told me about your past, Leo not talking about the incident, and that odd lady... I'm so sorry if it looks like I'm rejecting you. It's not at all the case. It's just... I need some space so that I can work out how I fit into your picture. I'm exhausted, to tell you the truth.'

'I know. The phrase that is haunting me time and again, day and night, is, *I can't believe I did that.*'

'Did what?'

'Well, I can't believe that I bought into my ex's charade and gave her so much of my life really.' I looked at him, each word he had uttered seconds ago slowly dropping into my mind.

I heard the music from a movie that was playing out on the TV for Leo and I walked over to check that he was indeed still watching it, rather than accidentally listening into our conversation. He looked up when he noticed my shadow standing in the doorway and we exchanged our usual warm smiles and winks. I brought him a mug of hot cocoa and his little 'thank you' made me deliver a peck on his head, before I told him that we'd be sitting outside on the terrace for our cup of tea. He nodded but, before letting me go, he jumped up for a cuddle and a kiss. I walked back through the kitchen and out onto the terrace where, in the meantime, David had pushed two chairs together. As I sat down, watching him pour the infused tea into two separate cups, a strand of dark hair fell over his forehead. I noticed his beautifully toned arms holding the heavy teapot. I felt warmth for him and put one hand on his forearm. It was a balmy night and we'd been through so much talking and listening that my head felt heavy. I just wanted to relax and gaze up to the moonlit sky.

'I know you're shocked by what I said but I don't think I should be telling you half-truths for the sake of protecting you. It would distort things. Leo is very fond of you. It would be a shock for him not to see you.'

'David, I wasn't implying that I wanted to leave you ... how can you say such a thing?' I retorted, taken aback by his words. The thought of being separated from Leo was like a painful jolt of electricity shooting down my spine.

'I was just saying, women are usually not that keen on looking after my child ...but you're different.' He reached over to pat my hand and smiled.

'What do you mean about other women?' I bit my lip, annoyed about sounding jealous.

'Nothing Sophie, nothing at all. I've not been a saint but, believe me, I've been too busy to have time for more than one girl.' He chortled.

'Yes, sure,' I replied weakly. I was simply his girl then. To avoid further embarrassment, I changed the topic.

'The reason why I'm surprised about your story is that I find it strange you knew about your ex's cheating but didn't walk away.'

'That's not completely true. I did try twice but she managed to make me come back. I gave her chances, but I regretted it each time because she twisted my words in such a way that she made me feel I was partly to blame for the near break-up *and* her infidelities. I could never do anything right.' I watched as tears pricked the corners of his eyes and he rubbed them away with the back of his hand.

'Impressive.'

'Yes, impressive indeed. She'd even told her lover that I'd been to emergency services for attempted suicide, which of course was ludicrous. But you see, she had a way of presenting the matter with tears and convincing arguments. For years I'd been a ghostly shadow of myself because I sacrificed my time and energy to save the marriage. People would have looked at me and thought, *well, no wonder she's looking somewhere else for attention*.' He laughed sadly. With his tanned face and arms and healthy glowing eyes, it was very hard for me to imagine a drawn in, unattractive and insecure David.

'I thought you said she looked terrible?'

'I looked exhausted because I worked too hard. I wasn't getting enough sleep and felt tense and guilty the majority of the time,' he said, as if he'd been reading my thoughts.

'You're working too hard now, may I remind you.'

'I've got no choice, have I?' His expression changed from bright faced to one of almost stony quality. I was startled.

'I meant well, you know.' Moody people make you feel like you have to walk on egg-shells. David was particularly good at that. One wrong word or a tone slightly out of place and he could send me looks that pierced through me. It was unsettling.

'Well it's easy for you to say. You have a job you love, your parents have helped you with buying you an apartment and you're young ...' I didn't let him finish his tirade of *you've had it so much easier than me* and intercepted.

'Excuse me, I may be *Miss go lucky* in your eyes because I've not encountered abuse like you, but you have no right to dismiss my life and wave your hands above my head like that.'

David's head had dropped into his two hands and he was groaning.

'I'm sorry, babe. That wasn't called for. I admit that I'm envious of people who haven't wasted years of their life on the wrong person.'

'No, it wasn't called for. I could say that you're the lucky one. After all, you have Leo, you have a fascinating job that gets you around, you stay in nice hotels by the sound of it and ...argh, whatever. I hate situations like this when people say, "you have that and I don't." It's tiring. At the end of the day, there's hardship for everyone - deadlines, worries, conflicts. It's pure luck if you haven't had to defend yourself in life against a bully. We've all met them in one form or another. They pounce on you when you least expect it. *My* luck, if you want to call it that, is that so far I must always have gotten away in time. I truly have a solid, normal and well-balanced family to fall back on as well.'

'I know. There are bullies at the best schools, in the nicest neighbourhoods and the slickest of firms. They come in all sizes and disguises. I just … I just sometimes can't believe how I could have done what I've done all these years. I feel I've been dealt a rotten card in life. That's why I move so often. I don't want to stay at one address for too long because I never ever want her to find me again. I feel that I'll always need to watch my back, in case she's there to finally give me the last push. The mad cow.'

I was taken aback by his harshness but remembered that his anger was undoubtedly still raw. Then again, Leo was six and he'd never seen his mother.

The conversations I'd had with David left me very confused. Thoughts would literally jump into my mind at odd moments and make me drift back to things said between us. I couldn't put my finger on it but I was starting to realise that I only knew half of the story. I had once read a thriller that had me gripped for the whole weekend because the underlying theme of the book was a strange psychological phenomenon called Stockholm Syndrome. A group of hostages had started sympathising with the hostage taker, despite the fact that they had suffered physical and psychological abuse. The hostages had started to interpret certain perceived small kindnesses from the abuser as the presence of 'normality' and potential for ordinary humanity. Witnessing small considerations, they would believe that the hostage taker wasn't that bad after all and that someone capable of kindness and even limited human compassion was therefore redeemable - despite the harm they'd done or were doing. The book had described very well how one's perceptions could change his or her perspective or point of view on what was *really* happening around them. It had been a fascinating novel, based on true facts. David would have been in a similar situation because he explained how his wife had gradually worn down his friendships as well as his relationships with close relatives. He had become increasingly isolated and, through his participation, had even encouraged the further break-down of his already very low self-esteem. The fact that many of his friends had not spoken to him since would have to have something to do with it, I concluded.

I now also understood why his parents had shown some reluctance towards me during our first encounter, just prior to our holiday. I only wished I had known a bit more then. Their attitude had almost been one of embarrassment. I felt increasingly torn between wanting to believe David, especially since he'd opened his heart to me, but equally so, as a woman, I couldn't help secretly having some sympathy for Leo's mother, who I understood had given up her own child. Could it be possible that she had willingly abandoned her own flesh and blood, her own baby? Were we not genetically programmed to love and protect our offspring, at absolutely all costs? Remembering Stockholm Syndrome had thrown an extra puzzle into everything.

I decided there and then that I was going to propose the topic during my next editorial meeting with my colleagues. The syndrome affected people in so many different types of situations – the abuser could be a hostage-taker, a parent, a teacher, a husband or a boss. I realised the extent to which emotional bonding could result in selfless cooperation, purely as a survival strategy. Victim and abuser became accomplices. This also explained why abused children and wives repeatedly returned to the one person who was intent on destroying their capacity of knowing what was right and wrong.

I was dozing on the sun lounger in the garden the next morning, taking in the warm rays, when I heard David and Leo coming through the door again. They had gone for a final stroll down the road, to hang out at a local playground. We had made the most of the last days and ended up relaxed, sun-kissed, and feeling fully rested.

I pulled myself out of the seat and started going through the house to pick up the last of our belongings. Despite all the stresses, late nights and revelations, the holiday had turned out a success. I was checking the last cupboards and drawers whilst Leo and David were kicking a ball in the garden, when I heard something drop through the letterbox downstairs. The sound made me stop in my tracks. I shook my head, slightly irritated that I'd felt startled.

'It's just the post,' I muttered to myself. I was going to check it on my way down and leave the item in the hallway, visible for the landlady to collect.

When I was finished and all the rooms were checked and our picnic was ready for the journey home, I remembered the post. I skipped down the hall and picked up an envelope. Strangely, it was not addressed to the landlady but I saw that someone had written three letters on the front. I instantly felt a chill as I read the word "Leo" on the front. I exhaled and slumped onto the seat behind me. What we had been pushing out of our minds for the last few days and successfully avoided talking about, was the stranger who had abducted Leo in the shop. Leo's reluctance to talk about the incident and the fact that I'd come across an oddly behaving woman, had been sufficient proof that something peculiar was going on.

What on earth was this letter about? I heard Leo's

happy laughter and David's teasing voice coming from the garden and impulsively decided to rip open the letter there and then. Next, I gave out a sarcastic laugh, noting that I was holding a set of identical looking leaflets in my hand. Irritated, I slipped them back into the envelope and stuffed the item into my handbag. There was no urgency for alerting David now when he and Leo were so carefree and joyful and the post only appeared to be a pile of nonsense. There would be a better moment to read it or pass it on. At best, I'd be able to avoid one of David's angry outbursts.

Leo's cheeks were red with excitement and David was lying on the grass roaring with laughter when I finally stepped out onto the terrace. I was hoping then that one day, our unusual holiday would simply become one of those stories we told others about around a dinner table or at a party.

I was thankful that my concern went unnoticed because both David and Leo shot me glowing smiles as I sat down on one of the garden chairs. I sighed with relief and raised my face to the sun, stretching out my legs and relaxing my shoulders for the remaining fifteen minutes before it was time to finally gather our packed bags, jump into the pre-ordered taxi and leave for the train station.

oOo

I picked up my ringing mobile phone from the small wicker coffee table in my living room. I had been nestled into the corner of my sofa, browsing through the long list of emails that had greeted me on the night of my return from Brighton. David and Leo had decided to continue on to his apartment after dropping me off. We had embraced and laughed and I made myself believe that the week had brought us closer together. David had whispered a big thank you into my ear for being his partner as well as his friend. So, I was relaxed and happy when I took the call.

'Hello, Mum. How are you?'

'Hello my darling. Are you home yet?' she asked chirpily.

'Yes, I've been back for about an hour. I'm just looking through all my emails for tomorrow. I have a busy week ahead.'

'Oh, what a shame – thrown right back into the deep end, eh? How was your holiday?'

Upon hearing the question, I realised that I hadn't thought about what to tell my mum, or rather, what not to tell her. Having a young child snatched from under our noses, a stranger haunting our holiday and a sleepless night chatting to my partner, where I found out that his past was less then rosy, well, what would my mother think of all that? I knew her pretty well so I guessed she'd voice concern and quite rightly, because if someone had told me their holiday events and it had entailed these unusual ingredients, I'd have been alarmed, too. It would have taken a lot to convince my mother otherwise.

'I'm tanned, rested, and had a great time just hanging out with David and Leo. The weather was amazing, too!' I had summed up our holiday in one sentence instead of spilling the beans. 'I must admit I'm exhausted though,' I added, laughing.

'Yes, I won't keep you for long. Just wanted to make sure you arrived back safe and sound. Travelling is tiring, so run yourself a nice bath, then hop into bed.' I loved my mum's genuine attitude, so maternal and caring.

'Yes, Mummy, I'll do just that. I'll call you later in the week for a proper chat, OK?'

As if my mother could detect something in the sound of my voice, as usual she didn't mince her words and asked me outright. 'How was it spending 24/7 with them both? It's different than spending time with someone in between jobs and commutes, school drop offs and pick-ups, isn't it?'

'As always you're right, but we got on really well actually, and sitting here all alone in my living room, I feel a bit strange to be honest.'

'Aww, that's good to hear. I'm pleased you had a good time. I'll let you go, darling. Call me if you want to talk. Kiss, kiss.'

I did feel a bit guilty because, all things considered, I did have a very nice time. Still, the holiday had left me with quite a lot of thinking to do, and I wanted to do this by myself first. I was a methodical person after all, so trusted in my instincts and knew I'd reach a satisfactory conclusion somehow.

Following a relaxing bath, I made myself a cup of herbal tea and read for a little while in bed, before turning the light off. Despite my good intentions, I had a fitful sleep with phases where I saw the scruffy lady staring at me over the seats and tables in the train, her smile a yellowish-brown grin with gaps where her teeth should have been. When I eventually woke and sat up in bed irritated, I recalled parts of David's story in my head and then wondered again who the person had been, taking Leo by the hand and guiding him away in a middle of a bookshop. I couldn't help but feel shocked again about the weirdness of such events and felt the blood in my face literally drain away, down towards my feet. My hands were shaking when I lifted the duvet and reached over to the bedside table lamp to light the room and get up.

'The Leaflet!' I said under my breath, suddenly

remembering it. I had successfully concealed its existence from David and Leo and, by the looks of it, from myself as well. It was still tucked in the side pocket of my handbag. I had completely forgotten about it until now - 5 o'clock in the morning – and I knew that in just under two hours I'd have to get up and look like I'd been on holiday and not bleary eyed and tired. However, I walked over to my bag knowing full well that I had to read it again right away.

As I reached into my handbag and retrieved the envelope, I wondered if what I'd done had been acceptable. This was like trespassing. What had entitled me to open a letter addressed to Leo? Despite the fact that I was looking after him as if he was my flesh and blood, it should still have been David opening it first. It was too early to call him though, and I decided that after everything I'd been through, it had been completely within my rights to open it. In any case, I would tell him the truth later and that I had been acting out of good faith when I'd popped it into my bag, trying to protect their bubble of happiness before we left, and who was to say that this document was in any way contentious anyway?

My clammy hands smoothed the crumpled envelope down and I looked at the scrawled cursive letters again, trying to imagine an invisible hand tracing the name. Then I retrieved the two identical double-sided brochures of what appeared to be an advertisement for a religious organisation. On the front I could make out the picture of a man opening his arms with a broad smile on his face and the words printed above saying, 'Love knows no boundaries'. I turned the leaflet over a few times, shaking my head in disbelief. Was this it? Then again, I knew there had to be more to this than just a bunch of flyers tucked through the mailbox at a rented cottage in Southern England. It dawned on me now that the person who had been stalking us on the train and then later outside the house and possibly the one guiding Leo away from us in the bookshop had to be the same person. She also seemed to have a religious penchant, to round things off. But why had the envelope been addressed to Leo? Where was the connection?

oOo

'She said that God is great and that through him there is always a place I can meet my real mum.'

'Yeees, and did she say where this place was?'

'In a church.'

'Why in a church?'

'My mum is in a secret place. She has to hide from me. She goes to a place where people can take messages from her to me.'

'A church?'

'Yes, the lady told me that Mummy is a really nice person and that she loves me.' Leo's eyes betrayed sadness and I knew not to prod further. I was stunned by the apparent resourcefulness David's ex seemed to have been able to come up with. Leo was of a perfect age to believe in the supernatural. The brochures were meant as a reminder that all Leo needed to do, was believe.

'So, as for that mysterious lady - have you met her before, Leo?' He instantly started twisting in his seat, lowering his eyes, then slipped his hands under his thighs. He was clearly uncomfortable, which answered the question for me. Children are bad liars and they are very easy to expose if you are observant enough to read their facial and bodily expressions.

'Please, don't tell Daddy,' he pleaded, and I

promised that I would be very careful about what I said.

'I really appreciate you telling me, Leo. Thank you. Just tell me one more thing. Did she say anything else, for example that she'd look out for you again?

'She always does.'

'She always does what, Leo?'

'Find me.'

'Oh. It's always the same lady?'

I watched Leo's face intently for any sign or reaction to what I was implying.

'Yes, I'm not to tell you …'

'I know, but I think that it's wrong for her to follow you.'

'It's always the same lady and she's been giving me messages. She tells me to close my eyes and just believe that there is a link between Mummy and me. But, but …'

'But what?

'I don't feel it anymore. It's rubbish. She's just telling lies.'

'Yes, I think you're probably right. Please, let's agree that whenever you see her again you tell me about it. I'd like to talk to her and sort this out for you. People can't just go behind Daddy's back and ask you not to tell anyone, and you should never ever walk off with people me or Daddy have never met. OK?'

'OK.' He hugged me and I could feel a mixture of

relief and uncertainty in his embrace. When he unhooked himself, he turned his big eyes towards me. 'But you used to be a stranger and now you're my best friend. How can I tell the difference?'

'Oh Leo, you're right, of course. It's so unfair of me to tell you that you should never talk to strangers and yet I put you in that position. To be honest, I think your dad was foolish to have left you on your own at the gym and believe that no one would notice.'

Leo shrugged his shoulders and smiled up at me. 'I'm used to it.'

I just stared, hearing his words.

oOo

I would not have passed as Leo's mother. I was tall, blonde, and my green eyes and freckly skin easily gave away my Gaelic ancestry. Even a colour blind or myopic person would have been able to tell that I was not Leo's mum, despite his affectionate behaviour, his hand clasping mine firmly when we crossed roads, and even despite of my obvious love and care. Darwin would possibly know what to say about the importance of parents recognising themselves in their offspring. As far as I was concerned though, I could not imagine loving my own son more than I loved Leo. These thoughts surfaced in my mind once in a while, when I pondered over my role as a parent and partner.

A few days after settling back into our routine, I decided to meet up with my friends for dinner and finished off the evening with a stroll through Covent Garden. We watched some street artists and browsed through shops and I noticed how much I'd neglected my need for independence. Applying make-up prior to our rendezvous, the thought of an evening with my two best friends had felt childishly exciting. It had been that long.

I boarded the last underground train back home, my head filled with my friends' voices and laughter. I knew that going home at this hour meant that I would not be alone. The wagons were packed with commuters who had been out for drinks, out dancing, or been to a show, or those who had simply worked too late at the office. I managed to stand in the middle of the carriage, holding on to one of the railings, my body tired from walking and having consumed a few glasses of wine. I was eager to get home. A man with a heavily scarred face was staring past me, his head occasionally drooping, probably due to a mix of drunken stupor and exhaustion. I sympathised with him and hoped it hadn't been loneliness that had caused his apparent desolate state.

From a distance, I started to feel that I was being watched. The person's head was partly hidden under a hoody. It had gotten colder lately. This year's summer had resembled a Mediterranean climate. People would talk about the long evenings spent on terraces and having barbecues, which had briefly made them feel as if they were in Australia rather than central London. A young woman suddenly leant into my shoulder, her ears closed off with small ear phones. I could tell she was listening to a Coldplay song and concluded that she'd be kitted out with hearing aids if she wasn't careful with the volume control. She would bear the consequences of spending hours in an encapsulated world of sound and noise. I looked up again and noticed that after leaving the last underground station, the person with the hoody had vanished. This was London for you, I thought. So many faces, so many lives, so many stories.

I thought back at how my life had changed in such a short time. It seemed ages since I'd sat in the gym café and spotted my little guy, his big eyes watching me. What must he have thought about me when I first smiled at him and tried to coax him into a chat? I suddenly felt the weight of my naiveté push me down. David had told me so much, but there must surely be details and parts of the story missing that were essential for me to truly understand him? I shuddered as my thoughts wandered back to the moment that I found Leo again in the back room of a bookshop.

I finally stepped out of the wagon at Tufnell Park, taking a deep breath as I felt a cold breeze blowing over the platform. You learnt to breathe shallowly when you were a London commuter. There were so many viruses and other unpleasant micro-organisms waiting to be picked up on the tube, that you had to learn to avoid them as best you could.

I was surprised to notice that very few people had stepped off the train with me. I decided to walk home especially briskly, so that in just under ten minutes I would cross the threshold to my apartment. You could never be too wary about being followed. I quickly ascertained that another two ladies were also walking in the same direction as me, which was reassuring. We passed a night shop where a bleary eyed, serious looking woman stood behind the counter, turning her gaze towards me, while her right hand was turning the page of a ruffled magazine. On the other side of the road I saw two men lurking at the traffic lights and I felt a sudden unease. I cursed myself. I hadn't jumped into a cab like most sensible working women in London just because I loathed my hard-earned money disappearing as soon as my salary was transferred each month.

I walked past a noisy pub, feeling invigorated by the presence of human beings standing in groups, chatting and sipping at their pints and glasses of wine. Next, I reached the part of my walk home from the tube station that I disliked the most, as it was partly shrouded in darkness. The two ladies that I had hoped would both still be following in my footsteps were now reduced to only one. I knew because one of them had been wearing high heels and I had heard the sound of them recede a while back. I was left with one female companion walking through a tree-lined back street and hoped she would be adding to my feeling of safety until I reached home. I heard a faint sound of a message arriving on my mobile but decided to check it later.

I saw my front door from a small distance, when a voice made me jump with a start.

'Hey.'

My heart was struck with fright and I sucked in the evening air and convinced myself that the question had not been directed at me. Why would someone call out to me?

'I need to talk to you.' The voice was strangely muffled and I did not like the sound of it at all. I turned round, terrified to see she had come closer to me. I remembered in a flash that not long ago I had set eyes on just that lady. We were close enough to a street lamp so, I could also make her out as the person with the hoody in the tube. My face felt like it had drained of its blood and I called out to her to leave me alone and raced to my front door.

I had been holding my bundle of keys since exiting the tube, an old habit so that I never had to search for the front door key in the dark. The key slid into its hole without a problem. I pushed the door open and stepped inside as fast as I could, attempting to push it closed behind me. I quickly realised that I'd not been fast enough, and looked down and saw the top of a dirty trainer wedged between the door and the frame. My heart sank and I suddenly felt such anger. I opened the door and screamed with rage.

'How dare you follow me! Get away right now or

I'll call the police!' I fumbled in my bag to retrieve my mobile. I hoped that my screams would be loud enough to alert my neighbours but I could not hear any movement from next-door or from above. Before I could race outside to ring a doorbell, the woman had clasped her grimy hand around my mouth and was eerily whispering into my ear.

'Don't fight it. Don't fight it. I only want to talk to you.'

She wants to talk to me? About what? This late at night? Who was this lunatic?

oOo

The woman is sitting in a waiting room. Her hair is wet, her cheeks flushed with what may be fever or she is simply feeling too hot under too many layers of clothing. She is in a room filled with people, all waiting for their turn to be seen by the local GP. She is sweating, and although it would be easy to simply stand up and take off her thick coat, her scarf, and the woolly jumper with the hood she is wearing underneath, she decides against it. Sometimes these actions come too late. She is afraid that her body odour will make people turn away in disgust, or worse, make them get up and swap seats. Then again, there are no other free seats so it would make things even worse because people would be forced to stand if they could not bear sitting next to her. She feels drops of sweat running down her temples and knows that under all the layers of clothing she is wet, as if she has just come out of a swimming pool. She shuffles uncomfortably and prays that it will soon be her turn to stand up and walk over to the doctor's room. She looks down at her hands and watches as her fingers fold and twist. It is as if they have a life of their own because she is now having to will them to stop fidgeting. She rubs her palms over the top of her tight jeans and reluctantly picks out a magazine from the middle of her handbag, noticing with dismay that one of her shoelaces has come undone again. As she leafs through the magazine, her vision occasionally blurs and she struggles to focus on the colourful pages. Her gaze settles on a picture of a woman laughing, her arms flung open to reveal a translucent, sensual blouse with pink and red flower patterns tracing their way around her waist. Her long brown hair is flowing in the air next to her oval face, as if magically suspended. The strands are set in perfect harmony with her porcelain skin and big hazel eyes. On one wrist she wears a heavy golden watch, its time frozen in the moment. If only she were able to capture happiness like that for herself and prolong it for a stretch of time that could sustain her. She has tried, and lately it has worked well enough. It has been such hard work to reach this feeling of happiness. The thought has made her eyes prick with tears and her vision is blurred, a small puddle settling at the corners of each one, wetting her reddened cheeks and causing streaks in her clumsily applied make-up. She rummages in her bag and is surprised to find a pack of tissues. The little set reminds her that she is able to do normal things, such as buying tissues in a shop – an ordinary task for most people yet an achievement for her. She yearns desperately to become that person again who can hold down a job, watch a series on television, sit with a friend in a café chatting over a cup of coffee and a slice of cake, and do an ordinary shop in the supermarket. When did it all get out of hand?

She had been to the rehabilitation clinic where everyone had been so helpful and kind and where she had found a special friend. The woman had told her the whole story about being a mother of a child but she had never been allowed to hold or care for her beautiful little boy. Her heart had started breaking upon hearing her say these terribly sad words. She had started crying with the woman and soon they were hugging to comfort each other. As the weeks unfolded, the woman would seek her out, usually during their outings to the park or at lunch time, guiding her to a table in the corner of the room. There, she would reveal more and more of her personal tragedy, the depressions she had stoically endured to fund her husband's extravagant needs, working long hours and barely keeping track on expenditures that were beyond their means. It had been a thorn in their relationship, her suspicions of infidelities evidenced by his numerous long absences and, later confirmed, when she'd stumbled upon a flirtatious text message on his phone. No wonder he always looked tired and overworked.

She presses the tips of her fingers to either side of her temples to ease the pressure that is so suddenly building up in her head again. She quickly checks that the tablets are still safely tucked deep in the pocket of her coat. Just in case, just in case, she tells herself over and over. I have what I need to ease the pain, just in case.

There were moments when she wondered why and how her friend had been driven to the brink of madness. She knew feelings of desperation and her way of coping was by taking drugs that lifted her back into semi-normality. It had been her escape for a long time, whereas her friend had been driven to madness by someone else.

She had felt extreme empathy for her. She was very receptive of the emotions of others in general. You had to comfort people in distress, avoid hurting anyone. Yet, the only way to avoid falling into people's traps was to avoid them altogether, leading to inevitable loneliness. She'd started with her habit to ease her sadness by taking pills. She knew that an overdose could kill her so she would learn to control the chills and ill-feeling for as long as she could, then swallow the pills that increased in number over time, until she almost forgot about taking breaks in between. That had been the first time she'd sought help and was treated for pharmacological dependency. Then came the phase that she remembered as numbing and disconcerting. It made her want to scream and shout all day, so she was prescribed calming tablets. She managed to get up in the morning, dress for work, mechanically say her hellos and thank yous, smile and go home, only to go through the same pattern again the next day.

She shakes her head about wasting all these opportunities she had to stop herself from taking the pills. Worse, she had given in to a different temptation. She was by then living in a bedsit in a rough estate. Of course, she vowed to do it only once, then quickly it became the reason why she did get up in the morning, greeted her colleagues at a part-time job, went out with one of them for lunch and concluded each day with a chirpy, 'See you tomorrow,' or, 'Have a nice weekend.' It was perfect really, but by the time she switched on the television and had eaten a meal and drank a big glass of water, she was desperate to sniff the meth up her nose again. It worked for a while but she'd been warned that if she didn't eat and drink enough, her teeth would start to rot and that the drug made people age before their time.

Needless to say, she did slip up, she did lose her grip on the daily routines, despite her smart phone - when she was still able to keep it topped up - reminding her about what to do, and post-its stuck to the fridge, telling her to eat and drink. Nevertheless, she ended up in a psychiatric clinic again. She had been lucky collapsing in the middle of a staircase where someone noticed her and called the ambulance. Yet again she had been saved and directed to a clinic. That was when she'd met her friend. Or was it before, some other time, some other place? What she remembers for sure is that she'd been so chatty and the only one who was persistently able to lift her out of her usual gloom. Her jokes had her in stitches and, before she knew it, she was getting more and more annoyed with the fact that her friend had never been allowed to see her own child and that the fault must entirely lie with her manipulative ex-partner. Thank goodness they'd both found solace in their belief and that a church community had taken them under their wing. She vowed to reconnect the boy and his mother through God's strength.

Her friend had given her sufficient information, almost vivid enough to picture the husband in her mind. It took her a few attempts and searches on Facebook, but she eventually managed to track him down and watched as his little son was regularly abandoned at a health club for hours on end. It had been like being absorbed in a good novel that was drawing in the reader's imagination to such an extent that one felt involved, a silent bystander observing the scenes unfolding and participating through empathy and sympathy. Through her friend's story, she'd come alive again and had been given a new purpose in life ... to seek out beautiful little Leo and connect him with the mother who loved him with all of her heart. She never told her about it and was embarrassed now about the lengths she took to achieve her goal. She'd even begged on a street corner on many occasions, so that she could pay the fares on the train and underground, but the one thing that she had on her side was *time*.

Oh, her head is spinning now with all these memories and the feeling that she cannot find a way out of the jumble and maze of words, expressions, and conflicting emotions rushing through her veins. Where were the years of ordinary life that she always hoped would fall into place for her? Where was the married life, the children, the putting up of a Christmas tree in winter?

She recoils from allowing the hopelessness of her situation to invade her mind. She's been denied what so many people take for granted. It's like shooting yourself a dark look in a mirror. There are so many doubts nagging at the edge of her consciousness and it hurts. She admits that having a purpose had filled her with energy and a reason to get up in the morning, even to keep her small bedsit tidy and clean, drink and eat regularly, and keep track of the pills she had to take as well as her check-up appointments. Initially, she only planned to track them down, not more, and then along the way she'd somehow felt she had to do more.

It dawns on her that she isn't sure what to tell the doctor. How does she tell a complete stranger that despite her medical history, today's chills are not due to withdrawal symptoms? What she has come to tell a professional is that she cannot hold it together any more. She had been so sure of her friendship but had to admit that the people she'd been observing looked like a perfectly happy family. Maybe she had given the little boy too much hope because she had increasingly felt compelled to hold back what she came to tell him about his mum. When she had started to edge closer and spoke to the boy at the playground and took him for a walk in the bookshop, she had had a sudden nagging feeling that what she was doing was wrong. To influence an innocent child and swear him to secrecy lest his mother would be kept away from him even longer could not be right, no matter how much her friend had been wronged and how big the suffering she had endured.

She folds her hands, clenches and unclenches her fingers painfully, and barely hears the lady's concerned question.

'Are you okay?'

She cannot help but stifle a laugh because the question, coming from the lady in the next chair, is so absurd. She does answer.

'Thank you, I'm OK, just feeling under the weather. That's why I'm here.' She smiles weakly. The words do stumble out of her mouth and she is amazed at how well she does by appearing normal, and by simply proffering a few platitudes. But within her head it's another story. She wipes her face with a tissue and smiles apologetically to other people looking at her, hoping that the agonising wait will soon be over.

She tells the doctor everything. Her teenage years spent with the wrong people, parents who did not notice if she was there or if she wasn't, and then her encounter with a special friend and hearing of her unfair separation from her son. She vowed to unite them. When she eventually found him, she started feeling increasingly unsure of her plan. The boy looked so happy with his 'new' mum, so happy to chat and play with his dad who also seemed a normal kind of fellow. She recounts taking the boy on a walk through a book shop and leaving him in a safe place, and that she'd been lucky that the summer was unusually hot with nights that allowed her to camp out at the beach near Brighton with a thick blanket and her change of clothes in a bag as a pillow. She admits to dropping a letter through the box with brochures. What dreadful reproach she had to endure over the phone thereafter, when she eventually revealed her clever plan to her friend.

'What on earth are you trying to achieve by being so silly and suggesting that God can bring us together?' she'd said.

'What was the reason for sending you on this wild-goose chase?' the doctor asks, interrupting her flow.

'She never really sent me ....' Her eyes are darting around with unease. 'She said that through sharing her story with me, she had created a connection. I felt that I could maybe find her little boy and create this connection for real.'

The doctor looks at her and smiles encouragingly, even though he looks like he'd rather pick up the phone and alert one of his colleagues working in the psychiatric ward.

Before saying another word, he studies her face as if looking for symptoms of a hidden disease.

The doctor then asks if she would like a glass of water. She nods and he fills a cup for her from a dispenser.

'You know, taking other people's stories and feelings literally is what is causing you this trouble now. You are being pulled every which way because you empathise with a woman who was maybe using you to continue manipulating her partner. It has a psychiatric term, but that isn't important here. It matters more now that you get the help you need.' He pronounces the words carefully and calmly, then adds, 'You know that it's wrong to follow someone?'

Her head cowers between her shoulders, but he decides to continue.

'I know you genuinely seem to believe that you were helping a friend. You know the world is full of people pretending and lying and it's very hard to tell the difference sometimes,' he says, trying to reassure her.

Tears are now running down her cheeks and he walks over to her, sitting down at the edge of the table.

'You were very brave coming to see me. I think you knew yourself that something wasn't right.'

His words are strangely soothing to her and she somehow feels that she is in good hands. She needs to be able to trust someone and not left to her own devices with post-it reminders and jobs where people are inclined to avoid her, after work hours are done. She knows that she is clumsy and she can tell by the way people look at her that they are afraid to get too close. This doctor seems to understand her and he may be able to untangle the thick jungle of words that is knotting up her mind. She falls back

112

into her chair with a big sigh of relief, wiping her cheeks with the back of her hand, and nods thankfully as the doctor holds a pack of tissues up towards her. Despite her eyes starting to blur again, she can still hear his last words before she nods in ready agreement with him.

'The first thing you need to do is completely break off your relationship with your friend. She has her treatment and therapy to complete and so do you. There are many things in life that seem one way and we believe them so intently that we absorb them as facts and not as mere possibilities. You need to learn that people can make up stories on the spot and so can you, if you are not careful. People do this very well but it is only a way to justify their actions to themselves and others. It doesn't mean that they are telling the truth.'

He looks into her eyes and she knows that their blankness betrays her incredulity. She is smiling, though. Then she remembers with a jolt why she is really here, in this doctor's practice, talking to him and hoping for relief from a burden that has become unbearably heavy and weighs on her shoulders like a pair of thick hands pressing from above by some giant ogre.

'But, you see I forgot to tell you ...' Her words come out stammered and her voice is trembling.

The doctor looks up sharply from his file, eyebrows raised. He had already been rifling through a pile of notes, indicating that he still had half a dozen other patients to see. Yet, his attention is focused back on the lady in front of him, his attentive eyes looking over the rim of his black-framed glasses straight into her worried face. *What now?* he probably wonders. She wishes that she was as unflustered as him. Wasn't it bad enough that she'd admitted to stalking a family?

'I ...I told the lady that she was evil and that I

knew she had taken a child that wasn't hers. And ... and I threatened her that the real mother would find her and that no one could replace a real mum,' she says, watching a deep frown appear between his eyes. 'I jumped on her last night outside her front door. I didn't hurt her but only told her I had to talk and get this off my chest... I was very angry.' She bows her head forward in shame. 'It felt wrong, so wrong, and she was so upset, screaming and scared. I really didn't mean to hurt her, just set things straight ... I had no idea, you see.'

'No idea about what?' His voice is steady, yet she can detect a weary undertone.

'That she had not taken the man and child away from my friend. She met them only a while back. I must have gotten a lot muddled up. Oh, I'm so confused, so confused.' He looks at her and before he can say anything, she adds, 'I'm so frightened!'

'*You* are frightened?'

'Yes, my friend must be getting more and more impatient with me. She tells me that she should never have told me about her past. She's avoiding me but oh, she is all I've got ...'

'Have you at all considered the possibility that you were acting against her consent? All she did was share her story with you. Did she actually ask you to get involved like this?'

'Not in so many words, no, but I felt the craving so acutely. She often said that she wished someone would stand up for her and bring her ex to justice. Her powerlessness was heart-breaking.'

She has covered her face with both hands and is shaking her head, unable to stop the tears from running down her cheeks, misting up her vision yet again. She is so tired now with the turmoil, and her loneliness is hitting her straight in the centre of her stomach. If she has lost her only friend because she is unable to keep her trust, who is there left to talk to?

She is shifting her weight around on her chair, visibly uncomfortable, then wipes her face and rubs her hands over the top of her thighs. She takes a pause and whilst wringing her hands compulsively, says, 'I did tell her that Leo's mum would kill her if she continued to see him. After that I ran out of her apartment and I've been so confused ever since.' She reaches for another tissue on the doctor's desk and, while she is blowing her nose, he gets up to inform the receptionist at the main desk that he will not be available for further appointments. His patient requires urgent assistance. He is calm and collected when he sits back in his seat, looking determined to help her.

oOo

All I can say now is that I didn't want to be a rival mother, trying to prove to anyone that I was the better Mum. I had no right. I knew somehow that David never expected that much any way. At best I was an amazing babysitter, nanny, au pair, you name it, amazing because I did it all willingly and for free. Yet, the frightening encounter with the mad woman haunted me for a long time. My emotions felt like they had tumbled from a great height, crashing on to sharp, rough rocks below. I started to doubt my own intuitions and judgements and there were some days when I was left feeling like an empty shell. No matter how irrational the stalker's threats had been, how upsetting her crazy insinuations, I decided to move and reported everything to the police. I was scared that I would turn into a person who looked over her shoulder every time she left her home. I was concerned that this insecurity would become necessary, repetitive, and obsessive. But my move also involved me suggesting, after a series of heated discussions, that David and I needed a break. His angry reaction to my request for some 'space' was to move away to Horsham, leaving me utterly bereft of Leo's company. I missed him so much and I knew that he would be upset, too. Our relationship therefore ended as abruptly as it had started and I knew then that I could never forgive David for this.

As for the other woman who'd been drawn into the twisted net – she was apparently receiving medical attention. She had completely endorsed David's ex's point of view, without checking whether her friend's feelings really rang true. By then, I actually believed that we'd both lost track of who'd been pulling the strings all along.

You might rightly wonder why things did not work out. After all, we did seem like the perfect little family. It all made perfect sense, didn't it?

First of all, I must concede that it may be difficult to comprehend that a woman could ever love another's child as much as she would her own. I felt that for Leo, I could, and it had also been a question of timing. When I started going to the gym and noticed the boy in the café, my spontaneous feelings had coincided with a great loss that I had experienced just a few months earlier. My pap test had twice come back positive and after research, further tests, lab results and many tears, it was confirmed that I was in the early stage of aggressive cervical cancer. I opted for the inevitable hysterectomy. So, the truth is, I have no womb in which to carry my own child, no possibility of ever knowing where the difference actually lies between loving your own or loving someone else's child. When I saw Leo for the first time, it didn't seem to matter anyhow. It wasn't that he was symbolically filling a gap, but I had simply jumped over one. To fall in love with a child who could already walk and talk was far better and easier, I told myself, than having to endure stretchmarks, labour pains and sleepless nights. I eventually told David about my hysterectomy a few weeks after returning from Brighton. Never did I think that this revelation could cause such animosity. Why had I not told him before? What were the pills for, which he had seen me take daily at bedtime? Hormone replacement therapy, I had answered dryly. He had laughed, and that one sarcastic laugh switched a lever inside me. No one, not my family nor any of my closest friends would ever have laughed that way. What until then I had called trust, was shattered into thousands of tiny pieces.

It was like a spell had been lifted from my eyes, revealing the landscape around me in new, more realistic colours. The biggest sacrifice was leaving Leo, which still festers like an open wound to this day. It made me realise why mothers are able to fight tooth and claw to defend their own flesh and blood. But Leo wasn't, and so I saved my own skin first, mourning the ensuing loss of the boy's company ever since.

As for the second matter, the question why in the end I decided to completely step away, withstanding many bouquets, phone calls, and attempts to win me back, can be answered with a letter I received just prior to moving house. The letter changed everything I had previously thought.

Dear Ms. Kenneth,

I hope you will read this letter before you are tempted to rip it to shreds. I am David's ex-wife and provided you have not been asked to marry him yet, I would like you to at least consider the truth you may have been told about me. I am not the manipulating, hysterical, deceiving witch he undoubtedly tries to make me out to be.

Yes, I did threaten to kill our baby. I will admit that much and it has cost me dearly, but the motive for my desperate threat was that I could not contemplate the idea of that poor child having such a nasty, selfish father as a parent. Nor could I ever imagine raising an innocent child with him. He had turned me into an angry, frustrated, emotional wreck. I was desperate by then to cut the ties and even asked a friend to tell him that I wanted a divorce. Yet, everyone could see that I looked like the one who'd let herself go and seemingly wasn't putting all her efforts into the relationship. So, I ended up being labelled as crazy.

David is very clever indeed and many therapy sessions have given me an insight into the psyche of a manipulative abuser. Even though he does not really care for Leo – he is a mere tool, a toy for him – taking him away from me was the punishment for wanting to leave him. Because, I eventually did cave in and he succeeded in making me go crazy. I completely understand now how, in the not so distant past, wives were easily shipped off to an asylum on the basis that they'd gone mad and were hence useless for society. I didn't have any close family when we first met, which was convenient for someone like him. At his mercy, he dismantled me gradually and consistently. For now, he is still charming you I suspect, making you his ally, his son's gullible babysitter. Believe me, sooner rather than later this will change.

I am in good hands now, even though I had been sectioned for a short while and my clinical depression and addiction to pain killers involved my son being taken away from me. There are professionals who now believe me, that I was and am the victim. There is not much hope for me to be reconciled with my son yet as David keeps changing address because he needs to avoid the letters that arrive, the debts, the questions from those few people who actually have also understood his macabre game.

Leave while you can and thank you for the kind

attention you have given to my son. Fighting to see him again is what gets me up in the morning. I would never ask for help and, believe me, my former neighbour at the clinic is a kind woman at heart but I never encouraged her to stalk you and David, or Leo for that matter. She calls me when she is desperate, then never stops repeating herself. I had no idea that she was stalking you until I heard about the incident at your home that I sincerely regret. I should never have told her my story knowing how vulnerable she must still have been then.

Kind regards,

Hanna Roberts

I suppose one could lose their innocence either through their own actions or through what others do to them. My innocence led me to talk to a young child in a café, and I was oblivious of how my actions would later influence the way I'd interpret my intuitions and allow another person to take advantage of me. I could not shake the feeling of unease which was telling me that truth, in any shape or form, is like a slippery wet fish that we normal humans are unable to catch with bare hands or, at least only for a second, until its inevitable twists and writhing give it a new lease of life, new waters to swim in, and new horizons to explore with new experiences to add to.

What I have learned, if anything at all, is that if you ever come across an expert at catching fish, you should get away as fast as you can, because they will change its habitat and keep it at their mercy at all times and for as long as they can.

I know because, for a short time, I was that fish.

H.A. Leuschel

RUNAWAY GIRL

She was sitting on top of the bunk bed, her legs crossed, smiling contentedly. She tucked her long hair behind her ears, a gesture which helped her focus and usually marked the start of an important occasion. She was ready.

One thousand five hundred and two pounds was the amount she counted and then diligently noted down onto a piece of paper in front of her. She could barely stifle a scream. She had conscientiously stacked away lunch and pocket money, payments for babysitting and neighbourly chores. She had saved every single coin or note that reached the palm of her now 15-year-old hand for what seemed like forever. She felt the heat of excitement rise to her cheeks. This was it, she muttered under her breath. She had given herself the target of one thousand five hundred pounds because she worked out that she needed that sum to cover her initial expenses – a train ticket to Scotland (she'd listed all the potential relatives strewn around the country who might be able to help and thought her aunt living in Ullapool the most appropriate and welcoming contender) and the costs for all of the basic necessities. She planned to make a new beginning after sitting her GCSEs and turning 16. She would probably be allowed to claim an education allowance in Scotland to boost her budget. She'd offer to work part-time in her aunt's B&B, sign up in a training course and show her true commitment by contributing to general expenses. They'd received so many kind letters and postcards from her relatives in the Scottish Highlands, urging them to visit and she hoped turning up on their doorstep for real would go down well. From there, she believed that things could only get better. Her dream was that after a month or two, she'd maybe be able to afford her own small place and then she'd be truly independent and in charge of her life at last. *I can run away*, she whispered to herself, her fists clenched in a gesture of victory. She felt an invisible door - that would lead her to freedom - opening up right next to her on the top of this narrow bunk bed. All those times that she had abstained, resisted and stood firm from spending her money on treats or on outings with friends, had finally paid off. She had kept the cash hidden in a small black plastic bag inside her mattress. She was the only person who knew of a hole in the side of it. It was the only safe place in this entire two-bedroom flat she shared with her siblings and parents. She had been making her bed since she was eight, so no one could ever have noticed. Then there had been her deep admiration for the Dutch sailor Laura Dekker that had kept her going through doubts and hesitations. The girl had circumnavigated the globe in her little sailboat all by herself, leaving at the age of fourteen and returning a sixteen-year-old independent and self-sufficient teenager. Holly had watched the movie documentary, mesmerized and inspired. She'd felt some kind of kinship with her because of her own craving for autonomy.

The latest version of her plan had been prepared meticulously and secretly printed in the school's ICT room. At last, she could get away from her annoying brothers, her mother's kiss that reeked of alcohol ever since she could remember, and from her Dad who tried to compensate for their poverty with his infuriating kindness. She unhooked her legs and let her feet dangle over the edge of the bed. Now that she had reached her goal, she felt an unusual tightness in her throat. She could barely swallow and felt light-headed, switching between a feeling of achievement as well as a contradictory sense of apprehension. Deep down, she did love her family but found the lack of space and privacy in their small apartment disheartening at the best of times. Whenever she opened a window, she was greeted by the pollution and noise coming from the nearby busy main road. Her mother worked long shifts in a local supermarket, lending her hand to anything and everything, whereas her Dad had impossible working hours, guarding a deserted office building in Canary Wharf. Needless to say, it took him a tediously long time to commute there and back from Croydon.

She pressed her fingertips against her temples and forehead, giddy with confusion. She had heard of many teenagers leaving school prematurely and unexpectedly for reasons not always disclosed to the other students. *Why do I want to leave so desperately?* she asked herself. *What will I do?* Now that she had reached her goal, she scowled at her own indecisiveness and naivety. So far, she had always moulded her behaviour around others' behaviour - her parents, brothers, teachers and friends. There was no way of knowing which of her past decisions she had truly made on her own and for her own sake.

She was still lost in thought when she heard a text arrive on her mobile phone. She retrieved it from the pocket of her jumper and noted that the message was from her friend Tina. She took a little time to read it, almost reluctant to be pulled so quickly into another person's world again.

Hi Holly – u wouldn't believe it!

She frowned and then typed back quickly.

Tell me!

The response was prompt.

Sara did the test. She is ...u know?!!!!!!

Her heart was racing faster with the realisation that her friend Sara was in trouble.

OMG. How do u know??

She waited anxiously for Tina's reply.

I'm at Saras. You've got 2 come over! Please b kwik.

She was still holding her phone when she heard her Mum's voice calling her from the hallway. The unexpected diversion was a welcome sidetrack from her latest doubts about her plans. It had all seemed so enticing - the allure of freedom and independence, but now she had reached her first goal, she just wasn't so sure about carrying out the next step.

'Hi Holly, you alright?' Her mum sounded weary and stepping out of her room, Holly saw that her hands looked moist and were shaking slightly as she peeled off her coat. Holly guessed that she was desperate for a drink but probably she had no money to buy some.

'Yup – I'm nipping out to Tina's quickly. I won't be long.' She answered, still busy texting until she had to peel away her eyes from the screen to pull on her black boots, slip into her coat and grab her scarf. She was out of the door without once properly meeting her Mum's eyes.

oOo

As the door closed, Holly's mother was suddenly aware of how mature her daughter had become, both mentally and emotionally, over the last year. It had taken her a long time to realise that Holly was somewhat unusual. Sweet, childlike in looks, yet very bright and mature for her age. She'd read more books than she and her husband had, put together. Then again, when it came to boys, she seemed either completely oblivious of them or was possibly just very good at hiding everything from her. She shrugged, giving out a tired groan. Her feet felt like lead as she dragged herself into the kitchen and put the kettle on for a cup of coffee. She stretched her arms above her head and gave out a groan of exhaustion that she was determined to shake off. Why, oh why was her life so tiring? She sat down on the chair, which creaked slightly under her weight. She remembered that she needed to put the washing on but her feet were sore and heavy from standing all day and her back was tense and stiff. She pulled all of her remaining energy together and decided to make a special effort. She knew that if she didn't move out of her seat right then, she'd be stuck there until the rest of the family would eventually trickle through the door, demanding to be fed. It would be too late again to show them what a real home looked like – smelling fresh and clean and with the aroma of grilled chicken wafting through from the kitchen. She decided to strip the beds and wash the linen. Then she'd mop through the apartment and give the bathroom a little sparkle, the kitchen a tidy look, setting the radio to Jazz FM while puffing up the cushions and straightening the curtains. She remembered that she had a few candles left in the kitchen drawer that she could light on one of the window ledges in the living room. Going through this simple yet effective plan had always managed to lift her mood in the past, on the few occasions that she had actually succeeded to put it into action. But the beautiful picture of serenity of a tidy home had remained mostly in her imagination because she was simply too downhearted, exhausted or filled up with alcohol most of the time to turn it into reality. Today would be different. *They will all see a new me*, she told herself. She lifted her long wavy hair out of her face, tying it into a ponytail, then rummaged through the pile of kitchen towels on the sideboard where she extracted a semi-decent looking apron and, whilst putting it around her waist, started humming to herself. *This feels good.*

oOo

Meanwhile, at her friend's place, which was very similarly laid out as her own home, Holly was greeted by two tearful teenage girls. Tina and Sara were her best friends. The trio had known each other since year six and, despite differing temperaments, Holly thought that they complemented each other well. Tina was the tallest of them all with an impressive size of 1,80m. Her friends kept urging her to apply to a Top Model agency competition. She had wavy long brown hair and dressed in the craziest of colours when she was out of her school uniform. If you mixed pink, blue, purple and green you had Tina's wardrobe in a nutshell. She was very confident and didn't have a care in the world about what people thought of her. Even the school uniform was not an obstacle for elaborate hair-dos, big earring loops and shiny shoes. Sara, however, loved everything dark and mysterious – from charcoal hair, thick black eyeliner to high leather boots and patterned tights. She'd recently had one of her nostrils pierced and Holly was still mesmerized each time she looked at the slim black arrow precariously sticking out at the side of her friend's nose.

Holly felt that her friends were the best thing she had in her life. They knew that she'd wished to save up money for a special trip. She'd pretended that she was dreaming of faraway places such as New York, Paris and Rio de Janeiro. Yet the destination that she really wanted to visit - and was too shy to admit even to Sara and Tina – was a place like Bora Bora where she could sit outside a little hut on a beach, watching guys with six packs walking past. She was the voice of reason to her friends, the dependable daughter and sister to her family, the hard

126

working student to her teachers, yet deep down she dreamed of the same as every other teenage girl. She swallowed the rest of her thoughts. She pictured herself instead, sitting on a Scottish beach that also came straight out of a postcard image, clearly etched into her mind. Ullapool was the most plausible place to start off from and could come the closest to initially fulfilling her dream to travel.

Tina had gone on many all-inclusive holidays to Spain and Sara had even been to Turkey. Holly knew that her parents could have done the same, had it not been for her mother's addiction. She'd been too little to remember meeting her aunt, but knew that after she'd moved to Scotland to open a B&B with her husband, she'd sent enticing postcards that would lie between the bills and leaflets coming through their letterbox. Holly'd kept one of them which had depicted a scene that had taken her breath away. It had shown an open bay at low tide with rocky outcrops and a sandy beach strewn with pebbles of all sizes. The shot was taken on a sunny day and she had pictured herself right there sitting on one of the big stones and gazing out to Loch Broom, watching the seagulls dive for fresh fish and lifting her face towards a vast, open sky. She'd already been to the odd place on the southern coast of England – day trips that had left a blur in her memory. She yearned to have the leisure to just sit and watch the open expanse of water and hear waves crashing on the shore. She imagined it as an intoxicating sound - sick and tired of noisy, stinky London. She wrinkled her nose at the thought. Having said that, nowadays the perfect combination of a faraway destination would be the sight of handsome boys on a pristine tropical beach and, of course, a big pile of books tucked away in a seaside cottage. She giggled to herself about these fantasies. She hadn't had one single boyfriend yet, just a few very awkward tussles at a party and a wet kiss during a school outing and that had just been a silly dare. A handsome boy with strong muscles on a deserted beach holding her hand … and more, yes, that image was better, she thought.

She was confused about her ideas of happiness and realized with a deep sigh that leaving home as soon as she reached the legal age of sixteen in a month, without telling her friends, would hurt them badly. Yet, it was the perfect opportunity she thought. The government was planning to raise the age for leaving school to seventeen and even eighteen over the next couple of years. She saw it as some kind of a sign that she was one of the last teenagers in the UK to be allowed to make her own decision when she turned sixteen in the spring. It would certainly only take her as far as her auntie's place, far away from tropical Bora Bora, but in essence heading north had the potential of bringing her closer to freedom and happiness. Argh, she thought, if she had to be perfectly honest, the one place she felt happiest and most resembled a beach setting because of the peace and quiet was …. the school library. Books, other people's trials and tribulations, just seemed to make her feel less alone. She had not spent much time in the quiet, warm interior of the library lately because of all the odd jobs that she'd picked up in the neighbourhood. She had been so busy running errands, completing chores and changing nappies to increase her savings that her studies and reading had taken a backseat. Holly remembered with regret that her English essay was late and that she had probably done poorly in her GCSE mock exams.

She was grateful for a diversion being handed to her right this instant. Something serious had happened and her help was needed. If she was to run away now, she'd be really letting her friends down. They had been so patient with her saving every single penny, knowing that each had to fend for themselves and find their own way in life. After all, whatever you got others to do for you, the less you ended up doing yourself. She remembered this idea from her English class. It had been one of many clever phrases coming from Jane Austen's pen. She must have known what she was talking about, because she remembered her teacher saying that the author had worked for a meagre living but that, on the face of it, she'd been independent in every other way. *I want to be free,* she screamed in her head. *Free ...*

Anyway, if she was to run away, she'd find new friends, Holly thought, and was instantly shocked by her feelings. How could she be so cold-blooded? Was this really how she felt? A teacher once said that she was the most independent young pupil she had ever met. She remembered that all she'd said in response was, 'You can only rely on yourself, really.' She could also remember the exasperation in her teacher's lowered eyes and shrug of shoulders. What had been wrong with telling the truth? Teachers just didn't get it.

Holly's thoughts were interrupted by her friends, waving her over to settle with them on Sara's bed. There was no reason for envy between the girls, regarding where they lived. She could be in her own home right now, come to think of it – it was so similar in build and lay out. The only difference was the thick lettering that someone had painted on the wall leading up to the landing where her friend's home was situated - *Eat your cartilage and run.* Moreover, the lift hadn't been working for months, so Holly could not help but shiver each time she came across the graffiti. She couldn't avoid reading the words, staring right into her face as soon as she came round the bend. The person must have been hallucinating, drunk or stupid when writing the phrase. Or maybe even all three.

Before offloading all the wretched details, Sara and Tina first made Holly swear to secrecy, their faces grave and serious.

'Guys, you know me, I wouldn't say a thing. Ever,' Holly reassured them, slightly peaked that her discretion was in doubt. 'Why would I?'

She was also a bit irritated at how the girls had dragged her into Tina's room. There was no one else in the whole apartment until late in the evening, hence this was the place they came to whenever something secret or unusual needed to be discussed in private.

'Are you sure you are pregnant?' she asked out loud.

'Shhhhhhh,' Tina responded, while Holly heard Sara gasp at hearing her friend say out loud what she hoped was just some terrible dream. She could tell that Sara was choked up and close to tears again. She lowered her voice and snuggled up closer to her friend.

'Okay, okay, calm down. Why do I have to be so quiet?' she whispered, clasping Sara's hand and rubbing her back. Holly looked up trying to hide her exasperation and quickly checked her hair in the mirror propped up at the other end of the room. Should she colour it a shade lighter so she'd look like a blonde? She was tired of being called 'interesting, different, or exotic'. She wanted to look attractive, cool, and stand out for the right reasons. She flicked her long red mane down her back and felt instantly guilty for bothering about her looks in the middle of discussing Sara's major problem. She looked at her friend's tummy and couldn't imagine her with a big bump. Come to think of it, she couldn't imagine anything growing there right now.

'Are you really a hundred percent sure?' Holly asked, looking at Sara doubtfully.

'Yes Holly, no doubt about it. My parents are going to kill me,' she said, her voice filled with dread and her eyes welling up with emotion. The liquid of her tears was visible just at the rim of her eyelids; beautiful little pearls of fluid. Holly had what she called one of her odd moments, where she imagined things that could not be. It was a habit that always managed to soothe her nerves. What she imagined now was a tiny, perfectly formed baby swimming in her friend's teardrops, smiling and playing with her umbilical cord. The baby was so happy that shortly – in one blink to be precise - she would be rolling down a person's cheek, having the ride of her life. She then pictured the baby closing her tiny hands around the cord, preparing to slide and be gone.

Sara looked up at Holly who was trying to look at her calmly.

'What?' Sara asked wide-eyed.

'Nothing! Just take it easy, will ya? I know it's a shock. But anyway, you're not planning to keep it, are you?'

Holly was smaller than her peers, her silhouette slim and light with looks that gave her an air of delicate apparition, like a porcelain doll from times gone by. She had been told before that she could have featured in a fairy tale because her skin was so pale and her copper red hair a surprising contrast to her green eyes, now firmly set on Sara's thoughtful gaze.

'Come on Holly, you are so clever. What do you think I should do?' Sara picked up an already tear sodden handkerchief from her bedside table, blew into it and gave another tragic sniff before continuing. 'One moment, I feel like I want to rip the thing out with my bare hands and then I see myself holding a soft smiling baby in my arms.' Her tears were welling up again and Tina was quick to hold her friend's shaking hand.

'Sara, you can't be serious. Remember Casey? It happened to her a few years ago. No, I don't think babies are all soft and cute.'

'I know; I know - chill; I was just saying ...'

'You don't want to push a pram around, do you? Change shitty nappies?' Holly's voice was firm and Sara shook her head. With her flushed cheeks and swollen red eyes, her shoulders hunched in a pink sweatshirt and her sporty, lean legs tucked up in black leggings, Sara suddenly looked a few years younger than her soon to be 16-year-old self. Her vulnerable looks were heightened by her dyed black hair, sticking up every which way. She told them that she'd showered for half an hour after school until the hot water had literally run out.

'I really hoped that the hot stream pouring all over me would wash the stupid, tiny cell away. I emptied the whole bottle of shower gel. My parents will be well happy. Not.' She raised her eyebrows. 'It just made me feel so much more stupid instead. How could I have been so silly?'

'It's always easy to say after. Don't beat yourself up over this.'

'Thanks for coming over to help me guys, I really appreciate it,' Sara answered.

'I know it may be a teensy little problem right now but very soon it'll be a big one,' she added, instinctively smoothing her T-Shirt down over her tummy. 'I don't want to get fat.'

'You won't. We'll help you,' Tina said.

Holly dropped her coat and scarf next to her friend's small bookshelf at the foot of her bed, as she felt the heat of emotion rise to her cheeks and warm the hollows under her armpits. With a sideways glimpse she could make out a few scribbled lines under the title question of their English assignment, lying on one of the lower shelves. So, Sara was late as well, she thought. For a moment her eyes lingered on the sheet of paper and she wondered what her conclusions should be regarding the set question: *What do Jane Austen, George Eliot and Simone de Beauvoir have in common?* She liked the ring of the last name and was keen to find out who the lady was, what she had written and also what indeed she had in common with the other two well-known English writers. Like many times in the past, she had the feeling that she was the odd one out in her family. She had never seen her parents read a book and, on the few occasions she had met some of her relatives, she wasn't struck by the realisation that, *Ah! I get my love of books from them.* It was not the first time that she wondered whether she had actually been adopted which, she knew was a bit unfair. Who knew whether her mum and dad would actually have enjoyed reading, had they not left school too prematurely or simply had more leisure time? Whatever lay in their past, she'd never been given sufficient details to piece together a picture of her parents' youthful selves.

'I mucked up completely at the party. I always think the first few hours being drunk are fun but afterwards it's just horrible … and now this. Argh.' She heard Sara's muffled words and Holly was immediately pulled back into reality.

'My face must look like a mess. I'll have to pretend that I caught a cold when Mum comes in,' Sara added. She'd have to hide the fact that she'd actually been crying about taking a major risk walking back to Billy's place. Both had been downing the various alcoholic drinks available, laughing and giggling. She buried her head in the crook of her elbow. She must be desperate, Holly thought, because she knew that you could not turn back the clock. She remembered Sara's panic when her period hadn't started as usual, waiting another week, the girls standing anxiously outside the toilets. Sara had 'checked' ten times a day, in case her period was just late. Finally, she'd given in and bought a pregnancy test. She'd spent a fitful night tossing and turning in bed, prior to going through the procedure after school the next day.

'I was so shocked to see the test was positive,' she exclaimed, wringing her hands in frustration.

The three friends were huddled together on Tina's bed, quiet for a while.

'Okay, this is what I think.' Holly eventually broke the glum silence. 'I watched this TV series a while ago and there was this young girl who decided to have an abortion. She'd called a helpline where someone ran through all the options. Depending on how far gone you are, you'll be able to either take a pill or go through a medical procedure.'

'I guess that's a good idea. I should do this. I want it to be my decision. So, don't tell anyone, okay?' Sara replied, looking at her friends gravely.

'Were you planning on telling Billy?' Tina asked, her freckly face gently inclined, as if talking to a bereaved relative. Sara shook her head energetically, and then carried on.

'No, no, no …I don't even particularly like Billy. No offense, but he doesn't even have a six pack and since the party we've hardly said two words anyway.' She looked glummer than ever. 'I feel so stupid.' She closed her eyes and shook her head as if it would somehow make the reality go away. She gave out a big puff of air.

'What's done is done. We'll back you up. Soon you'll see, it'll be over and forgotten. Here, drink something. You'll feel better.' Holly said, and Tina nodded, offering a glass of coke to her miserable-looking friend.

'Yes, Mummy,' Sara said, batting her eyelids, her mood improving slightly. She took a mouthful of coke but instantly wrinkled her nose and retched. 'Oh, this is awful. I can't even stand the smell of my favourite drink now.'

Shortly after, they sat at the kitchen table, all sipping lemonade. There was a moment of silence, interrupted by a sudden gust of wind rattling at the window. Holly dreaded the idea of having to trudge back home through the cold weather.

'You have a choice and it's safe,' Holly said. 'Remember what our teacher told us in history? A hundred years ago, women would die trying to have an abortion or worse, they'd have to marry the guy.'

'Yikes! Yeah, cool, thanks for the info, Miss Encyclopedia. You can be so annoying with all the stuff you remember. Billy as a husband? No, no, no. I can do better.' She rolled her eyes. 'By the way, please help me with the English essay. I'm so behind again and what with everything that's going on, I'll probably get a fail.'

'I'm late too, but yeah, we'll sort it out, don't worry,' Holly reassured her.

'I've started on mine, so feel free girls,' Tina added.

After an hour of discussion and with no more tears left to shed, all three girls snuggled back together on Tina's bed, when Holly suddenly felt as if the entire colour in her face had drained away. She was no longer her pale porcelain-like self but had turned ashen. She jumped off Tina's bed, grabbed her things and, as if stung by a bee, rushed through the apartment with a quick, 'Don't ask, I've got to run, forgot something *really* important. I'll call you later,' and was out on the street where the chilly, damp evening greeted her. She was so shocked, it felt like steam could have poured out of her ears any second. *How on earth could I have forgotten to hide the money?* she screamed in her head, her heart pounding in her chest. By now, her two younger brothers would have come home, jumping about the place noisily and snooping around for anything that remotely looked like a distraction from boredom. She was imagining all kinds of scenarios as she rushed over the zebra-crossing, narrowly avoiding a cursing cyclist as well as bumping into an elderly lady who was bent over her trolley bag, barely able to set one foot in front of the other.

'I'm so sorry; please let me help you with your bag. I didn't see you coming.' She offered. The lady did answer but Holly was not able to make out the words because of an ambulance's siren a short distance away, momentarily drowning out any chance of a conversation. The woman seemed to grab her bag more tightly and Holly realised that she probably thought she was a thief rather than a helpful teenager, keen to get her safely across the road. She decided to nod and smile instead, and then rushed off home as fast as she could.

oOo

A few days later, Holly's feelings were pulling her in all directions. She was on her way home from school and after splitting from her friends, she decided to take a detour.

She was tucked up in her coat and her pink woolly scarf was snuggly wrapped around her neck when she climbed up the stairs at the local train station. Her hood was too big for her but she liked the feeling of being hidden from view. Her small headphones were set in her ears and she was listening to the radio DJ announcing the next song. As she stepped onto the overpass to change platform, she heard a gentle ballad starting up. Instinctively, she slowed her pace and had the impression of her feet hardly touching the ground. She barely noticed the other commuters walking past and for a moment forgot why she was there.

Holly stopped in the middle of the bridge and pulled a folded sheet of paper out of her pocket. It started fluttering and flapping around her gloved hand. She leant over the railing, having to stand on her tiptoes in order to comfortably lean over far enough to see the train tracks beneath her. She swiftly threw the piece of paper into the icy wind and watched as it was tossed and turned, just as she had felt tossed and turned in her life so often before.

She remembered the disappointment in her tutor's voice as she learned of her mock exam results and the tears suddenly pricked at the corner of her eyes. Within her big coat, she could feel her skinny shoulders sink forward and the weight of the news came flooding back through her mind. She felt frustration and anger rise in her chest and the emotion made her knees go weak. Most of all she was angry at herself. All this time she had focused on saving up money. She should have focused on her school work, aiming to improve her skills rather than looking after snotty little toddlers. They could be cute and she liked their big innocent eyes, thankful for every attention they got from her, but what had she been thinking of really? It had been a goal, but now what should she do?

Why not finish it once and for all? Take a one-way ticket to the centre and throw herself into the murky, ice-cold River Thames that was flowing through a city that offered so much she could not afford? That would punish her mother for wasting every penny on alcohol. Disgust and anger rose to her throat. She hated her mother's weakness. Maybe she should have left there and then, with her few belongings and the cash in her bag, ignoring Tina's message. Pff, she knew the answer too well. Dreams didn't usually carry you the whole way.

She awoke from her dark thoughts, picturing her body lying on the grimy train tracks, as another popular song started on the radio. Yet, upon repeatedly hearing the same word – runaway - she felt annoyed and pulled the headphones off. Her hood had fallen back and now revealed her long, thick red hair. She didn't care about being exposed now; she even raised her chin and let the tears flow. Somewhere deep in her coat she could still hear the sound of a male voice singing. One day she would show everyone that there was more to life than instant gratification. She didn't know anyone who could delay it as well as she could. Her money was in a savings account now – oh, those raised eyebrows from the bank clerk when she'd brought out her black bag. She'd been convinced that if her Mum had found the money that day, she would have run off with some of it to buy alcohol. Her heart sank again with the memory, feeling hurt as well as angry.

She had seen with her own eyes what it was like being a pregnant teenager – her friend's eyes had been wide with angst, fear and confusion. Now she understood her mother that little bit better and realised why it was the circumstances that somehow would have strongly contributed to her way of living. Despite their hardship, she did care for her family. Come to think of it, she would always vigorously defend her parents and siblings in front of her class mates, teachers or friends' parents. She could not bear the thought of revealing to anyone the conflicting feelings and emotions that truly lay within her. She was momentarily stunned by the realisation that what she would like more than anything was a soft hug from her Mum and Dad. A warm feeling came over her as she thought of their soothing voices and pictured them tickling her seven-year old brother. She softened at the thoughts of memorable moments and decided to hold on to them for as long as she could. Saving up money felt like a door to freedom, liberating her and giving her the impression that she was in control of her destiny.

She sighed, then turned to go. Her toes had gone numb in her boots so she sped up her pace. What she could

138

not run away from was her thoughts, always her thoughts. You'd think that there could be an end to them and yet there never was; they constantly invaded her mind. They seeped through her daily life and sometimes even hijacked her sleep as if they had a life of their own. They seemed merciless in their intensity and capacity to influence her behaviour.

She walked past a young couple, kissing passionately, oblivious of her presence. Trudging down the road, she longed for such an embrace herself and she hunched her shoulders deeper into her coat, convinced it'd never happen to her. She wasn't the type for anyone. Then again, her mum had been attracted to a red-head once.

Oh, her mum, she thought with mixed feelings again. What she would have liked to wipe away - more than her own insecurities and attempts at freedom - was the look her mother had cast on her the night she had run back home, cheeks flushed with panic and apprehension. She had hurried to her room, throwing her shoes off in the middle of the hall, and with dismay had seen the black plastic bag had gone. She had jumped on top of the bunk bed, cursing herself, and searched under her duvet, her pillow first, then the corner of the mattress where her hand had settled over the small lump in its hiding place. When she had retrieved the bag, the sheet of her plan neatly folded and, as usual, safely tucked away inside, it had dawned on her that she had been found out. She knew that she had made a grave error of judgment. That was also the moment when she felt someone's presence nearby. Her mum had been standing in the doorway, her eyes sad and dull.

'Holly, I understand you,' she'd told her later, after a long discussion at the kitchen table. Holly had asked many questions, demanding answers, irrespective of her brothers' whining in the hall.

'I was stupid to get pregnant with you when I was fifteen and it was certainly more than a punishment for my foolishness to be stranded with a tiny infant I had absolutely no idea what to do with in a lonely council flat.' She paused, twirling her wedding band, and probably adding things in her head which Holly would never know.

'Don't get me wrong. I thought the world of you and you were such a beautiful little one.' As much as Holly loved hearing these words, she knew that they were not true. She had been a scrawny baby, crying with gusto day and night, feeding badly and quick to pick up a virus. She'd overheard that much. Oh well, mothers seemed to either delude themselves or others. She imagined Sara in the role of a parent and frowned at the thought. Children were the last thing on their minds. It was enough that she had to help look after her two younger brothers. They were good kids but still they needed to be fed and bathed, their clothes needed to be cleaned and she had to check they'd done their homework. She felt competent enough to know what needed to be done, but she wanted to find out what it was like to be in a boy's arms without any side effects - witnessing Sara's distress being one of them.

'Oh, I had such grand ideas of freedom and independence and you seemed to be the ticket for them. Stupid really, to think that having a kid would make me an adult. The ticket really though, was meeting your Dad. He literally saved me from drowning.' Her mum looked as if she'd drifted off to another place, talking aloud to herself.

'He can't mend it all, Mum.'

Holly's remark brought her mum's attention back to where they were, sitting at a kitchen table that was too small to hold all family members for a meal. They had always eaten at different times and in different corners of the apartment.

'It's not really the lack of money that bothers me so much or that we all live in such a small place. It's that we can't really count on you. You're either exhausted or drunk or hung over. I know people who get help for this. You should, too. Please, Mum.' Her words almost came out in one breath. Not for the first time, she wondered which of them was the grown up and which one was the child.

'It's been wrong to hide the difficulties of my addiction from you. The alcohol has been a substitute but, really, I'm not as desperate for it as you think. I really feel I'm OK. Thank goodness Dad managed on his own before.' She lowered her eyes, now twiddling with the edges of her cardigan.

'Mum, he still does and you are not okay. You've got to admit it. Look, this may sound harsh, but I'm so relieved that you didn't take my money to go off and get drunk, as usual. It's horrible to see you being dragged back by Dad and then it takes you ages to get back onto your feet. I really can't take it anymore.' Her mum's cheeks turned red with embarrassment and she cast her eyes onto her interlocked fingers. She was tense and, Holly thought now, it was probably because she was ashamed. Holly managed a weak smile and, after squeezing her mum's shoulder, put her hand over hers.

'I love you and I know you try doing what you can but I was convinced you'd take some of the money.' She watched her mother's unease and put it down to the fact that she must have seen her elaborate running away plan.

'Come on, you look so sad. Is it because of my plan? Well, don't worry about that … I won't leave as yet. It was a stupid idea in the first place.'

Upon hearing the words, her mum stood up and walked over to the kitchen sink. Her jumpy gestures should have made Holly suspicious. Instead, she was convinced that her mum was simply embarrassed or even hurt that Holly could have contemplated running away and, worse, had imagined that she could steal from her own daughter.

She took the cash to school in her bag the next day, determined to deposit it in a safe place. When the bank clerk eventually counted out the money in front of her, it had dawned on her *why* her mum had suddenly been unable to look her in the eyes. The cash left in the plastic bag amounted to one thousand pounds. She had recounted it a few times in front of the astonished bank clerk and then just nodded in resignation adding that, yes indeed, that was the amount she wished to have payed into her savings account.

Leaving the footbridge, she was overwhelmed by her need to trust and understand her mum, yet unable to forgive her for taking the money and being unable to own up to her dishonesty there and then. Holly had been surprised about her own lack of anger when she'd confronted her mum about the missing cash. Her mother had looked at her as if electricity had struck her, unable to speak. Rather than release her frustration, Holly had simply shrugged her shoulders and decided to walk away. In reality, she'd just been weary of hearing yet another list of her mother's usual excuses and empty promises. They were the last thing she'd wanted to hear and had resigned herself to the fact that a thousand five hundred and two pounds could not buy her the freedom she craved for anyhow. How silly had she been to believe it could? Her elaborate plan was now being ripped to shreds on a dirty train track, rain water seeping into the paper and disintegrating what was left of her dream. She would confront her mum, demand her money back and ask her *how, oh how could you do this to me?*

She had been so deep in thoughts that she was only now fully aware that her tears had dried up and that she had turned into her road, heading towards the apartment block. She could see from afar that her window was lit. Her brothers were home already. A lady with her dog walked past and gave her the smallest of nods. People didn't really greet each other much here but she did know this lady so nodded back, vaguely remembering taking one of her previous canine friends out for a walk. As she reached into her pocket for her key, she heard the characteristic tone of her mobile phone announcing a new text message. She read it quickly while looking for a corner to shelter, in case she needed to answer straight away.

Thank u for ur advice. I took a pill because I'm still under 9 wks. I'll call you when I'm back from the clinic tonight. My parents think I'm with u. Plez cover if need b. I'm so relieved. xxx

Holly swallowed hard a few times as the familiar lump was back in her throat. What if that had been her mum's decision sixteen years ago? She slid the key into the lock and let out a small but distinct sigh of relief. Maybe the five hundred and two pounds' difference, even if only symbolic, was worth her life. *Count your blessings* was what also came to her mind. Cheesy? No, she thought, definitely not today.

She decided that it was time to put pen to paper and write her essay. Holly had puzzled over the question long enough in the library during lunch break, looking up the names on the internet. All three women had been writers and each had gone against the odds in different ways and at different times in history. What all of them seemed to have fought for though, was independence.

oOo

The next day, Holly went to school early to put the finishing touches to her essay, determined to start working harder again. Yes, her mother had admitted to taking the money, the shame written all over her face. She had said that while she had been tempted to drink, she'd paid an outstanding bill with it instead. She'd also promised that she would sign up with a detox clinic and get rid of her addiction once and for all. 'Please,' she had pleaded, 'Trust me, I'll make sure you see every single penny again,' and then she had apologized again and again until Holly's knees went weak with exhaustion and she had slumped down on the sofa, shrugging, giving in.

She settled in one of the seats of the school's ICT room, tucking a strand of hair behind her ear. She had taken some time today getting her wild mane up into a ponytail, brushed until it looked as shiny and slick as a real horse's tail. She'd applied light make up and accentuated her big, bright eyes with mascara and a little eyeliner. The powder and a pale lip gloss finished off her delicate appearance.

She was comfortably settled in her seat and had opened a word document when after typing out the first three lines, her body sensed someone's presence. The small hairs at the back of her neck instinctively rose in response to her heart beating faster. She thought she'd been alone all this time. How strange to find yourself in company when you least expected it. Had she picked her nose, done anything untoward that would have made the other smirk? You couldn't be too careful at school, or you'd get laughed at. From the corner of her eye, whilst slowly lifting her head, she was startled by the cheeky look that was directly aimed at her. Luke, one of her classmates, was staring at her. She blushed in response. He was slumped in one of the corner chairs at the back of the room where no one could see the screen he was working on. He was looking past the monitor and his unflinching stare made her shuffle nervously in her seat before she could manage to straighten her back and throw out a question.

'You scared me. Why are you staring at me like that?' she finally said.

'Oooh, someone's being a bit touchy. I'm looking at your beautiful face, of course,' he retorted, charming as he would normally be with his many female admirers. Holly gathered that it came naturally to him, however, she could not help enjoy the attention.

'I've waited for a chance to be alone with you for ages,' he said seductively.

Her eyes widened with shock.

Did he just call me beautiful? Me? He wants to be alone with me? What on earth has gotten into him? She wondered what she should say in response. She was a headstrong girl, able to fend for herself but had, as yet, not ventured properly into the boyfriend-girlfriend territory. Luke was the most handsome boy of the class, confident, cocky, arrogant, you name it, but he had so far never set eyes on her. He always had a girl hanging longingly around his neck and all he needed to do was swat her away like a fly if he wanted a change. Holly admitted to having secretly watched him, his dark blond hair cropped into a sporty cut, gel at the edges, and those eyes, dark brown and intense that were … still staring at her right now.

'Sorry, I say what I think. I've just never had the opportunity to be in the same room with you without anyone else staring and listening in. I hate school. Can't wait for it to be over.'

'Oh! So, why are you here this early then? Are you doing some homework?'

Her thoughts were racing through her head. This was unbelievable. Since when was he interested in spending time with her?

'Yeah, I'm just finishing the ICT homework. I've been late with the stuff yet I kinda like it and maybe wannna do something with web design later. What about you?'

'I'm typing up the English essay. I'm late too, but I really want to get it done. It's the one subject I really like.' She started typing, pleased that she had to keep looking between her notes, the keyboard and the monitor, rather than having to meet Luke's eyes again. Her fingers were shaking slightly under the pressure and she noticed with great relief that Luke had turned off his terminal and was gathering his stuff. Surely, he'd be out the door before she knew it. But instead of throwing his bag over his shoulder to leave, he casually walked towards her work station and slumped into the nearby chair.

'You're really cute.'

'Oh stop it, will you? You're just winding me up.'

'Sorry, I knew you might think that but, I mean it! Let's meet up after school. I'll take you for a drink and a snack at Body's if you like. That's close to where you live, no?'

'Yeah.' *How does he know where I live?*

'Is that a yeah, you'll be there?' He cocked his head and was up in a flash walking over to the door and said, 'See you later,' looking over his shoulder. As he left, a group of girls walked in, chatting and giggling.

'He is soooo cute, don't you think?'

'Yeah, he looks better than any of the boys in One Direction.'

'Did you hear what he did to Philippa though?'

'No what …?'

146

'She deserved it, I'm sure. She's a bit of a slut…God, I wish he took the slightest bit of interest in me.'

Holly was annoyed that most of the discussion was lost on her. *Arrgh, I must have dreamt this whole thing*, she thought. *Surely he's not wanting to meet me after school. And what did that girl say about what he'd done to Philippa?* She vaguely remembered the girl crying in one of the girls' toilets but then, a girl crying in the toilets happened every day for one reason or another.

She managed to finish her essay and sent it to her tutor just in time for the bell, which calmed her agitated nerves. She'd felt out of control lately, what with her friend's abortion, her mum's deception and her school work being late. The last thing she needed was a boy playing with her feelings. She desperately wanted a boyfriend but Luke seemed way out of her league. Or was he? It had felt good to be the focus of his attention, even if only for a short time.

She was content and it was only at lunch time, sitting and chatting with her friends in the school canteen, that she properly thought back to the encounter with Luke that morning. She was both elated to have been given such a lovely compliment and at the same time had a wary feeling about it. *What if this is just a trap to make fun of me?* She decided not to say a word to her friends and had just bitten into her sandwich when she caught a glimpse of Luke sitting three rows down from her. He was in deep conversation but one glance in her direction confirmed that their earlier encounter had indeed taken place. He quickly looked up and winked at her, a cheeky smile etched into the corner of his mouth.

'What's up, Holly? You look like you've seen the Queen; you're all red in the face,' Tina said, sitting opposite her and now leaning over the table, amused and inquisitive.

'No, there's nothing at all. It's just a bit hot in here.' To demonstrate that she was feeling warm, she slipped out of her school blazer, sensing that Luke was fixing his intense eyes on her all the while.

'You've not said much all morning. Is there something?' Sara added, brushing bread crumbs off the front of her jumper.

'No, how could I say anything when we've been sitting in class all morning? I'm just tired. My brothers don't give me any peace these days. And I got up really early to get to the ICT room. I managed to type up the essay and send it off at last. What a relief!'

This was a bad excuse and she couldn't believe that she had not found a way of telling them what had happened. It was because she couldn't believe it herself, but now that he had sent her another secret wink, she knew that she hadn't dreamt up their chat. Just then, Holly's mobile beeped. She reached into her bag and quickly opened it.

Hey gorgeous, at Body's at 5 – B there X

Wow he's crafty, she thought. How did he get her mobile number? She quickly glanced in his direction over the tables but was surprised to see that the bench where he had sat just a moment ago was now empty. She didn't know what to answer, whether she should go or not, or if she ought to tell her friends. What a dilemma! She slipped her phone back into the bag and swung it over her shoulder, telling them that she was nipping to the toilet before the next lesson.

Her heart was racing fast and she ran into an empty cubicle, sat down on the edge of the lid, thinking and breathing as if she'd drunk too much coffee in one go. She slipped her hand into her bag again and read the message a few times. What was holding her back from answering with a straight, 'Yes, okay' was the fact that she could not believe someone like Luke would really be in the slightest bit interested in meeting up with her. Something didn't add up. She wondered whether she was just being insecure or he was just making fun of her. Knowing his reputation, she was more inclined to believe that he was playing cat and mouse with her. Yes, her friends kept telling her what an exotic beauty she was, with her long, wavy coppery hair and her big bright eyes. She could feature on the cover of a magazine for looking ageless and innocent. She was as skinny as a thirteen-year-old though, whilst the string of girls Luke had so far devoured had mostly been curvy in all the right places. She decided not to answer his text but instead walk past the café on the way home. If he was there, she'd pop in – if not, she'd carry on. She smiled to herself approvingly. After all, a girl could not be too careful these days.

oOo

'Are you playing hard to get then?' He was right there, slumped in one of the chairs in the far corner of the café, watching her walk through the door. The accusation was written all over his face and she instantly felt guilty. She had not been able to see him through the café window but, rather than completely give up on the possibility that he had turned up, she decided to enter and give the place a quick scan. He added one of his irresistible winks to his reproach and lifted his hand to indicate the empty chair next to him. His legs were confidently spread open and for a brief moment she thought that he looked like a younger version of Theo James. He had the same brown eyes and full lips, thick blond hair that seemed to style easily and a lean body which looked good in any clothes. Added to his appearance, he knew how to disarm a girl with an assertive, deep gaze and a smile that conveyed cocky self-confidence.

Her knees felt like jelly and her heart was racing so fast now that it felt as if it was on the brink of bursting through her chest. She grabbed the handle of her bag to settle her shaking hand. She wondered what her friends would have to say about all of this. She had never exchanged a single hello with this guy ever since he joined the school last year, yet a brief chat in the morning had now meant they were looking into each other's eyes as if they'd always wanted to be together. This was what falling in love at first sight must feel like, she thought. The only thing was though, she told herself in an attempt to sober her excitement, that this was not first sight. Next, she felt his hand reach out to hers, patting it gently. It made her feel like an inexperienced little girl, which she knew she was. *Don't spoil this Holly, pull yourself together*, her voice muttered in her head.

'What would you like to drink?'

Holly sat down on the empty seat he had kept for her, placing her bag at her feet and shrugged her shoulders, suggesting a 7 Up.

He returned to the table with a glass and a can and she was amazed about how confident he was at starting a conversation, talking about himself and how soon they were engaged in general chitchat. It was when her mobile beeped with a new message that she realised the time and that her mum would wonder where she was. It was her job to look out for her two brothers until her parents arrived home for dinner.

She gathered her bag, giggling with him now, already more at ease and relaxed.

'Sorry, I've got to go,' Holly said, but before she was able to get up and say good-bye, he was by her side, leaning towards her ear and whispering.

'Don't ever make me wait again, babe.' She looked up in shock, and then sighed with relief when she saw him smiling and blowing her an air kiss and reaching his right hand to her cheek to stroke it with his index finger.

'Wow, I've never met a girl with such perfect skin.' Her cheeks prickled just hearing his words. Compliments did seem to come easy to him but they felt wonderful, even though he was clearly quite full of himself. Don't make me wait again, he'd said, as if he was some kind of VIP.

'Oh, and best not tell anyone we're seeing each other. They'll just make fun of us. OK? See you tomorrow.' She nodded and before she could say anything else, he winked one more time and was out of the door.

She was almost out on the pavement herself when she heard a gruff voice coming from the counter.

'Oi, you've not paid for your drink, young lady.'

'Oh, I'm sorry, I thought my friend paid for me.' She ruffled through her bag and fished out a few coins, handing them over the counter to the lady's outstretched palm.

'A right friend that is then, eh?'

'Ah, he must have forgotten. He was in a real rush. I'm really sorry.' Her cheeks were crimson, this time with embarrassment.

'That's alright, pet. You watch who you go out with.' The lady shook her head slightly and her forehead was still set in a frown as Holly left.

She was fuming with anger. How could he have forgotten to pay? He seemed to have made it so clear that he'd invited her for a drink. Or had he? Maybe she had been assuming too much. He was just a student too, and it had been their first date.

She was still unsure what to make of this strange day when she walked into the apartment and her mother poked her head out of the kitchen.

'All good, sweetheart? What took you so long today?'

'Sorry, I just hung out a bit with the girls after school. I didn't see the time go.'

Her phone beeped with a new message so she slipped out of her shoes and coat and rushed into the bedroom, trying to find a place to chat in peace.

Soz - I had to rush off. Can't wait to see you again. Xx

As much as she had been annoyed by his failure to pay for her drink, she was sucked into the warmth that his few words generated in her tummy.

Meet me in the ICT room.

He did seem to enjoy giving orders, she noticed, and was slightly annoyed yet at the same time there was a feeling of pride nestled in the centre of her chest. *I'm the centre of Luke's attention*, she thought.

The next day, Holly was back in the ICT room, her hair flowing over her shoulders and two sparkly ear rings accentuating her light eyes. Like the day before, Luke was nowhere to be seen until she spotted his bag leaning against the chair in the corner of the room. She decided to walk over when, mid-way past the tables, she felt two arms wrapping around her waist. The adrenaline rushing through her veins almost made her stumble but Luke seemed to have anticipated her reaction because he was already leaning into her, holding her firmly, nestling his soft mouth into her neck and whispering in her ear. He expertly turned her round and without her being able to either escape or resist his strong grip, their hips and then their lips joined. He emitted a slow groan that she hoped was a genuine sign of desire and her whole body felt like it was floating with a pleasant ache coming from the centre of her stomach, travelling all the way down to her pelvis. The palms of his hands felt warm where he was gliding over her shirt and she noticed his expert touch. He seemed to have taken her to another place in time, away from her struggles, her disappointments and frustrations, and even away from the future that at times felt like a concrete wall crushing down on her fragile frame. She didn't remember when she had last felt so light, secure and carefree. Had she ever? The fact that their story was a secret added to the tingling that she now felt travelling up and down her spine as his skilled hands explored the edges of her bra. She was literally swept off her feet, lost for words, lost to the warm body that was holding and exploring hers. They were out of breath, their cheeks flushed and hair ruffled when they finally disentangled and flopped onto the nearby chairs, stifling giggles.

'We can't be seen together yet Holly,' he finally said.

'Why? I don't understand.' She raised her big eyes to his, but Luke seemed to be staring into space, looking at something she could not make out.

'The girl I used to date is dead jealous and watches my every move at the moment. It's so annoying. She can't get over having been dumped and in any case she can be very nasty, she bit right into my arm once. I can't risk her having a go at you.'

'Oh no, that's awful. Why did Philippa do that?' She was secretly touched by his protective behaviour and curious at the same time to find out the true story behind his disastrous liaison.

His head jerked round to face her and as he grabbed her shoulders, his eyes were fiercely set on hers.

'What do you know about Philippa?'

'Ow – you're hurting me, Luke. Calm down, will you?'

'Sorry babe, but honestly, she is the worst of the lot that I've met since joining this school. Well, I suppose the whole school has talked about it. But really, she's the stupid one here.' He almost spat out the last sentence and suddenly broke out into laughter, not laughter caused by a joke but, to Holly's ears, it sounded like he enjoyed the thought of Philippa's loss of fame. She shuddered.

'I don't think much was said at all. I just overheard some girls mentioning her name. That she's been crying and that she got hurt.'

'Hurt? The one who got hurt here is me. What a bitch.'

'Maybe it's nothing to do with you. I don't know really. So, just leave it will you?'

'You're right. She goes out with so many guys, that slut, that you wouldn't know who was hurting who anymore.' He gave her a sideways grin and just shrugged, visibly already past thinking about his failed relationship.

'Luke, I need to ask you something. Don't get all annoyed but I need to get to the bottom of this so, just tell me what happened, OK?'

'Sure, about what?'

'The lady in the café made me pay for the drink yesterday.' As soon as the words spilled out of her mouth, she realised how silly they might sound. But with their morning passion having confirmed that Luke was truly interested in her, she was more than sure that he simply had forgotten to pay up. She scolded herself for even mentioning the embarrassing situation. She was intent on holding on to the fact that the most handsome boy in the whole secondary school was chasing after her. She only had herself to blame.

'What? I paid for that drink! That silly cow, I shouldn't have left you so quickly. She took advantage of the situation to rip us off.' He puffed with irritation and his cheeks turned red with anger. Before she could say anything, his warm soft lips were cupping hers and he lifted her off the floor in a melodramatic swoop. He looked down at her and smiled enticingly.

'She seemed genuine, Luke. Are you sure you paid for *both* drinks?' She instantly felt like a mother scolding her naughty little boy but he took the queue and reassured her.

'Of course, and in any case I didn't drink anything, remember? Anyway, are you implying that I'm lying now?' His brown eyes looked innocent, wide and hurt.

'No, of course not. It's just a misunderstanding.' She sighed with relief that after all, he had meant to pay and probably just forgot, or worse that they had indeed been cheated by the café owner. It was just a soft drink for crying out loud, she scolded herself for the umpteenth time.

'I'm sorry Holly, but you need to be more assertive. Do you honestly think I wouldn't have paid for your drink when it was me who invited you?' For a short moment his eyes looked like they could stare right through her. He instantly softened his gaze, probably reading the anxiety in her face.

'Don't worry, if there's something I hate it's dishonesty and that lady cheating you really pisses me off. Let's meet somewhere else today, OK?'

'Luke, I've, well … we've got a lot of studying to do. Maybe we can do something on the weekend.'

'Come on, I hear you're a good student – I don't think I can wait until the weekend to kiss you more.' He stepped closer to her again and wrapped his arms around her back, pressing his hips into hers. She could not believe that all she was able to do in response was emit a quiet moan of pleasure and a nod. Sara and Tina hugged her all the time but to be held seductively by a gorgeous boy was different, very different.

He looked deep into her eyes, then folded his two hands together as if ready for a prayer in church, but raised his eyes pleadingly up to the ceiling. Her knees felt weak and the butterflies in her stomach fluttered about wildly. She felt like a little girl again, not like the independent teenager she normally was and she was annoyed with herself.

'Okay - but today I can't be too late or my Mum will get suspicious.'

'That's my girl.' He mimicked an imaginary high five, picked up his bag and was off, leaving her standing in the middle of the ICT room, making her feel slightly lost and forlorn. *I wish I was that confident,* she thought as she lifted her bag and raced down the corridor to join her friends outside the classroom. He was right; she should be more assertive and sure of herself. The last thing she wanted was to spoil the amazing feeling of being desired. Her heartbeat must surely have been as loud as a drum as she recalled the entanglement with Luke. The temptation to tell her friends was itching on her tongue all morning, desperately wanting to spill out the news that she had a second date with him.

The next morning, the same meeting took place, just this time shortened by a group of pupils entering the ICT room earlier than expected. They both gathered their bags while Luke threw a cheap comment over his shoulder.

'You'll be fine with the ICT test. If you follow my tips, it'll be easy.'

Before she could think of what to add, she lifted her bag and nearly tripped over the foot of one of the pupils.

'Oooh, got yourself an eager student, have you Luke?'

'Well, yeah, you've got to help the needy ...' came the sarcastic reply, and all broke out in laughter as she rushed past them down the corridor.

Her cheeks were flushed red from the running when she reached her friends. They exchanged their usual hellos and how are yous but she could tell that Sara and Tina did not quite believe the reason for her excitement. She knew that they should rightly be suspicious because she was pretending to be excited about their next cinema outing, distracting them from asking why she had been late again. After all, the English essay had been safely handed in. What other excuse could she concoct? It was difficult to contain herself and for a split second she considered telling them everything.

'I'm finished with my essay by the way. What about you?' she stuttered slightly.

'I thought that's what you did yesterday?'

'Yes, yes, but I quickly added another paragraph. Now it's done and dusted. No more changes.'

'Riiight,' Tina commented with a frown and a sideways glance.

Holly was mortified about her lie and determined that it would be her first and last one. She had always been so angry about her mother's excuses and evasions, so made a mental note never to do it again. However, how could she tell her friends without breaking her promise to Luke?

'You're acting a bit weird lately,' Tina said, and Holly noticed the quick glance that passed between the two girls. They would have spoken about her, she was sure of it.

'Well, I've actually not been sleeping well. Both my brothers have a cough, so annoying and Mum is practically on her knees when she comes through the door. I'm so fed up living at home.' Tina's eyes softened, and Sara immediately wrapped her arm around her. Holly almost believed the lame excuse herself, which at least was the truth but not the real reason for being flustered. She felt even worse now not telling them the whole truth. She had been charmed by a boy whom she believed every girl was dreaming about kissing. She cowered slightly at the thought but luckily had turned towards the classroom door where their English teacher was standing tapping her feet, looking at their little group impatiently.

'Good morning, your majesties! Whenever you feel like it, could you please get to your seats, so I may start the lesson?' She said, her face was set in a frown. The inseparable group of girls walked towards three empty seats muttering a 'sorry'. Their English teacher had proven to be one of the more observant teachers. She commented on her delight that the girls had handed in their essays, albeit a bit late. She'd also questioned Sara about her looking a bit pale and whether she could be lacking in vitamins. She'd reminded them of the impending GCSEs and that they should try and goad each other on, adding that she believed they could achieve good results.

As soon as Holly slipped through the door, she could see him slumped at the back of the classroom, in deep conversation with two of his friends. She initially averted her eyes but the moment he focused his intense stare on her, Holly could not help but gaze back. Her heart was beating intensely and she felt the heat climbing up her face. Just as soon as she was sitting in her seat and had opened her books, she felt his eyes piercing through her spine, willing her to turn round and look at him. The small hairs on the back of her neck were raised and she felt so flustered that her pen fell through her fingers.

'Holly, are you alright?' Tina whispered.

'I'm fine, don't worry,' she answered under her breath.

When she saw Luke again later that day, she suddenly realised that she'd moved from having never been noticed by boys before to being the centre of attention of the best–looking specimen in school. He sent her one of his secret winks and she felt giddy just thinking about the early morning kissing and embracing. She had heard girls mention before that things could move fast in a relationship, but from a quick chat in the ICT room to a kiss and passionate entanglement in the space of a few days was overwhelming, probably a record, she thought. She was also astonished about how quickly she'd accepted Luke's advances, yet decided that it had felt really good and that she enjoyed the view from cloud nine.

When the next message came into her phone, she had almost forgotten the awkward exchange in the ICT room.

Soz for this morning. xxxx

oOo

When they met again, he was agitated and restless and their conversation was nowhere near as relaxed as the previous times they had got together. He was still all over her and when their lips met she could sense his passion, yet he could not hide his moist palms and an underlying tension.

'What's up, Luke? You seem a bit upset.'

'Never mind. I'm okay.' He lowered his head and it was the first time she noticed dark circles under his eyes.

'You know you can tell me. If there's something I can do, I will. You just have to tell me.'

He looked bashful and his eyes had lost their usual shine that afternoon. He was visibly preoccupied about something.

'I'm a wreck, Holly. My stepdad is giving my mum hell and I overheard their conversation last night.' He stopped, subdued by what he was seemingly unable to tell her. Holly's heart melted just seeing his face so downcast.

'Well, at least I have you,' he said, raising his face up to her, and she was overwhelmed again by his beautiful eyes looking at her. 'I can't tell my friends about us for now, though. They think I'm a tough guy and only after girls for one thing.' He looked at her in a meaningful way. 'You've not mentioned anything either, have you?' He was watching her closely now.

'No, I haven't,' she answered quickly, keen to

loosen up his intense stare.

'We best keep it a secret, don't you think? It feels so good to be with someone so gentle and honest ...' His thoughts appeared to drift off and she watched his eyes scanning the room and his hands moving frantically again. 'Would you mind paying for our drinks today? My stepdad told me that there's no pocket money this week. It's so embarrassing.'

'No, it's not embarrassing at all. Would your parents not let you work? I've done lots of babysitting and different jobs in the neighbourhood. It's really quite easy to earn a bit of cash.'

'You have no idea what my parents are like. I'd love to work. I actually think I could make some money with web design or something. Babysitting doesn't sound very appealing.' He pursed his lips, amused. 'Unless it was sitting next to you watching a baby, yeah.' He moved over to tickle her.

'Ahh, you're so silly.' She wriggled out of his grasp, laughing. 'Web design sounds good, sure. I wouldn't know where to start, but yeah, it sounds brilliant.'

When his mobile beeped with a message, he jumped up as soon as he'd read it and gave her a quick peck on the head.

'See you tomorrow ... I've got to run. I'll be in touch later, okay? You said you had to rush home anyway, yes?' Without waiting for her response nor another glance in her direction, he was out of the café, leaving her to feel an emptiness as well as a yearning for more. Being in love was an amazing sensation and after she paid for the drinks, she was sitting on her cloud again, a smile etched on her face all the way home.

Before she managed to open the main entrance door, her phone interrupted her thoughts and she decided to answer the ringing first. It was Sara. In a few words she told Holly that she and Tina had been following her after school.

'You've done *what*?' She was shocked and angry to know that her two best friends had spied on her and were intruding on her secret relationship – surely that's what it was, after all the intimacy that had passed between her and Luke – but she noticed that her outrage was coloured with a sense of relief. She remembered that, had it not been for Luke's reluctance, she would have boasted about having her very first boyfriend to the whole wide world from the very start. She took a deep breath and, after a moment of silence, decided that she would probably have snooped as well if one of the other girls had been acting strangely. They could not believe what they'd seen, Sara told her then. Holly was proud hearing the words. Yes, it was amazing, she replied, and quickly urged her friend not to tell, that it was all still a secret for fear that they'd be the laughing stock of the entire school. Yet, what her friend said next upset her. Had she been okay about kissing Luke? From what they could see, Luke had seemed to hold her so tightly, that they'd feared he had actually forced himself on her.

'Oh Sara, how can you say such a thing? He'd never do something like that. The attraction is completely mutual.'

'When did this all start and why didn't we know about it?' Sara said crossly.

'He surprised me in the ICT room the other day.'

'When?' Sara was practically screaming down the phone now. She could hear how appalled her friend was by the news and felt hugely disappointed.

162

'Now I know why you were late all these mornings. Did you not think we'd suspect something?'

'Of course, but it just went so fast and he insisted from the beginning that I shouldn't tell anyone about us.'

'Holly, what are you talking about? Don't you know about his reputation?'

'Here we go. You're just jealous,' she answered lamely.

'Sure, he's a hot guy. Of course he is, but that doesn't mean I'm jealous. Anyway, his looks are probably why he gets away with being a bastard. You know that Holly. So, no, I'm definitely not jealous, just worried about you.'

'How can you judge someone without knowing him? He's so kind and attentive with me. He's got a lot of problems, you know.' As soon as the words were out, she felt doubt creeping up her spine. Did he really pay for the drink during their first date and why had he suddenly been out of cash? Worse, why was she defending him?

'Yeah, he's got problems alright. From what I hear, Holly, he owes some people a lot of money.' Sara sniggered into the phone.

'You don't understand, Sara. He told me all about his shitty life with his stepdad and that they're struggling to pay the rent this month. He was really vulnerable today.'

'I can't believe what I'm hearing, Holly. You must really have fallen for him.'

'What's wrong with having fun, Sara? You of all friends …'

'Don't get me wrong Holly, please just hear me

out, will you?' Sara interrupted, then after a small pause, continued. 'I know you. This isn't about having fun ... we just spoke to one of his ex-girlfriends and she burst into tears just hearing his name mentioned. She told us that she still has a massive bruise on her arm. He said that he'd done it 'by accident' but she told us it was because he didn't get what he wanted.'

'I can't imagine that he'd be able to hurt a fly. What was it he wanted from her?' Holly asked tentatively.

'She couldn't tell us. I think she was too upset, embarrassed or something. I'm not sure.'

'See? You don't know. I just can't imagine him doing anything bad to anyone. He's so gentle. You know how nasty and jealous girls can be. Please don't spoil this for me. It's the first time someone has really taken an interest in me and ...' Her voice broke up as she recalled his warm touch and the flow of compliments that surely no one could say unless they'd really meant it. He'd be a candidate for drama school if this had all just been a charade. And why would he waste his precious time on her if he wasn't truly attracted? No, her friend was mistaken. No one had ever spoken to her like that before and it had felt truthful and good. Everyone deserved a second chance.

'Holly - be careful! You know *us*; we're your best friends. We'd never be jealous of you, ever.' Sara was pronouncing every word carefully as if they were as precious as gold.

'I know but really you have nothing to worry about,' Holly replied.

'I'm not so sure about that. Let's speak at school tomorrow, okay?'

'Yeah, sure, but in the meantime do not tell *anyone*

please. I promised that we'd keep our relationship secret.'

'Isn't it a bit early to talk about a relationship?' Sara gasped at the other end of the line. Holly's answer came out as cold as ice.

'Sara, you have no idea what goes on between us. He's amazing. If you gave him a chance at least, you'd see. Nobody is perfect. Well, sometime soon I'm sure he'll want everyone to know about us and then you'll feel sorry for saying this.' She bit onto her upper lip, trying to hold back tears.

'If it wasn't you saying this Holly, I'd dismiss what you just said. By all means, if you think this feels okay I'll stand by you, but don't let him rob you of a normal life.'

'Pff, you can speak. What's a normal life?'

'Look, I already told you. Luke's good looking and his charms probably irresistible, but that doesn't change the fact that he stares at girls in a sleazy way. He's so secretive and I've seen him loads of times in intense discussions with people. I know that some girls bring it on themselves, I'm not denying that for one second. But …' She sighed.

'Exactly, Luke told me that he got bitten by Philippa. Well, maybe there is jealousy and that's why he wants to protect me by not telling anyone about us. Don't tell anyone. Again, he made me promise not to say a word.'

'Of course, I'll keep it to myself but, I don't know Holly. I don't like the sound of all this but as I said, I hope you're right. I really want you to be happy, you know that, don't you?'

'Yeah, of course – see you tomorrow okay? Got to go.' She hung up and as she slipped the phone back into her pocket, a little emoji popped into view on the front screen. It was a smiley face from Luke with a kiss set on the edge of its mouth. She smiled, convinced that all would be well.

oOo

The next day, they were both back again in the usual early morning meeting place. He looked upbeat and if there had been any kind of worry and sadness the day before, it all seemed forgotten.

'Nice to see you're happy again, Luke.' She beamed at him as they greeted with a passionate kiss.

'Well, it's my birthday today and I'm holding the most gorgeous girl in my arms.' Before she could answer, he closed her mouth with another kiss.

At some point, he reached for her tie and slowly pulled her towards him, kissing her cheeks, her lips, then moving his warm breath towards her neck. The pull was getting stronger when his other hand slowly drew her shirt out of her skirt. She squirmed and tried to speak, but he stifled her words with a kiss that was getting increasingly persistent. His hand travelled up her hip and his fingers were slowly lifting her bra underneath the strap at her back. Within seconds his hand was cupping her breast and she was moaning with shock and pleasure at how good it felt. Next, he disentangled himself from her, telling her that it was time to make a move. She pushed her shirt hurriedly back into place and tried as best she could to smooth her hair out of her face and appear dignified.

Next, he was holding a delicate golden necklace in front of her astonished face. He held it dangling from his index finger, watching her surprise with amusement.

'It's your birthday and you're giving *me* a gift?'

Without another word, he turned her around and hooked the chain around her neck, then leaned towards her ear, whispering.

'You're mine and I wanted you to know that.' His words made the small hairs on her neck tingle.

'We should celebrate your birthday…'

'I'm sorry, I can't make it today after school, Holly. Tomorrow, same time, same place. Can you last until then, kitty-cat?' He was out of the room within seconds as usual, without a backward glance.

Later that day, she faced her friends' inquisitive stares and reassured them that there was nothing to worry about.

'What makes you think this is okay, Holly?' Tina said, touching the necklace hanging from her neck.

'He was all over me and I feel this is special. He's been disappointed in the past. Just imagine, he's given me a gift on his birthday.'

'Because he wants something,' Tina blurted out.

'You're joking, right?' Holly replied.

'I'm sorry, that wasn't called for.' Tina leaned over looking bashful. 'Let's talk about something else.' She added, giving Holly a little nudge and offering her a piece of her chocolate bar.

Later that day, she was proudly twirling the chain around her finger when her mobile bleeped. It was Luke.

Hi, can u meet me downstairs?

You're outside? she answered, her heart thumping with excitement.

Yes, kwik, think of something.

She wriggled into a warm hoodie, jumped off her bed, and sneaked past the living room where her parents were watching television. She made some noise in the kitchen, put the kettle on, and while the bubbles were creating a roar she slipped into her shoes, fetched her keys, and slipped out.

'Hi Holly.' Luke's face looked dishevelled.

'Hi, what's the matter?' She was immediately concerned, seeing his puffed up eyes.

'I had a fight with my parents. You see, I found this great job the other day, working in a trendy shop in the west end, but I really need new trainers.' She looked down at his feet and had to nod in agreement. Luke's shoes did look tatty.

'My mum and dad promised I'd get a new pair for my birthday, but they let me down again. I really need this job, Holly, and you know what it's like in these places, the staff have to look the part.' He picked up one of her hands, then looked into her eyes intently. 'I hate to ask you a favour.'

'Tell me, Luke, what is it you need. Your birthday, of all days.'

'Yeah, well, I'm used to it.' He looked self-conscious. 'I just need a hundred pounds so that I can get a decent pair of trainers. The great news is that I'll get paid a week on Friday and, well I thought to make it up to you … and of course to spend a bit more time together,' he moved towards her, embracing her and kissing her neck gently, 'I'd like to treat you to a day in Brighton, on the Saturday.'

'Luke, a hundred pounds …that's steep.'

'Seventy would be okay, too. I saw a cheaper pair,' he said swiftly.

She swallowed, then thought about the necklace, reassured that his feelings must be genuine.

'Okay then, I'll see you tomorrow morning and get the money out before school.'

He hugged her, then kissed her on the head.

'I knew, we had something special going. I'm really looking forward to starting work, although the downside is that I just won't see you as much over the next week or so, but at least it'll be great to have some money. I'll pay you right back and start treating you a bit more.' He smiled, pulling out his mobile that had started ringing. 'Right, you better get back inside. It's cold out here. See you tomorrow.' He walked away, chatting to the caller, without as much as another glance back at her. She shrugged, stepping back inside, shivering.

They were lounging on Tina's bed on the following Sunday, just like old times. Holly was hugging her legs, sitting up against the wall.

'I've been seeing Luke for over three weeks now and he's offered to take me to Brighton next Saturday to celebrate his birthday. He's got himself a job and all,' she announced proudly. 'I need you to cover for me, please. I'm so excited about spending a whole day with him at last.' She'd get the opportunity to gaze at the sea properly again, she added in her head. 'I didn't tell your parents about you know what. So, I expect you not to tell on me now, okay?' Holly looked at Sara intently and regretted her threat right away. When did she learn to manipulate her friend like this? Why was she so desperate anyway? After all, she would actually like to tell them how good she felt lately and that she was head over heels in love and it felt amazing. What was holding her back was the memory of his suspicious nature and deep down her intuition telling her that somehow, all this was surely just a dream. Her thoughts were pulling her every which way. One moment she got a tingling feeling in her chest just thinking about his soft lips touching hers, the stroke of his hand above her knee, and another moment she wondered whether her emotions had robbed her of forming any rational thought.

What she hadn't told them was that Luke owed her money now.

oOo

She looked right and left again, but Luke was nowhere to be seen. With the two tickets in hand, she decided to jump into the next carriage closest to her. That was when the mobile bleeped at last.

Hi babe – I'm sorry I won't start the journey with you. Will hop onto the train from the next stop, so keep my ticket safe. Something's come up. See you shortly. Xxxxx

She barely had time to consider the meaning of the message, when another one came in. It was from Sara.

Are you on the train yet? Is he looking after you?

Holly swallowed painfully and as the train left the station, the lump in her throat was getting heavier and heavier. Why she was so uptight, she was not entirely sure.

It suddenly felt as if hundreds of needles had been stuck into her tummy. The pain of the cramps was so severe that she frantically looked along the aisle up to the area where signs would indicate the whereabouts of the bathrooms. She spotted the sign lit up at the furthest end of the carriage, walked over and waited outside the closed door. She hated public toilets with a vengeance because of the smell of other people and the way many of them disregarded the person that would step into the cubicle after them. The thought was enough to make her want to retch but she managed to stifle it, reminding herself that she had no choice.

Stepping into it, she could barely manage to look at her reflection. That morning she'd been so excited, getting ready in front of Tina's mirror, being coaxed and gloated over by her friend. As soon as Luke had sent her his first message about getting her to buy two train tickets, she had felt like a balloon which had lost its air in a single swift whoosh. She knew that she had lost track, lost her sense of self and was wondering where the sensible, rational Holly had gone. He insisted that he'd pay her straight back, apologising profusely. Despite his reassurances, she felt let down.

At the next train stop, she let her eyes travel over the platform and with a little flutter of hope spotted the familiar crop of short hair and his worn leather jacket amongst the crowd waiting for the train to stop. They were expected to let the flow of passengers out first, so that new ones could come on. She watched as he was the only person bold enough to try and squeeze past the exiting flow of people, being cursed and cursing back. She sank back into her seat, suddenly unsure, a cold sweat sticking to the back of her neck and lower spine. What on earth was she doing here? What should she do next? And then he was there, by her side with that customary wink, hands searching and prodding and grabbing, and he must have realised that she was not responding.

'You're not telling me that you're upset about me being late, are you?' His breath smelled of alcohol and something else – she couldn't tell what because she'd never smelt it before. 'Come on, what's up?'

'Nothing. You're the one who planned this *surprise* trip, so...'

'So, I made it in time to take you to the seaside. I don't see where your problem is!' He put on a pout and blinked with his eyes innocently. She laughed, punching his shoulder playfully, his distorted face mimicking pain in response.

Despite the change of mood, she felt guilty and angry all at once, two emotions tugging at opposite sides, which lately had become a familiar sensation. She was unexpectedly swept up by the realisation that what she had been looking for all along was love and tenderness. Someone to care about her, hold her, and tell her things would be alright. That was when his next words reached her through a mist of confusion.

'I'll show you the sights and sounds of Brighton. You wait and see – it'll be unforgettable.' There was the wink again, which was starting to irritate her, and she decided to pretend having to head for the toilet again, if only to collect her thoughts and take a few breaths at the end of the carriage. When he was not next to her she felt like a void had opened up, but when he was right next to her it was like he was smothering her. And even though it had felt good to be desired, it was less so now. She scolded herself that she was acting like a spoiled brat, someone who didn't know what she wanted. She brushed her hair back, put some lip gloss on her dry lips and subtly tugged her padded bra into place. She was determined to have fun today, her first day out with her boyfriend. She looked at her reflection in the mirror one more time, rolled her shoulders back and returned to her seat with a sense of purpose and excitement.

They arrived at the train station and he was all over her when they walked into the main hall.

'Babe, I'm skint, I've got to get some cash out of the machine first, so I can treat you.'

'Yes, don't forget the train tickets and the seventy pounds. I can't afford to pay for all of this, you know.'

'Now, now are you pleading poverty? You told me that you worked!' He looked at her expectantly.

'Still, I ... you said you'd treat me and the money was to help you buy shoes.'

'Oh, stupid me, and I secretly hoped it was a birthday gift.' He focused his brown eyes on her, his head tilted slightly.

'Luke, that's not fair.' Her face felt hot with confusion.

'Don't worry. I'll pay you back, calm down.'

They walked towards a cash machine where he inserted his card a few times without success. His anger and irritation was palpable. Within seconds his mood had gone from jolly and casual to annoyed and concerned.

'Let's go and try another machine. This is a nightmare. My money probably didn't arrive yet. They promised that I'd have it every Friday.'

'So, your parents are okay with you working now?' she asked, puzzled.

'You're not the only one making money here, you know. Just don't tell anyone. If my parents knew, they'd demand half of it for rent.' He brushed his hair back and before she could ask any more he was dragging her out of the train terminal. Her tummy was rumbling and she suggested that they go for lunch first.

'I just told you, I'm skint. Could you get some money out? Please, just this once.' He begged, batting his eyelids. At that instant his mobile went off and he stopped in his tracks. Before he answered the call, he managed to touch her golden necklace ever so lightly, then suggested that she should get some cash out for now and that he'd pay her back straight away, as soon as they found another cash machine. She felt as if her body was stuck in a puppet show, someone else holding the strings attached to her arms and feet and guiding her head into the wrong direction. Next, she sensed his hand giving her a shove and saw his encouraging nod, and she slowly headed back to the machine he'd just left. It was as if her stomach had dropped to her feet, she was so hollow. When she turned around one more time, he was already on the phone, talking intently with someone on the other line, completely oblivious of her presence now.

She may have come to Brighton to enjoy the sea view but was aware all of a sudden that it didn't matter anymore. She picked up her feet and ran, scanning the departure board for the next train back to London.

oOo

'You let me down, you bitch. I was stranded without a penny, miles away from London.' He was practically spitting the words into her face. He seized the top of her arm and pulled her harshly towards him.

Holly's eyes were cold with anger. Luke had cornered her in one of the school's halls but she was

174

determined to ignore his insults, waiting for the best moment to retort. It was so outrageously unfair that she felt like punching the living daylights out of him. Her fists were clenched and she was about to answer when he carried on.

'How dare you treat me like that? You left me standing there, pretending to get cash out for us.'

'And how dare you talk to me like that? You disgust me. You made me buy the train tickets, were late, and then had insufficient funds in your account to even buy me a sandwich. Do you think I'm stupid? I saw the screen. You're overdrawn by a huge amount. There was no way that you'd 'treat' me to a day out in Brighton or give me the money I *lent* you. Pff, you're pathetic. Let go of me.' She tried to shake him off but his grip hardened, making her draw breath with the pain.

His eyes darted from side to side and his fist clenched with rage. What seemed to stop him from punching her was a group of students walking past them.

'Oh well, I never thought much of you, just in case you hadn't noticed.' He let go of her, pushing her away as if she were a piece of junk, a look of disgust on his face.

The words stung. She was taken aback by the hurt she sensed in the centre of her stomach, despite all the determination she had built up over the weekend to face him confidently. She was prepared for this, considering that he'd phoned her mobile a hundred times and texted like crazy. She knew that his words should be meaningless but they still hurt.

'You're so weak, after all. What a waste of my precious time. And don't think that I'll give you your money back. You let me stand there all by myself. I deserve better than that.' Then he started laughing and with his usual arrogant gait walked off with a swagger that she would have liked to crush, squash and exterminate from the surface of the earth. He turned one more time, pointing his finger at her menacingly. 'Don't think you'll get away with it. You'll pay for treating me like that.'

The rage she experienced was the same rage all the other girlfriends must have felt at his inability to acknowledge his pathetic, selfish game. She was utterly stunned because there was absolutely nothing that seemed to make sense any more. He said that he was in love with her. He said that she was gorgeous and that all he wanted was to keep her to himself with no one looking, no one knowing. Yet, over the last forty-eight hours she had had to keep reminding herself that this had been a ploy all along. She had not seen the real Luke, had not wanted to see the real Luke, come to think of it. He must somehow have known that she had put savings into a bank account or at least he would have overheard her telling her friends that she was babysitting and being paid for doing lots of odd jobs. Well, she actually recalled now proudly telling him herself. Her face turned ashen, her arms now hanging limply by her sides.

If moments ago she had felt able to kick his head in and stamp him into the ground, now she didn't think she had any strength left to even pick up her schoolbag. She shuffled over to a seat in an empty back room and slumped into the chair, burying her head into her hands. All she was really left with was wondering how on earth she could have believed a single word he ever said to her. Actions spoke louder than words, everybody knew that and still – pah, there was the old wisdom staring into her stupid face. She felt so utterly dejected as her eyes blurred with salty tears and she hadn't even got the strength to wipe them out of her face. Her thoughts trailed every which way now. She wanted to disappear into the depth of the earth, ideally sitting on a flow of lava and being swept away into the abyss. She knew then what it was like to be used purely for someone else's benefit.

Luke knew exactly how to trap her and make her think that she'd been chosen by the most attractive boy in school. He had seen her blush, her looks of adoration, and he had calmly watched as she had fallen right into the trap that he'd prepared just for her, the same way he'd designed clever ploys for all the other girls before her.

Her eyes were red and sore when she walked into the nearby girls' toilets. She splashed water over her warm red cheeks and dabbed the puffy skin under her eyes. So much for love and excitement, she rebuked herself. She hadn't noticed a person stepping into the bathroom whilst she leant down to pick up her bag and was startled to see her English teacher standing behind her.

'Oh sorry, I didn't hear you come in,' she said, and was about to walk past her when the teacher touched her arm lightly.

'I was actually expecting to find you in here. I saw you and Luke in discussion and quite frankly I didn't like the look of it. Is everything okay? Well, I should rephrase that I think. Do you want to talk about it?'

Holly's eyes welled up again upon hearing the words. She thought that all her tears had dried up and that she could face the world again. But no, there was so much grief to get rid of.

'Come, just follow me and we'll find a quiet place to sit,' her teacher added calmly.

The words were soothing and Holly thought that they were exactly what she needed to hear. She followed with a small nod. On their way, she was relieved to notice that Luke was nowhere to be seen. His anger had spoken volumes about what he was capable of and the memory of Philippa's bruises came to her mind.

They finally settled in the empty art classroom where her teacher encouraged her to sit down and, after fetching a glass of water, pulled up a chair and sat down in front of her. She listened closely to Holly's description of events and after taking a deep breath commented.

'You know there are people who actually enjoy inflicting pain.'

Holly's eyes darted up in surprise.

'I've been watching Luke for a while. I can't give you the reasons but you know yourself that he's only been at this school for less than a year.'

Holly's cheeks blushed instantly as she realised that she might have been fooled by a person whose behaviour had been noted.

'Is that because of what maybe happened to Philippa?'

'Yes, partly because of that. Unfortunately, she was really hurt. It's so difficult to collect evidence though. On the one hand we are responsible for providing all of you with an education and on the other we need to ensure the safety and wellbeing of every pupil in our care.'

'I feel so stupid for falling for him,' Holly said.

'It's natural for you to feel like that, Holly. You're so young and it's very difficult to see the difference between genuine affection and someone who maybe just pretends, yet has an ulterior, selfish motive. I'm not saying this was the case with you and Luke. By what I just saw, I guess things are not too good though. You both looked very angry.'

Holly shivered at the thought.

'He cheated, lied to me, and he owes me money,' she replied, then decided to blurt out the whole story, happy at last to off-load her strange relationship with Luke. 'I really thought he meant it,' she concluded, sniffing back tears.

'Holly, I'm so sorry. I'm very pleased you spoke to me and, by the way, it's great to see that you're working hard on getting good grades. You kids are so fragile at this age and it's so hard to help you when you most need it. I can only imagine how much you yearn for a better future but let me tell you that you're a lucky girl, having Sara and Tina. And you're very clever. Look out for each other and you'll get through it,' she said, then paused briefly before resuming.

'As for Luke, I'll keep an eye on him. It looked like he was hurting you out there.'

'Yeah, he grabbed me really hard. It still hurts.' Holly felt like crying again, remembering Luke's harshness.

'Unfortunately there's not much I can say regarding the money, Holly. My guess is that he won't pay you back or he may even deny you ever gave it to him. What I suggest though, is that you should make sure you don't walk home alone and that your mobile is in your hands if you need to call or send a text. If you ever want to speak to me again, you know where I am at school.'

Holly's eyes were sore and puffy and a hiccup interrupted her whispered, 'Thank you.'

'Don't thank me, dear. Thank you for coming forward with this now and for being so brave to open up. It's half the problem out of the way. We all make mistakes about misjudging people's behaviour or true feelings.' Holly nodded and smiled softly. The teacher's voice had been gentle and soothing.

Holly's knees were weak when she finally stood up, feeling wobbly but otherwise relieved. Her school tie was squint and her teacher leant over to set it right. She gently brushed a few strands out of her face and placed her warm hands on Holly's shoulders.

'There is one more thing, Miss.'

'Yes?'

'Luke has cheated and I can prove it. He told me that the reason he went to the ICT room early in the morning before class was to copy essays. For the last one, you know the end of year project, he just took passages from the internet.' She said it all in one quick breath, the weight of the knowledge visibly tumbling out of her mouth.

'How can you prove this Holly? It's a serious allegation. We're talking about plagiarism. You're not saying all these things to get back at him, are you?' The teacher's eyes focused on Holly.

'Well, I know where he copied texts from for the essay we had to hand in recently. I told him it was wrong. He said that he'd only done it this one time because he was late. He also said that he was dyslexic and that it wasn't fair to ask the same of him.'

'I see, well, I can assure you that Luke is *not* in the slightest bit dyslexic, just … well, leave this with me and I'll see what I can do.' She sighed and shook her head.

Holly nodded and after thanking her teacher again, made her way out the door.

She stood in the hall for a while, sending a text message to her mother, then rummaged in her bag for the bottle of water she'd bought earlier in the day. As she took the first few refreshing sips, she heard her teacher's muffled voice from the art room. From the snippets that reached her ears, it sounded as if she was reporting back to the head teacher. She couldn't help but move back a little closer to the door.

'Yes and no. Whatever it is, he may possibly admit to having done wrong but it's usually a farce, to rope you back into believing anything he says. We know he's got a conduct disorder and causing so much pain among the girls here. It's hard to help them, you know. By what Holly is saying, he also owes her money.'

There was a pause before the teacher carried on.

'I know, she's lucky nothing worse happened. After Philippa ...'

She couldn't hear the rest of the conversation as it sounded like her teacher was walking around the class room.

'Yes, I'll make some enquiries and see whether we can initiate some kind of counselling. He'll not believe he needs it but at least if we instigate the procedure, it'll distract him for a while. I'll get the ICT teacher to inspect his file.' The sound of her voice was coming closer to the door, so Holly decided to call it a day. She'd heard enough.

A few days later as Holly was walking home, her thoughts as heavy as lead, she was taken out of her reverie by the familiar sound of a message arriving on her phone.

Hi Holly – Have u heard?

About what? she answered.

Well, Luke of course – he's been called into the

head's office. News r spreading fast and furious so I'm not sure exactly what is true or not.

oOo

'What I found out is that Luke is what they call a 'manipulator'. It's quite something to get your tongue around. But if you look at the list of characteristics and the way they deceive you, it fits him like a glove,' Sara exclaimed. Holly wrung her hands in response while Tina wrapped one arm around her shoulder. She felt ashamed, unable to make eye contact, then simply shrugged, saying nothing. Tina continued to comment on the amount of information available online, pointing out that a victim was likely to feel ashamed for defending the manipulator.

'We know that it's normally you who's the brainy one. But we thought we'd look up the information available about 'manipulators' on the net, and you wouldn't believe the amount of stuff that's been written about these people. Women can be like that too, but they tend to have a different style. The main strategy is that they are really charming and good with words. And they tend to act fast and pretend that they can't be without you,' she said, watching Holly all the while.

'Well, I can confirm that,' Holly said bitterly.

'So, don't feel bad about what happened. He had us all fooled until we heard about Philippa.'

'Yes, Sara's right. It looks like we'd all have fallen into his trap. He is good looking, after all. So, please don't beat yourself up over this. It's not like you got pregnant along the way … unlike some silly person in this room.'

'Yeah, look at what an idiot I've been. What would I have done without you girls? Really, Holly, we should go on a special diet. Not talk about boys, not look at boys, not even think about them. Imagine they're an alien species we have to avoid at all cost.' The girls burst out laughing but a sudden bang interrupted their giggles. Holly and Sara looked at each other in surprise. The only one who wasn't startled by the noise was Tina.

'What was that?' Sara asked.

'You wouldn't believe it, but my brother is actually, seriously, honestly, really …' Tina rolled her eyes.

'Yes, yes … what?'

'He's practicing for Britain's Got Talent.'

The girls' eyes widened. 'And what is it exactly he believes he could contribute to the show?' Holly asked.

'Well, actually he's not that bad but still, he'd have to practice an awful lot before auditioning, I think. He thinks he can belly-dance better than a woman.'

'He can *what?*'

The giggles that rippled through the girls' bodies was causing tears of laughter to wet their cheeks and they were soon rolling all over each other, bellies aching and exhausted from a roller-coaster of emotions.

That's when Holly knew that she'd recover, that soon Luke would only remain as a dark shadow in her memories, that indeed actions spoke louder than words and that you had to forgive yourself for being foolish.

oOo

'You did what, Mum?' Holly sat at the kitchen table, looking up to her mother's face.

'I took a picture of the two of you kissing, embracing and well …gazing into each other's eyes.'

'WHY?'

'I did it because I needed to know what you were up to after school. I just had an inkling, which made me follow you. Sorry, I just didn't like what I saw AT ALL. I remember being a teenager. I may not be a good parent but I do have a nose for fishy situations. You've been consistently late coming home, your clothes smelled different somehow, and your eyes looked absent most of the time over dinner. I could tell you'd been hiding something from me and I could tell it was because of a boy.'

'This is incredible, Mum.'

'I know. As I already said, I know I'm not the greatest Mum on earth – you don't have to tell me that - and who am I to talk anyway? I've done things that are terrible, despicable, but the one thing I cannot bare is … someone taking advantage of my baby. I got my phone out and zoomed into the scene. I know at the time you'd have killed me but there you go, I've been there before, you see.'

'What do you mean?'

Without answering Holly's question, she continued.

'When you came home upset the other night, I knew I had to act fast. I knew also that you'd not tell me what happened. So, I walked up to him yesterday and told him that if he as much as looks at you or threatens or touches you again in any way, he'll have to deal not only with me but with the evidence I've got. I said that I'd send my pictures to some of your school mates so that he'd have to explain himself to them. Sorry, sweetheart, I think you're gorgeous but you know just as well as I do that he wasn't serious about being with you or has never been serious about any girl. All he was after was your money. So, he'd be mortified and he'd feel exactly what his type hates feeling – being exposed in front of a crowd.'

Holly's eyes narrowed and for a few moments she was literally lost for words. Was this really her mother talking to her or just a very bizarre dream?

'I don't understand.' She finally managed to say, articulating each word very carefully. Her right hand had moved to the middle of her chest as if she now braced herself for more unusual comments.

'Oh Holly, it was so obvious to everyone that you were saving up money. You're paid for babysitting, jobs in the neighbourhood, and if I could tell, of course your friends could and ... so could someone like Luke. He just had to have his feelers out for the 'worker', you know what I mean? The person that works hard and is too busy to notice when someone is on the lookout to benefit from them. These people can smell you out from a long distance.'

Holly was slowly nodding her head as her mum's words sunk in. How could she ever have thought that Luke was remotely interested in *her*?

'For some reason we all dream about meeting the charming prince in shining armour but, trust me, he doesn't exist. It's all bullshit .... utter bullshit. And you know what? It's okay.'

Holly's eyes shot up and she was now gazing

straight at her mother whose face was glowing with passion and determination, her brown wavy hair slightly out of place above her right ear and her slim hands imploring her to listen and accept.

'I know. I'm okay Mum, really.'

Her mother reached over and Holly was surprised that there was no hint of alcohol on her breath. In actual fact, her mum had smelled different for a while and this possibly had something to do with the fact that during their conversation, the usual resigned person she had known for so long had been replaced by a more determined, almost belligerent character. She was defending her, had taken a clever step in protecting her and had gone as far as facing Luke with clear evidence. She couldn't help but feel a rush of warmth for her mother now, this vulnerable messed up adult who would have been hurt badly herself in the past. She sighed and noticed that the bright light of the kitchen's ceiling lamp was accentuating the circles under her Mum's eyes. She lowered her gaze, trying to focus on what lay ahead.

oOo

As she looked at him, his eyes dropped, a few strands of blond hair falling over his forehead. It was greasy and unkempt and his breath revealed a night of heavy drinking. She sat back in her chair trying to hide her discomfort and the need to cover her nose from the intense reek wafting over to her. He wasn't his usual confident self and she watched as he slowly turned away from her and hunched his shoulders in an oversized brown leather jacket, like he often did when he knew he'd been caught. He rubbed his moist palms on his dirty jeans and started tapping his right foot on the floor. One of his shoes had lost its laces and his socks looked a dirty grey, which once must have been white. She knew he was not going to talk first and that if she was going to make the first move, his excuses would come out mumbled and only increase his nervous twitches and his eyes moving wildly around the room. He had a demeanour of someone in need of saving and if it wasn't for the state of his appearance and Holly's recent revelations, he looked like a small child you would want to scoop up in your arms and cuddle until their tears and sadness subsided. She knew better though, not to believe his pretence, and asked him a few general questions. She had heard all about the fictitious step father, the dire conditions of living. None of that was accurate. His dad worked at a local bakery and his mother was a cleaner at the main hospital ten miles away. They both had long days and therefore very little time to gauge their son's whereabouts and various doings. She took a deep breath, trying to stay as neutral as she could by keeping her voice steady and calm.

'Luke, we're reaching the end of the school year. How is everything going?'

'Yeah, great.'

'Hmm. I've noticed though, that you appear very distracted lately.'

He looked up at her fleetingly but shrugged his shoulders instead of saying anything.

'Well, I wanted to talk to you because I've noticed that the style of your writing has changed … to the extent that I'm wondering whether you've been given help by someone else.' As soon as she'd voiced her concern, his mood shifted.

'Why? It's so typical that no one would believe that I can write a good essay. It's so typical,' he said angrily.

'I never said that you were not able to write a good essay, Luke. I'm just querying the style. It's just that I can tell that it's not yours, you see. It's okay to get tutored once in a while. I encourage it, actually.'

'Oh well, why would I go to school if it wasn't to improve my style?' She had to concede that his answer was clever and again could have fooled her, had she not known about his past and been able to prove his plagiarism attempts. She knew that it was one thing getting him to admit his deceit, but another thing altogether for him to admit that he was wrong to do so. He'd have an explanation or excuse at the ready.

'You know that we have CCTV cameras hooked up 24/7 in the ICT room for security purposes?'

The face that next looked up at her was ashen and she could detect a twitch at the corner of his left eye. He stared not so much in shock but with cold appraisal. He now looked at every move she made, any signs that her facial expressions could give away. He knew that she was aware of his life circumstances, that she knew about his past. He seemed speechless and probably furious, realising then that Holly must have spoken up. He swallowed and then arrogantly said.

'So?'

'Look, I'm not saying that all your classmates are angels and that this kind of practice doesn't go on right under our noses without us seeing it. I'd like to reassure you that I know you are just an ordinary boy with ordinary needs. We all want a girlfriend or boyfriend, to succeed in life, and to have enough money to buy us what we like.'

Where his cheeks had previously been ashen and pale, they were now visibly blotched with red patches and the twitch of his eye looked like it had shifted to his temples. They were pulsating with increased blood flow and with what she now saw as bubbling rage. *Gotcha*, she thought to herself and was ready for the tirade of inflated self-importance she had expected to hear all along. For a fraction of a second she was lost in thought, when the first punch hit her right into the face. The bone in her nose crunched as his fist made contact with it. She was momentarily unable to breath, the pain too much to make a sound.

'Look at what you make me do. Ordinary, you said? Pah, here's what you get for calling me *or-di-na-ry*,' he said, leaving the room enraged.

oOo

Holly walked hurriedly, crossing the road, avoiding the numerous puddles and motorists splashing the side walk. She was on her way home from school. She had managed the last of her GCSE exams and the feeling of achievement permeated every single cell of her being. Whether she would have scored well or not was of no significance. The very fact that she had sat them all and that she had prepared as best as she could, was proof enough that she could reach a goal – in this case to not give up. Never ever give up! Despite the miserable rain and biting cold wind that was taking her unawares as she rounded the corner, briefly winding her, nothing could stop her from feeling relieved, proud, and light as a feather.

She had almost reached the front door when her movements were forced to freeze. A hand had gripped onto her shoulder so fiercely that she winced with pain. Upon trying to free herself, she could see a hand reddened at the knuckles and then her assailant's mouth coming closer to her ear. The person had literally come out of nowhere, interrupting her private thoughts, her carefree footsteps.

Instinctively, she knew that the person holding a grip on her was Luke. She could smell him and when he finally uttered his words, spat out like bile, there was no doubt that she was right with her assumption.

'Are you happy now? You took advantage of me and then humiliated me in front of everyone... what a snake you are.'

'Shut up!' she shouted back, her anger stronger than her fear. Her voice had been so sharp that for a small second or two she could sense the grip on her shoulder loosening under his surprise. She used this opportunity to wriggle out of his clutch and reach for the doorbell of her apartment. With any luck her mum was already home and would query the call. She'd promised that she would be home early to celebrate the end of the exams.

'Don't waste your time. I'm not here to waste mine. Just thought I'd let you know that you meant everything to me. I was sincere, honest and genuine. You decided to destroy what we had. That was so stupid of you.' He barked the last words into her face and finally tutted at her with his head inclined, as if talking to a small irrational child.

'What on earth are you talking about?' She could not believe that Luke actually believed what he was saying. It was a tactic she knew all too well now.

'Just kidding. I came to tell you that every single person who lets me down has paid for it. So will you.' He laughed, turned his back, and walked away.

That's when she heard the steps of someone running down the flight of stairs, inside the building. Her mother was out of breath and her eyes wide when she finally opened the door.

'Are you okay, my darling?'

Her mother took her in, out of the rain and into the echoing staircase and they said nothing as they climbed the steps. When they settled on the sofa with two steaming cups of hot chocolate and sweet popcorn piled into a bowl between them, Holly's Mum looked up.

'Holly, I met Dad when you were just one. I don't know what he saw in me but I will always love him for who he is – a kind and loyal person. He protected me from the kind of guy that Luke is. He saved my life, and, yours actually,' she said.

'So, my other dad was like Luke?' Holly asked, stunned. Tears pricked her eyes.

'Yes,' she replied, looking glum. 'We'll get over this together. Luke will move on to the next victim quicker than we think. You'll go on to study a course, I'm sure of it, or why not travel to Scotland and stay there for a while? You've proven already that you can stand up for yourself and that you're focused. There's no need for boys or men in that context …yet.' She looked at Holly, who nodded.

Her mum flicked a strand of hair out of Holly's face and before she carried on, took her hand.

'Here's me talking about something I never managed to do myself but maybe you can. Girls are interested in boys and boys are interested in girls. It's natural … unless it takes over your life. Be selfish my lovely, and follow your dreams. Stand out, be different. God, I sound like a self-help book. Don't forget - you'll always be my little girl.' Holly rolled her eyes in response. 'I know, I know, but I must say - thank goodness you're not my Runaway Girl.' She winked, then focused on Holly's face, sliding an envelope over the table.

'Argh, you can be so cheesy, Mum.' Holly said, shaking her head, unable to hide an amused grin.

'Here's a special surprise for you, to change the topic. I hope you like it.'

Holly looked down at the envelope placed in front of her, an inquisitive frown narrowing her eyes, and then stole a few querying glances to her mum.

'C'mon, just open it, sweetheart.'

When Holly finally managed to look inside, she was so elated she jumped about the kitchen, embracing her mother, then jumping again with her arms held high.

'This is amazing!'

'I know how much you want to sit by the sea, digging your toes into real sand again – your dream.'

'Oh Mum - a weekend for the two of us in Brighton! I can't believe it.' Then she stopped in mid-air.

'But - who paid for this?'

'Well …'

THE NARCISSIST

The moment I wake up, the dismay and desperation are back. The knot in my throat is so big that I am sure, soon enough, I will choke on it. I cannot understand why I am lying in this tiny room attached to an IV drip with only a glass of water as my companion. My heart is beating fast with anxiety and when I try to lift my head I can see my emaciated arms sticking out from under my hospital gown. I know, yet again, that my attempt to get up is futile. Why am I here, and why am I all alone? A strand of grey hair falls over my forehead and into my eyes, pricking at the outer edges, and it costs me great energy to brush it aside.

I faintly remember a voice now. She was reading something to me. Confusion and fear flood over me while my eyes move wildly around the room. I note that the small window is still there with its curtains drawn. Is it winter? Is it daytime or night time? I have no idea. A small radiator stands in the corner and once in a while emits gurgling noises. The sound is strangely reassuring, but what I really want is a human hand holding mine, a human voice talking to me with kindness, a small smile, anything to take the dread away. I remember my family and other faces come crowding into my head and then ... my children. Oh ... my children. Where on earth are they, now that I am helpless and desperate?

My throat is dry, and when I turn my head towards the bedside table I see the glass of water standing next to me. I yearn for it and decide that I have to try and reach for it. I lift my bony and unusually broad hand off the bedcover but my fingers instantly start to shake. The simplest of movements now seem almost impossible to be carried out. I remember the voice telling me that I am dying, and deep and utter anger rises in my weak chest. Me - dying? That is ludicrous, to say the least. I am maybe ill and weak from some terrible disease, but never in a million years am I dying.

My anger is escalating when I finally manage to reach for the glass, only to make it topple and fall. The sound of it shattering has alerted someone in this forsaken place because, before I can turn my head, the door is opened and a nurse comes into the room, heading straight for me.

'Had a little accident, did you?' he says, as he walks over to the wet patch glistening on the linoleum floor. Inspecting the area that he will have to clean up, he throws a small nod over his shoulder. 'I will get you another one, OK?' He does not wait for an answer, just carries on as if talking to himself. 'I'll be back shortly.'

I seem to have lost all sense of time because the nurse is already back and holding my neck, while I struggle to lift my head towards the new glass of water. Is there something floating in it? My eyes strain to focus on the slight mist that is clouding my drink. They are poisoning me, I think, but my thirst is stronger than I, and I drink greedily. The freshness of the water lining the dry walls of my mouth and running down my parched throat is the best feeling I can remember having for a while. But keeping me company are painful thoughts, pulling me to and fro without making sense. I give a small nod as I lick my thin, chapped lips, trying to catch every remaining droplet of water, and sink back into my pillow, exhausted. A whiff of stale body odour reaches my nostrils. Argh. What kind of a place is this where I am simply left to rot?

The image of a spacious bedroom comes to my mind. The carpets are thick and my bare feet dig into the welcoming softness. The bathroom is heated, and the towel I pull off the rail to dry my wet hair is warm and soft. Only a 5-star-hotel can provide this kind of ostentatious comfort, a luxury they make you believe you deserve. I am addicted to being treated with such opulence. My mind has worked so hard to find a way to keep coming back to this haven. The food is layered delicately on porcelain dishes when I come down to the breakfast buffet. I raise my hand arrogantly to one of the waiters and order him to serve fresh coffee. The waiter says, 'Certainly, with pleasure, sir'. This is the way I should be treated.

With a sigh, I let go of the surrounding white walls and close my eyes, suddenly convinced that the hospital room must surely be part of a bad dream, one I need to avoid at all cost.

'Good morning. How are you?'

I don't remember hearing or, for that matter, seeing the lady now sitting next to me enter the room. She looks to be in her mid-forties and is dressed in black trousers and a buttoned-up, light pink blouse. She is wearing no jewellery, but a soft smile is etched on a small mouth, and her eyes are a mix of brown and green, gentle but with a gleam of determination.

'Another letter has arrived for you. Would you like me to read it?'

First encounters shape the impression we have of a person and can have an impact on how we predict and interpret them, I remember reading somewhere, a long time ago. I used to be good at that, excellent really. But now everything's too foggy and vague to make any sense. The lady sitting cross-legged next to me on an uncomfortable-looking plastic chair rings a bell, somewhere in the depth of my memory, but not more than that.

'I'm sorry. Have I startled you?' Her right hand reaches up to her dark blonde hair, tucking a lost strand behind her ear. She is an exact sort of person. Her appearance is tidy and she emanates an aura of confidence.

'I think you are experiencing more and more absences now.' She pauses to watch me and continues. 'It is normal in your condition.'

I notice that she doesn't spare me but I cannot sense any sarcasm or malice in her voice, which is calm, yet firm. She carries on introducing herself for what feels like the hundredth time, but she keeps her patience in check and asks me again if I would like the letter to be read out to me.

'I don't know,' is my answer. My mind is clouded and I just cannot come to grips with my lack of energy. Where is my unfailing presence of masculinity? The vision of something is niggling at the edges of my consciousness but I am unable to conjure up the full picture. My face feels sunken, my body weak and frail. What is unchanged, I hope, is the stubbornness in my eyes, fiercely refusing to align with my physical condition.

'The first one that arrived upset you very much.' I am startled by the comment; which I know she can tell by the widening of my eyes. She pauses briefly, takes a deep breath before carrying on. 'Do you remember it?' She says, observing me intently.

The memory does come flooding back to me. My daughter had sent me a few lines. Yes, I am elated to remember something but I am also struck at once with pain rising in my chest. I am lost for words, again something I have never – until now – experienced before. The anger and frustration is all that is left to feel and I am still good at that.

'Who is this one from?' I manage to ask.

She turns over the envelope that has been resting in her hand and reads. 'Emily Magady. You have so far only received post from her – your daughter.'

Oh, Emily. Hearing her name sends another stabbing pain through my heart and leaves a bittersweet taste in my mouth. After all these years she has not regained that innocent trust she'd had when she was small. It used to be so simple. All I ever had to do was show some emotion, or deliver an excess of compliments about her school work or some tender words, and her eyes would shine with love.

My mouth is so dried up that it cannot produce the insults and threats that I used to throw at her, first verbally then in writing. Why did I fail to convince her? How dare she question my integrity, jeopardise my position? After all, I was entitled to receive respect and admiration. I still am. Sometimes you need to tweak a few things, jump through some hoops. Yes, I did concede to that, but who doesn't once in a while? You can forget about things and just move on.

'Are you OK with this?' the lady says, still sitting there next to me and holding an unfolded sheet of paper in her elegant hands. I cannot help but notice she is wearing a wedding ring. I give another small nod.

Do you remember the painting I made for you when I was only six years old? The one I made because I felt sorry for you because you had to stay away from home for weekends on end, even two Christmas eves? You managed to convince us so well. Do you remember the rage you got into when you suspected the smallest lie, the smallest bit of deviation from the truth from us? Yet, you lied and lied and lied yourself and you did so for what looks like your entire life.

I know now that you are a deceiving individual, my own dad, a person to be ashamed of. You betrayed every single person who came your way and worst of all you believed it was always justifiable, always a matter of talking the other into accepting your own version of things. You were excellent at using every trick in the book.

'Would you like me to carry on?' She looks up at me and I can feel my cheeks flushing a crimson red. I nod, yet my eyes cannot focus. I feel agitated, trapped, like a wild animal captured in a cage.

How does it feel to be all alone now? Do you feel

guilt at last or are you still convinced of being irreproachable? Have you found a good explanation for why you are all alone?

'Is that all?' I manage to ask through clenched teeth.

'Yes, I'm afraid that's it.' She says drily.

Before I can sense another person entering the room, I hear murmurs coming from my bedside.

The lady has turned towards whom appears to be a doctor, and is quietly whispering into his ear. The man in white must be in his fifties, he has a sturdy, tall build and could pass for a southern European due to his black hair and olive skin. He is inspecting a chart but occasionally looks up with a neutral, detached look in his eyes.

'He doesn't remember much, it seems. Unbelievable, if you ask me, but then we never got anywhere with him anyway. He is deluded until the very end. He does seem to remember his daughter though, and his face betrayed some past shame. That's all really.'

The doctor nods while I listen, and occasionally looks up to the woman.

'These people never fail to confound me, really. The list of witness statements is so long, the accusation of fraud, deceit and intimidation should clearly be enough evidence for him to admit his guilt. But no, he carries on with an attitude of being wronged himself. I wouldn't be surprised if he still believes his stories right now.' The man suggests.

'It is the daughter that I am more worried about. She seems to have regained the anger that she experienced shortly after finding out that her father had led many double lives, lied to and threatened these women, and financially cheated a long list of people.' The lady says, then looks down at her notes and sighs. They seem to have completely forgotten that I am still in the room.

By the time they conclude their conversation I am asleep.

I spotted her straight away. She was a bundle of fun if ever there was one. Her bright blue eyes were shining with laughter and her hair fell over her flushed cheeks. From where I stood, I could tell she was well dressed and that the jewellery dangling down her ears was expensive. I looked down and immediately spotted that the golden chain around her neck was holding a pendant with a sparkling ruby set in its centre. My fingers started tingling with excitement straight away and my mood was improving with every step that I took, edging towards the beautiful stranger. I have a sharp eye and good nose for luxury and wealth and I'm proud of it. I am drawn to beautiful things. From that very instant, my goal was clear. I had to work out a plan on how to approach the lady, get my first impressions, and find out as much as I could so that I could work out a way to get really close to her. I never do things in half measure.

Ah, to reach that neck, to kiss the grooves of her cheeks and roll my fingers around the sparkling, golden filament. It was imminently clear to me that I had found a woman worthy of my attention. I quickly scanned the room to make a note of who was around or whether anyone had noticed that I was not really "one of them". I reached for a glass of wine and very quickly felt at ease as I spotted what I always call a "small mouse". The lady was standing uncomfortably next to the buffet, seemingly forgotten by those who had spoken to her initially. *She will be my introduction,* I thought. *Wrapping her around my finger will be a piece of cake and it will make me look like I'm a friend or acquaintance, so no one will be suspicious.*

I knew then, just as I know now, that I deserved being part of that crowd. They were the lucky ones. When you are born into a family with money and education, it is so easy to succeed in life. From the word go, I have had to live with scarcity because my parents struggled to pay for the weekly shop to feed a family of six. They were immigrants, people good enough for cleaning the streets of England's suburbs, good enough for being sent down the last of the remaining mines in the country and good enough, therefore, to sacrifice their health for the welfare of others. This was how I saw it anyway. My parents were idiotic enough to preach to us children the respect we should have for a country that had, in their eyes, so kindly taken us in, given them jobs and provided us with an education. Pah! I was going to be a part of the other group, the ones who felt worthy getting up in the morning because they were special.

I would never have tried the ordinary route, even though I had no choice for a while. My primary school years were filled with lots of well meaning, silly teachers and social workers – each and every single one wasting my precious time – trying to goad me into making an effort. The problem was that they would complement me on my talents and soon thereafter criticise or suggest how I could improve my projects. How dare they? It was boring, so boring that I had to bribe someone to finish them for me; I knew my parents would otherwise impose tedious chores or lecture me for hours. I learnt at a tender age that only very few people were worth listening to. Teachers and parents were definitely not in that group.

Except maybe one teacher! I must concede that she did try to amend for the advances that she had made on me. She had found my looks irresistible, and her smiles and the flicks of her hair had dazzled my innocent, young eyes. Her outfits had become more and more revealing as she flirted with me and eventually she had been unable to guide my urges and stop them when there had still been an opportunity. Oh well, at least she did help me forge a school diploma. Ever since, I have managed to hide from everyone the fact that I never managed to pass my school exams. She had had the decency never to reveal it because she blamed herself for my failures.

Later on, I learned precisely how to avoid uncomfortable questions regarding my schooling, or any other matters, by never directly answering them. The confusion in people's faces was very amusing. I know that they wondered whether they had misunderstood me or, when I pointed out that I didn't quite get their question, they would worry about the clarity of what they had said. People were so self-critical and apologetic. It was comical. I started filling in the big gaps that were dividing my different life stages with all kinds of stories, so people would let me get on with it. Luckily, my family wasn't proficient in English, especially my parents who stumbled on each English phrase, from the simplest of interactions with neighbours or local business owners to more serious exchanges, such as discussing my school reports with teachers. They never got to grips with it, and thank goodness for that. I do admit that I had to bend a few facts because I didn't want people to know just how embarrassing my parents and siblings were. They would never have endorsed the transformation I gave to my childhood experiences. Some remained true, yes, but others had to be made up in order to give the illusion of a different, more appealing upbringing. I simply had to give myself the chance for a new life. That also meant making up a story that would trigger the right kind of feelings in others. At least I had learned the most important skill in life – predict, control, and use others without them ever suspecting it. If they did suspect anything then avoidance, answering questions in riddles, or cracking a joke proved effective enough to put them off from further querying. The subtler I was, the quicker I would achieve what was duly mine. What did get into my way were those irritating people who insisted on challenging my stories, testing their veracity and focusing on the details, bending them until breaking point. This proved so annoying and such hard work because I had to keep twisting those stories back to their initial versions.

Still, all had been worthwhile as I was about to conquer what I believed was duly mine, right there, standing on the dance floor during a college degree celebration. I decided there and then that she was mine because I was going to do everything to conquer her trust and convince her that she would be able to repair my painful and unjust childhood. I remember the satisfaction I felt at that very moment. In the past, I had learnt that if you wanted to be happy you had to focus on what you wanted at all cost.

The girl I managed to entice before had turned sour on me. She'd even used her fists to stop my kind embraces. Why indeed should I waste my energy and precious attention on someone who was actually so below me and didn't appreciate how special I was? I made a mental note to stop harassing my ex, indeed any insignificant other girl. I deserved a breath of fresh air! I needed to focus on a new adventure, new opportunities and a new future. I smiled to myself about this clever move and, without thinking twice, made my way across the dance floor, holding the glass of wine and rolling my big shoulders back to appear stronger and more in charge. What this lady needed was a man who appreciated her, who looked good by her side and who could protect her from going astray. I would be her guide, her charming prince in armour. I chuckled to myself at the image and congratulated myself, yet again, for gate-crashing into the party I had not been invited to.

How easy it had been to pretend that I was one of them. All it took was for me to iron a shirt, get a decent haircut, invest in some fine, shiny shoes, look confident and speak nicely, ideally in riddles and with some clever jokes, so that the other person was inclined to believe that they were too stupid to understand me. Later, I would add the ownership of an expensive car that would heighten my image, delude those I most needed to trick – the neighbours, the friends of friends, and then also the people I unexpectedly would need to approach. They would trust me more because I would mention my grand projects and, therefore, show how hard I had worked, and why I deserved to be surrounded by luxurious status symbols. I could feel the weight of the expensive sun shades sitting on the ridge of my nose, hiding my shrewd eyes, on constant look out for the next prey.

After all, I absolutely love magicians and their illusory tricks. They can teach one so much about camouflage and fantasy. If you believe hard enough in your dreams and work on the props and devices that will shed the light on where you want them to look, you will dazzle and amaze any novice. Those whom are smart enough to work out a magician's tricks will just have to be avoided or, ideally, excluded from the start. No matter what situation you are in, it all depends on how you present your story to the listener, or on which details you reveal and which ones you leave out, then you have them eating from the palm of your hand. The trick is to appear that you are going with the flow while staying focused on what you want. The pleasure you then get from achieving your goals is exhilarating. Trust me, I've been there. The main thing you have to do is ignore the whimpering of others. When they cry or shout at you, make sure you shout louder and reap the fruits when you see them swimming in self-pity. As I said earlier, you have to focus at all times on what you want and tell yourself that it is not your fault if others are too weak to follow it through themselves.

For now, I must look like the artistic type: smooth, mysterious, and interesting, because I have an exotic appearance, and I could hint on a bit of emotional hardship here and there. *Let's see if she bites and believes me.* That was usually a good clue to knowing how gullible a girl was. You can cheat yourself out of any situation if you make sure that at least some of your allies stick to you like glue. Then you use your male attributes such as your strong, yet smooth voice, and determined stare; you make sure you set up a list of rules and regularly check on whether they are respected, and you make sure that people closest to you see you are a very busy man at all times. It is hard work to stand on top of an unshakable fortress but that's, after all, where I belong.

Suddenly, I felt dizzy and disoriented. It was as if some power had dragged me into a direction I did not want to take. Troubling images came to the fore and I tried to brush them aside but the dreams carried on, spooling out parts of the film that make up my life.

I was sitting on the sofa in what looked like a living room, my first born on my lap. The little boy was crying his heart out; born too early. I thought to myself that I didn't want this. The clock on the nearby mantelpiece was indicating that it was three in the morning. My father never did this for either of my siblings, or for me. He was too busy fooling around with the neighbour's wife. What a lazy, smug old git he'd been! I overheard him say that it was his lady friend who had approached him, pleaded with him. He must have been joking! As if anyone would plead to lie in bed with that ugly good-for-nothing. I wouldn't make that mistake. I was different anyway.

I was brought back to the screaming child but found that it was another tiny little face I was looking at. The cheeks were red and I'm sure that it was a little girl I was holding - my daughter. How could it be that I was here again, rocking a crying infant in the early hours of the morning, while the mother, my wife, was asleep? I didn't remember this ever happening at all. The children were entirely my wife's responsibility. Why was I staying up all night, making bottles, cleaning vomit, doing chores that, of course, were below me?

My vision blurred again and this time I was confronted with a weeping, distraught young woman, her face somehow contorted. I didn't understand why I had to put up with this. I tried to tell her that she was weak and needed to sort herself out, that indeed she had got to stop complaining.

Next, I found myself in a prison cell. Hours upon hours I tried to explain, to whomever wanted to hear, my account of events. The tricks didn't work though. My hands were red one moment, white another. When they turned red again, it was blood that dripped from the tips of my fingers. I jumped back and bumped into a grey wall, stumbled and slowly buckled under my knees. I was imploring God now, imploring and also cursing the only hope I seemed to have left for being heard. What had happened to my plans? The tears streamed down my bloated cheeks. I was stuck within myself, inside this foul prison, and the thoughts twirled around my head like a swarm of bees gone mad, because they had been robbed of their luscious, sweet nectar.

In my dreams I could see her clearly now. She had big eyes that could pierce through me with hatred and at other times look soft and defeated. These were the eyes of my wife. I didn't know which set of eyes I was most drawn to. What I knew was, at that moment, they were drawing me in again and again, like a spiral swallowing me right down into the blackness of her pupils. When I managed to recover and stand, the room was empty and I was completely and utterly alone.

As I felt my knees buckle, I slid to the floor and my daughter's stern gaze had replaced my wife's. Emily was my exact opposite. She could not lie; she could not pretend but, like me, she enjoyed giving people a piece of her mind. The effect was very different. Whereas I would tell people what I wanted from them, she would question each small morsel of information and straighten it back up if she deemed it to be inconsistent. How tedious was that? If I only gave you one piece of advice, I'd tell you - don't linger, just move forward, take what you like and take it as quickly as you can, before someone else gets it. I had siblings; I knew what it was like to get the last piece, or be ignored by my parents because they were too tired, or considered me annoying and worthless. It was the survival of the fittest. So, I had to jump on and enjoy the ride.

I wake up, blinking my eyes frantically. I see the white hospital walls greeting me; my limbs feel stiffer than ever. This is ridiculous. I've got to get moving. My back is so sore that I have a desperate urge to roll over onto my side. I try to will my legs to bend at the knees and after much effort and many failures and sweat starting to pour down my temples, I manage to get them poking up into the air very briefly. It is enough to allow me to drop to one side. What I am not able to anticipate is that I am too close to the edge of the narrow bed and I know, before it happens, that I will fall. Next I am lying on the floor like a discarded sack and all I am able to come up with is a mantra of, 'Oh my god, oh my god, oh my god …'

This time the lady sitting next to me is holding a painting in her hands. She is sitting patiently and when I acknowledge her, she gives me a little nod, closing her eyes briefly.

'Have you had a good day today?'

What an odd question. How can I ever have a good day lying here on a hospital bed, attached, incapable of getting up, unable even to raise a hand to my head, which is feeling itchy right now. I glare at her and say 'no, terrible.'

As if I haven't said anything, she continues.

'Would you like to see a painting your daughter sent you?'

My pulse is instantly beating faster and soon I sense it climbing right into my throat. I can barely contain my anxiety. What on earth has she sent me now? I give a small nod of approval and as the painting comes into view, my heart seems to stop for a few beats. The painting is undoubtedly made by a young hand. The strokes are thick and generous and they clearly show the artist's determination to get it right. A big green Christmas tree is stuck underneath a few written lines and the four sides of the A3 sheet are decorated with stars, presents and circles, which are coloured in with golden glitter pen. The words have faded a bit after all these years and the edges are bent but, all in all, it could be yesterday that my little girl made this painting for me.

Dear Daddy
I'm so sad that you have to work so hard and that even on Christmas you can't be with us. Mummy is very sad too and Matias says he will keep your presents safe until tomorrow.
We miss you lots, Emily
The words hit me right in my chest. They take me

to a place where I fear to tread. My thoughts drift back to another place, another time and another dimension, where I am standing at a cliff's precipice and a huge gust of wind blows me over. I am falling and it is a feeling of somehow losing my own stomach.

Am I dreaming or day-dreaming? I do not know. There is an image that haunts me, its contours are fuzzy but in the middle I can see myself sharply. Looking more closely, I can indeed make out my own five-year-old little face but something is very wrong about the image. I am dressed in a skirt and a frilly pink top. My wide feet are crammed into dainty black lacquer shoes. They hurt, actually the whole scene hurts. I have a feeling of unease. No, that term is not strong enough. I am ashamed. Again, that is not what I am feeling. I am inadequate. Yes, that's it. It is all my mother's doing. She used to play ridiculous charades with me. I am her third-born and another son at that – a boring, annoying, whining bundle of flesh. She desperately wanted a girl and what did she get? I brush the next upcoming thought aside. I remember all too well how little I was worth to her as a boy.

Then come the words, read to me through a fog I cannot see through, it is so thick and dense. The feeling of helplessness is so intense I am frozen in time and space. I am forced to listen to every single word.

I am so helpless, lost and sad. This is what it must feel like when you are drowning. There is nothing you can do because the air that is sucked out of your lungs prevents you from forming new words, planning new actions and making rational decisions or simply saving yourself. You drift from a state of desperation to one of resignation before you lose hold on reality. Before I reached this stage, I believed that you could fix anything, keep up appearances so you don't have to face the fact that nothing is what it should be. It worked quite well and I was even convinced it was normal, the way things pan out in life. But now I know that there are two realities, the one I vaguely remember being a part of and then the other – the one constructed by someone else who has placed me and moulded me into fitting into that odd space. I lost my bearings long ago.

'Do you feel like this?'

My voice answers as if guided from afar. 'Yes.'

'These are some of the few words left from your wife before she died. The way you feel now is what she had to endure for two decades.'

The shock is intense upon hearing these words. What is all this about? Am I being tortured?

'Just in case you were wondering, no, this is not an interrogation. I am your psychiatrist and talking to you is simply a way to show you that your failings to see the damage you have done are now catching up with you. By alienating, manipulating and controlling others, you have obviously never experienced what it is like to feel cornered yourself. There is nothing else to be said for now.'

When my tears subside, I notice that the chair next to my bed is empty. The lady and the painting are nowhere to be seen. I try to remember what the reader looked like and whether she said good-bye, but I can't piece together what happened between my day-dreaming and my regaining consciousness. My thoughts drift off again and a feeling of warmth settles in the centre of my chest. I close my eyes and new memories invade my mind.

I was wearing one of my finest black suits. It had been custom-made and therefore fit me like a glove. Underneath, I wore a white shirt, ironed to perfection by my wife just under an hour before. My tie was red and had a black eagle stitched onto the front. I had been called away for an important business dinner, as I often was.

I entered a restaurant and instantly felt at home. A mounted floral creation was displayed at the centre of a big room with a layout of tables, set with the finest cream-coloured linen and crystal glasses, that gave off a feeling of exclusivity as they reflected the flattering light of candles placed between the delicate porcelain plates. I absolutely loved these Michelin star places. Every single detail had been thought about, considered for the greatest comfort of the very special customer who could afford the bill, subtly concealed under a crisp-white napkin. The carpeted floor muffled my steps and the submissive glances of the staff gave off a sense of suspended existence. I was in a bubble of wealth surrounded by people of wealth and I was one of them. I always felt my chest rise in volume, my heart beating with excitement, and this was when I produced my best small talk and funniest jokes. This was also where I lingered that bit longer on an attractive woman's silhouette as she passed by, picturing where she lived and how thickly her wallet may be lined. And before I knew it, I sat in the most comfortable seats in town, thanks to lavish cushioning.

Without a moment's hesitation, I took out my mobile. I should not have been the one waiting. She should be. I was only faintly annoyed though, because my attention was swiftly diverted by a perfectly dressed young waitress approaching my table with a welcoming smile. Her attitude confirmed, yet again, how special I was. Her hair was smartly pulled up in a tidy bun and her make-up had been applied subtly so that every other lady in the room could shine. I knew that the aim was to look pleasing to the eye without stealing anyone else's show.

'Good evening, sir. Would you care for an Aperitif or would you prefer to wait?' she asked, whilst lifting off my napkin and setting it accurately over my lap. It was a perfect choreography and if it wasn't that way, I'd be the first to complain. Next I sensed the refreshing, prickly feeling of Champagne filling my mouth and sighed with relief that all was well and as it should be.

The lady who sat down opposite me was dressed in a classic dark blue suit and matching trousers. A silk blue and white scarf around her neck finished a picture of corporate perfection. She leant in to me and we kissed on the lips, both parting with a smile, hers overshadowed with a hint of uncertainty in her big brown eyes. Before she could protest – as I knew she would like to – I had already ordered the evening's five course menu. I couldn't stand other people being fussy and, in any case, I always chose what was best.

I was somehow determined not to let anyone spoil this evening. I knew she was tired and needed to get to sleep but hey, you only live once. She would comply and thank me for it later. I had ordered the most expensive dishes on the menu and I looked forward to indulging in the enticing smells of lobster cooked to tender perfection, the range of colourful vegetables and lightly browned potato cubes sprinkled with fresh herbs, and a bouillon made of lemon juice and aromatic spices. The range of artistically displayed starters and the smell of small buns tickled my senses. The bouquets of wines that accompanied the different stages of the meal added to the overall ambience of murmured conversations and laughter and a low, jazzy background sound track. This was heaven. I felt as if I had arrived exactly where I wanted to be. I briefly closed my eyes, swishing the different aromas of red Bordeaux in my mouth, before letting it run down my throat.

When I opened my eyes, I knew that something was different. My pulse started to quicken because I was suddenly anxious and uncertain. Then I sensed cold sweat running down my back when my lady friend looked up to me. She was blonde now, her hair tied up in a meticulous mound and pinned with glittering golden pins. Her blue eyes were staring at me and I noticed a gaping wound on her wrist. She was bleeding and I instinctively jumped up, raising the alarm. When an anxious waiter came to the table, he looked puzzled by my exclamations of panic and my insistence to call for a doctor.

'But sir, I don't understand. Are you feeling alright?' His head was leaning into me in order to encourage my voice to calm down and his left hand was gently placed on my upper arm.

I looked frantically back to the table and I could

not believe my own eyes. Another of my ex-lady friends was there. Her long black hair was hanging loosely around her shoulders. She was wearing a tightly fitting green dress that showed off her long, bare arms and she was holding a glass of chilled white wine. She looked at me with her head tilted and then exclaimed, 'Have you finally lost your mind?' She asked, then smiled, causing rage to mount into my throat and my hand closing into a tight fist.

I wake from this recollection with a start. What a nightmare. Why did it have to go so wrong when everything seemed absolutely perfect? I realise that I am touching white hospital linen instead of a crisp restaurant napkin and my eyes close with dismay. Why, oh why has this happened to me? Why have I fallen so low? Why is there no one to hold my hand or tell me reassuringly that this is all just a nightmare, soon to be forgotten? I, who have given so much, worked so hard, and have been so generous.

The Visitor

Today I sit quietly, observing him from my uncomfortable chair. I had been pacing the room yesterday, wondering about this man's impact on so many lives. My thoughts - if one was able to read them now - would reveal blank frustration. People like him should never be allowed in this world, I tell myself. And still there are worse versions than the one lying in the bed right next to me. Some of the most intelligent narcissists and manipulators are those leading big multinationals, governments, and yes, criminal organisations. It is useless trying to reach through the labyrinth of their minds, when their ability to sympathize with others is lacking. Why was it lacking in the first place? Was it some evolutionary glitch – some genetic outcrop of humanity? If there is a God, and I definitely don't believe there is, he wouldn't test humanity's kindness with deformed and twisted minds such as his. What a waste of everyone's life and time. No, there was no purpose, just the making up of one, and then pure survival for many in the world – each for herself and, if one was lucky, they got to meet kindness and someone to love and cherish, children to rear and cuddle, activities to enjoy. Every psychiatry book advises that the only way to deal with people like him is to avoid them at all cost. The pathway of affective empathy is lacking in them and because they cannot distinguish clearly between what their own and other people's feelings are, they are able to go straight for the kill. The other person is just another object among many objects in the world that serve the sole purpose of fulfilling their desires and aspirations. When others get hurt, they experience pleasure because they are like cats tormenting their prey, unmoved by the slow and desperate expressions of demise.

There were many circular conversations I've had with him but there is one I have committed to memory. The discussions had all been recorded at the time after his arrest but this particular one remains intact in my mind.

'Can you tell us what happened on the night your wife died?'

'We had a family argument. It went out of control because my son was lying to me.'

'I repeat - can you please tell us what happened on the night.'

'I just told you. Families have disagreements. Things got out of hand.'

'You call attacking one of your children and throwing your wife against the wall things getting out of hand?'

'I was provoked. I knew that my son was lying and I told them lying is unacceptable. You always have to be truthful.'

'So you call your serial adultery truthful?'

'My wife is severely depressed. She cannot be a proper wife. She is doing crazy things, tried to cut her wrists. There is just so much a man can take. I put …'

I interrupt his avalanche of broken sentences and calmly look into his face, while his eyes are unable to hook onto mine. I know he is lying, ranting, raving, but I will not let him get away with this attention seeking.

'You killed your wife. She is dead and there are no wounds on her wrists, therefore she cannot have cut them at any stage in the past. There are no files either, detailing that she was depressed or had ever been admitted into hospital for psychiatric treatment.' I take a small breath and watch as the man in front of me is hunching his shoulders, an invisible weight keeping them bent, and there is desperation in the way he is wringing his hands.

He is up in a flash. His right fist is clenched as he locks eyes with me now. If ever one body could stand for the word 'rage' it is synonymous with this middle-aged man now. That's exactly the message his appearance conveys and instinctively I nod to the two officers who rush to the interrogation table and hold the incensed man by the elbows.

'I didn't kill her. It was a family argument. It got out of hand. I told you already. Do you know who you are talking to like this? I have put up with so much. I saved her life so often. I did take her to the emergency rooms once and she spent time in a psychiatric ward. You haven't looked up the files properly.'

'You see, what you are saying now is interesting. You are saying your wife was depressed?'

'Yes, severely depressed.'

'She tried to commit suicide?'

'Yes, she slashed her wrist'. He is mimicking the movement with his right hand moving over the left one.

'So the children were not safe with her, would you say?'

'Of course not.'

'How come then, you left them with their mother, leading a double life with other women, all the while pretending that you were on business trips as well as travelling abroad, as soon as the opportunity presented itself?'

His face turns a crimson red and he looks like he is about to explode.

'I had to get away from that dreadful stress. I'm a man …'

I decide to intercept and answer the sentence for him.

'…and you decide to leave the severely depressed, suicidal wife at home with two children? That seems quite unreasonable to say the least. Why, may I ask, have you never sought help? We have also thoroughly checked your wife's medical history and there is absolutely nothing to back up your claim of her suffering from depression. On the contrary, she had been with the same GP clinic for over twenty years and all of the doctors that knew her said that she was a healthy and perfectly balanced lady. You killed your wife because you were confronted by two brave teenage children who had started to work out your lies and deceit. You couldn't keep the lid on, so to speak. There you have it.'

'My wife is the best thing that ever happened to me.'

'We know that. You exploited, deceived and cheated on a perfectly gentle human being. She happened to conveniently stand by her children first. We know from all the witnesses that have come forward that you threatened more than one of them verbally and physically.'

I have had enough of the chatter that can fill my head from all the conversations I have with inmates. It is tiring, exhausting, and in cases like this, downright gruelling to observe the human mind at its worst. Women were locked up for their tears or basic demands made, not so long ago. They were locked up for expressing their despair of simply not being heard, or nowadays they are maimed because they dare to speak up against conventions in countries that still hold on to strict, conservative rules. Things may stand better for the women in Europe. Yet many lives are still lost or wasted today to the manipulators of this world who cannot but pervert the truth, twist it and bend it so far that it becomes a new reality, one they enjoy and appreciate, and it is one they alone can see, hear and feel. Anything coming into the way of their path must be crushed or trampled. Any tools are good enough and it is so easy to come up with platitudes. They may be empty but they are effective. Guilt may niggle them at the edges of their vision or a remark stir uncomfortable recollections but, overall, using some mental glue, all discrepancies can get patched up. There is always a way to make situations appear different from what they are. Hence the reason why evidence is so important in a court of law.

I sigh and stand up, taking one last look at the remains of a human shell, soon to be forgotten. Just as people forget quickly that their head of state resigned a year ago in disgrace, linked to suspicions of fraud or deceit, they see the familiar face re-appear, only to be re-elected into power again, despite of all the past scandal. Time changes our perceptions and with the right marketing we forgive and forget. You are fooled daily and let's face it, you fool yourself. You could find an impressively long list of those professional hide-and-seekers. Knowing when to duck and when to dive is a skill.

Time to go, I decide. Maybe I will reach greater depth with the next patient. I stand up and lightly tuck my grey skirt into place. My knees are stiff so I take a few paces over to the radiator, rest my hands on the warmth for a few seconds and take a deep breath.

There is always a risk of turning into a cynic, so I reassure myself why I am here. When my hands feel warmer, I turn to take one last look in his direction.

The mind is flat, flat as a pancake, I conclude. I'd rather eat a pancake now though, than have to face another patient on the ward, only to come to the same conclusion time and again.

It's simple: you mix flour, milk and eggs together in a bowl. Then heat a little oil in a non-stick pan and gently spoon some of the cream-coloured blend into the middle of it. Disperse it into the round shape by skilfully holding the handle of the pan at an angle and letting the dough fill the whole circle. Stand by with your spatula and let the smell of golden crispy edges reach your nostrils. It is so simple, yet so effective, to take your mind off the complexities and intricacies that the human brain is able to conjure up through its millions of synapses. You have got to get the right mix though, or your pancake ends up a gooey mess that doesn't hold together.

It seems so simple for most of us to connect and mind read, empathise and be guided by our inhibitions yet, for some, it is an unreachable goal. It's a muddle of neurones that don't seem to work the same as for others. And who is to tell that in the bigger picture, within our evolutionary history, it isn't the clever manipulator of memories and lived events whom achieves the greatest heights? Who is to know if the human ability to empathise is here to stay? The man I have just left is on a lower scale of intelligence. He was more of a successful bully than a refined example of perversion. He is a Nobody, come to think of it.

I give him a polite smile and know that it will not be long now and that there is one more remaining task to tick off. I hope that I have picked the right words to introduce my last tour de force. After all, I made a promise and no matter what etiquette and ethics may prescribe, I convince myself that a transgression of this kind is vital for justice to be done.

Shortly after, I am out of the door, cautiously looking right and left, and walk down the corridor with my thoughts still busy when my mobile bleeps with an SMS.

Be careful – I don't want you to get into trouble because of me.

I step to one side to let a nurse pass. We briefly exchange a warm smile, then I lift the phone up to type a return message.

Don't worry. I'm done.

The Narcissist

When I come round, I feel unusually alert and my mind has momentarily lost its thick fog. If it wasn't for the realisation that I am still in a hospital bed, I would believe myself able to get up and move about. My hair is moist and stuck to my scalp and within a few seconds my mood has turned from calmness to annoyance again. I try to raise my hand in order to reach an itch that is tickling the side of my neck, but I give up half way. After a while I try once more and this time I manage to reach what now seems to be a thick piece of paper lying next to my head. I lift it down in front of my face. I am looking at a photo montage – I used to be good at manipulating pictures and documents so I can still recognise one when I see it – and I am in the middle of it, surrounded by cut outs of all the women I entertained whilst being married. At the bottom I can make out the faces of my two children and the copy of a newspaper headline: 'Man stabs wife to death in front of their two teenage children'. I can see it clearly now. That is me alright, and there are the women I met, and also there are my children who had to witness my delusional rage. *That was a bad slip up* is the thought coming to my mind.

What happens next is a strange feeling of being lifted away from reality, losing every connection there ever was. I am lost ...for words.

Then I hear my visitor's voice again, reading. I open my eyes to attempt looking at the person talking, but am startled by the burning sensation this action is causing. I shut my eyes again, and without being able to protest or make any eye-contact, I simply listen.

'There is one last letter that arrived. It appears to be a diary entry written by the woman you killed.'

She seems to make a point of taking a few soothing breaths before reading from the lined piece of paper held in her slender hand. She clears her throat a couple of times before she seems able to find the poise to speak up.

Inside me, there were things I wanted to tell my husband. It would not have been that hard after all. I could have done it in front of those who had warned me so many times, those who had tried to reach my isolation and break through my stubborn resistance to accept that my marriage was deemed a failure. I should have stopped him and said something, or at the very least exposed my pretence and spoken up, because I knew that I'd been fooled. Now I feel the chance is lost forever. I will write them down instead, the words that are so desperate to slide over my tongue, now falling onto paper via my shaking hand.

You are a nobody! You will die a nobody because no matter how well woven the stories are you tell others and most of all yourself, I know better than anyone that you are empty and dead inside. You are the weak one, not me, and you will be forgotten as soon as your last breath is drawn. No matter what happens I am sure you will die alone.

When the voice stops, I am caught by a sense of panic. I somehow know without having to open my sore eyes, that I am indeed alone. I find it hard to breathe now. Something must be wrong with me after all! And I know that it is futile to deny it to myself any longer.

Sometime later – I am not sure at all how much time has passed – I sense my visitor's presence. I am confused again. Did the lady leave and then return, or has she been here all along? And where is the photograph?

The Visitor

I look at him and say, 'Is there anyone you would like me to contact on your behalf? Remember you are not allowed any visitors but I can pass on any messages if you so wish.'

I see the patient in the bed raise his eyebrows and

although he does not say anything, I interpret his expression as yet another sign of demented memory loss.

If he is impatient, he does hide it well. I take a little moment before carrying on though, my lips pressed together in concentration. Finding the right words is essential, considering that the man is deluded and too weak. I cannot stop the pity and sheer frustration still rising in my throat but I will remain professional and explain the situation to the helpless heap of human that is left in front of me. He has been told this information numerous times, but I will repeat it again now.

'You have been kept under hospital order for a very long time. You were sentenced to life-imprisonment for the murder of your wife.'

I can tell by the blank look on his face that he probably doesn't remember.

'You killed your wife when she tried to stop you from attacking your teenage children. Well, you attacked your son physically and screamed insults at your daughter. You claimed later that it was a simple family dispute that had gone out of control.'

I take a deep breath and suddenly feel so tired. People who never take responsibility for their actions are the worst for wearing you down. Those that start apologising, those confronted with a surviving victim or meeting their family, manage to connect with the harm they have done and recognise the guilt. But when they don't, it is like banging your head against the wall – again and again. I remind myself that this man is soon dead, so I wonder why I should bother and therefore decide to cut the conversation short.

'It is quite simple really – when you didn't get what you wanted, you used every trick in the book to get it. It's one thing though when you are a toddler demanding a sweet and see it refused in front of your eyes. You may climb a ladder to get it but ultimately you have the excuse that you are a little being who cannot yet control himself and who has not yet developed the skill of inhibition that we share socially with others. It is quite another thing to be a grown adult and to behave that way. At some point your selfish plans take a turn and that's what happened to you.'

I want to add one more thing. It is the only thing that every single person adversely touched by this man needs.

'You should have apologised'. It is so ridiculously simple; I want to laugh out loud.

I look down at the man and am startled by the wide eyes staring at me.

Emily

I am sitting in front of a log fire. I have tucked my feet under myself and am wrapped in a thick, woollen, cream-coloured cardigan. My pink jogging bottoms complete my feeling of relaxation and comfort. The last log I decided to throw onto the glimmering ashes is now well under way of being consumed. I watch the greedy flames licking around the dark trunk. I recall my meditation teacher's instructions to try 'looking without judging'. I blow a soft strand of my hair out of my face. Most of my life – which spans thirty-one years so far – has been spent judging. A great part of this time, fifteen years to be exact, I have been verbally challenging anyone prepared to respond.

On the fateful day, all those years ago, I had been to school as usual, entirely absorbed by my studies, impending projects, and revisions. I had always thrived for the best by observing my teachers closely, taking note of their particular requirements in order to ascertain what they expected from a top student. For some reason I always wanted to stand out, and I liked to be heard and seen.

I'd had suspicions about my dad and those doubts dated as far back as when I was involved in a car accident. He was always blaming others and, where necessary, picking a fight because it was a tool to divert the attention from an obvious failing of his. The more intense his response, the more likely was the outcome that his opponent was successfully intimidated. Nevertheless, nothing had prepared me for what changed the course of my life on the 3rd of June, fifteen years ago. If I had read a news story relating the incident that radically transformed the way I would look at my parents, I would not have believed it possible. Surely, you notice something that would send out warning signals and make one imagine the worse? I was to learn over a period of time that those who had seen more clearly, could equally not have predicted the outcome. No single person had been in the possession of all the evidence and understood my dad's character flaws that created the sad plot I had been an innocent participant in. I feel like Roald Dahl's small heroine, 'Matilda'. How, in the book, the dreadful headmistress of her school gets away with the worst insults, intimidations and abuse because the children know that no one would believe their tales at home. Had it been the case for my mum? She was always the first to take the blame, iron the creases of any disagreement or act with fierce determination whenever someone criticised my dad's behaviour.

Am I happy to be who I am? Am I happy that my eyes are dark like his, my hands broad, and the colour of my skin yet more evidence that he was my progenitor? Yes, and no. 'What if?' is a question that has almost thrown me over the precipice of madness. What if my mum had not met this charming man at a student fete? How had he managed to get there in the first place? He had not been part of the student body. What if, on that night, he had come down with a fever and would have missed it? Or what if, after that first meeting, my young, kind, and naive mum had sensed something was amiss? She could have escaped. She could have met someone 'normal', someone who would have loved and cherished her and brought real happiness into her life. His lack of inhibition and outstanding ability to convince you that he was worthy of your full attention had overwhelmed the best of them. It takes time to work out a compulsive liar and narcissistic pervert and then most of the time … it is too late anyway.

I pull myself out of the reverie, back to my living room and back to the remaining glimmering heap of wood that is creating the enveloping heat on my face and body. I reach out to a mug filled with hot milk and honey, standing next to me on a small glass table. I am nursing a sore throat, a side effect of travelling on the London tube daily. The taste is sweet and smooth and I feel warmth spreading down my throat and stomach. I need to open the front of my cardigan now as I am starting to feel too warm. I enjoy watching the final pieces of the log disintegrating, looking like tiny caves lit by a friendly radiance from within. It is soothing to let my mind rest from all the thoughts and feelings that shape my daily ponderings.

The next thing that I am fully aware of is my brother's hand, which has settled gently on my shoulder. I vaguely remember his swishing treads coming down the steps from the top level of my small house. I had heard a muffled conversation reaching my warm little bubble. I know what he has come to tell me before he has time to form the words. Despite the heat of the room, my soft cardigan, and the balmy drink lining my innards, I feel a shiver passing through me now. I pull the front of my cardigan back together and cross my arms in front of my chest. Shivers are useful reflexes in the body that are triggered in order to maintain stable conditions. My scientific mind is focusing on that interesting physiological fact, distracting me once more from the obvious news my brother has come to tell me.

'He is gone.'

Gone with him is a connection I never asked for. At last, my role as guardian of memories is complete. I have kept hold of them for so long, so that there was no possibility for him to propagate his lies outside the prison cell. And now, at last, I can breathe more freely, move on with my life and find fresh connections, and they will only ever know that I am an orphan. I want to claim my own future now where I pick the fragments of the past that I can bear to hold, guarding the details until, together, they will form a history worth memorising.

Later in the evening, I reach for my mobile and tap a message that I have mulled over all day. I know that over the years, the psychiatrist had become biased to my grief. I never gave up hope that one day and, especially when my devious father was dying defenceless and lonely, there'd be realization at last, a small flicker of remorse.

I type, my head bowed to the screen, and without reading it again, press the send button.

Thank you. Please throw it all away —the letters, the painting, the photo and, come to think of it, the whole file. I have already put away what I need and I will try to only keep the memories worth treasuring.

MY PERFECT CHILD

I sit slumped in the garden chair, my eyes staring to the ground. What else is there to say or think? There has never been a perfect child; never. And I only realise it fully now. My eyes wander around the garden before my thoughts draw me inwards again, far into the past.

In the beginning

'Oh, look at him. Isn't he just the most beautiful baby in the world?' Lisa exclaimed, holding her baby wrapped in a soft, light blue blanket, beaming with pride and joy. She had quickly brushed through her thick blonde hair, applied a little layer of lip gloss, powdered her face and changed into a freshly ironed light cotton shirt, prior to receiving her first visitors. It was a day she'd never thought would come to pass but it finally had. At the age of thirty-nine, after one failed marriage, a string of boy-friends and a few fleetingly unimportant infatuations – each time with the wrong guy, as she'd announced to her family and friends – she had eventually met and married the father of her son. She had been attracted by his multi-lingual and distinguished English education, his background of many professional successes, and his ability to tell stories with wit and historical accuracy. And, most of all, he was a gentleman in the truest sense: charming and honest and always ready to acknowledge her need to look generous and be pretty. They seemed a couple made in heaven, she with a job in marketing, he with the sale of a clever investment in sunny Spain, some rental

225

properties and a small collection of valuable pieces of art. So far, their various occupations had kept them busy, never too stressed nor too worried. There had been no children in both of their lives until now, which had added to a lack of expense not to be underestimated.

'Yes, he is, Lisa! Gorgeous and … oh look, he's got your bright eyes. I'm sure they'll be green soon!' he said, and smiled.

'Oh, Allan, aren't we just the luckiest parents in the world? He's perfect!' she replied, giving her husband a list of things to buy and things to pack. Her voice incessantly centred the conversation around the new-born baby, his needs and wants, resolute in telling everyone time and again just how perfect he was.

She was determined to fill her son's first years with the love, affection and attention, which she'd told everyone she had always sorely lacked herself. Her own mother had been distant and cool. *Children should be seen but not heard,* her mother had thought, and very often she had made it clear that she didn't even want to see them. Lisa and her siblings knew that their mother's life had been primarily taken up by her busy social agenda, her appointments, her passionate love for their father and the hours needed to look the part. The children had been given very little room to voice their worries, their fears, and whenever they eventually did, she would wave her hand and say, 'Oh, don't you fret. Stand up for yourself and you'll be fine.'

Sometimes they would hear her mutter under her breath that children were such a pain, that she wished she had their insignificant little problems, and those comments would sting the most, remaining in Lisa's memory to this day. To keep them busy after school, she'd signed them up for riding classes, ballet and tennis lessons, extra French and maths tutoring, and of course there was a string of babysitters at the ready for the evenings, when their parents went out to dinners and vernissages. Their father hardly ever asked what they were up to unless their report cards had arrived and he'd have to listen to a quick summary of the teachers' comments. Their mother knew how to give him a concise résumé, not only to convince him to continue paying the hefty private education bills but also to get it over with as quickly as possible. Nothing could change the fact that they were content with the gap that they had created between them and their off-spring.

Lying in her hospital bed on the day of her son's birth, Lisa couldn't help but close her eyes for a few minutes, smiling happily. She'd done it, and what an achievement, she told herself again and again. At last, she had been given the opportunity to do things right, better than her parents could ever have done. And she was the centre of attention at last. All of their family and friends had paid a visit, oohing and aahing over little Lucas, then insisting on how beautiful they both looked, how motherhood really suited her, and did she mind that they took a picture? She had Allan's full attention, too. He was everything an attentive, loving husband and father should be.

She smoothed out the stiff, crisp duvet in front of her, disheartened by the look of the mound she had been left with under her ribcage. There would be no other child, she thought. Why should she have another baby when the one she had just given birth to was unique? No, she'd suffered enough. He was going to be her only baby, forever.

My memory still manages to conjure up that special day with unusual clarity. Specific conversations are etched into my mind as if I only need to press a button and the movie from the past spools out its content. After the birth, events were much less vibrant, interspersed with the faint sense of being on the move – day and night – and feeling exhaustion followed by elation and joy, then the hope that somehow what I had been doing was all right. Actually, if I hadn't created a collection of albums, I'd probably find it easier to cope with the past. Each picture now tells a completely different story to the one I wanted the observer to believe. Only a stranger could still be fooled.

Sowing a bad seed

It had been harder than Lisa had thought – to love unconditionally and protect her son in this world. There had been countless moments of confusion and doubt but somehow, seeing Lucas's beautiful eyes, the look of innocence, and then his tears that melted her heart every single time they wet his cheeks, had always brought out the lioness in her. Numerous fellow mothers had confirmed the same feelings to her - that instincts made them act in a protective way. Yet, she had mistaken her maternal instincts with the idea that she always had to act on them. It had been a mistake, at best a bad excuse, all along. Nothing and no one had managed to open her eyes to the fact that she had overindulged her son from the moment he drew his first breath. As much as she, herself, had lacked the real warmth and attention any child needed, she had given her son too much. A parent really could give too many compliments, too much devotion and too much credit. Then again, it was like the person with a sweet tooth who knew fine well that biting into his next piece of chocolate could very well give him diabetes. He'd read up on it, his doctor had warned him and there was his family history confirming that he was at risk, but nonetheless, he decided to ignore the sound advice and bite into the dense sweet delicacy … out of weakness. She felt that her relentless protection of Lucas had been weakness, too. She had been told many a time to take a back seat, to let him sort things out himself, to set clear boundaries, stop fussing about things that weren't there, and the list could go on and on. It had been impossible for her husband to even suggest she take a look at herself in the mirror. On the few occasions that she did, she only saw a mother in love. She'd also been convinced that children grew out of their bad phases, their tantrums. Surely, everyone could see that she'd waited so long to hold her little bundle in her arms and that, when the moment had finally come, she'd had to vow never to let go.

The day I eventually did, I found myself facing one - and only one - simple wish, and that was to throw the baby out with the bathwater, turn on my heels and leave. How had it come to that? I get up and prepare a cup of coffee, dark and bitter. It will help me be alert, think it all through again – maybe even understand. People who say that your core self remains the same throughout life are wrong. I look at my former self with disdain and shock now because I literally see things I couldn't see before.

One of the decisive moments when she realised that she had played, if not the main part but unfortunately a very big part in the making of a self-absorbed individual, was years after when she'd believed that her son was happily married and, numerous niggling suspicions apart, leading a respectable life. *'Pah!'* she thought.

She recalled the day she'd stood in Lucas's bedroom, clearing out a drawer, when she suddenly heard the phone ring in her next door bedroom and, rather than rush to answer it, she'd frozen in her tracks. The sound was not as muffled as she thought it should have been. The ringing had been so clear and her thoughts had trailed off to the many conversations she'd had from her bedroom; conversations Lucas would undoubtedly have overheard. How stupid had she been? Then again, she'd told herself that surely he'd have been too bored to pry on his chattering mother next door and remembered the countless times she'd found him listening to music with his headphones on, the volume set too high to hear her calls to come down for dinner. He would not have heard most of her exchanges - maybe some, but not all - she'd added in her mind, her cheeks feeling flushed with shame.

The truth was that Lucas had made fun of her all the

time, playing not only with her devotion but using it to make her a laughing stock. She'd felt stuck, unable to put an end to his denigrating comments, then on the rare occasions she did, he'd wave his hands in distress, assuring her it had all just been a silly joke, no harm intended. It had rendered her speechless. It had been uncomfortable but, yet again, she'd always found an excuse to make his behaviour look benign, and she'd brush it all under the carpet as quickly as possible and move on. Allan had been the most outspoken against their son's insolent behaviour but had eventually given up as well.

When did Allan throw in the towel as a parent? When I think about his role as a father, I can't remember why I side-lined him all those years ago. Why did I never stand up for myself? I ask now. Why did I simply stand there and watch as Lucas freely used me as a punch bag? He was a teenager and surely that was exactly what they did when they experienced puberty, I'd told myself. All the other mothers spoke about their children being difficult at that age, too - moody, rude and self-centred.

I sip at the remains of my lukewarm coffee and heave a sigh. If I'm honest, I know exactly what had been going through Lucas's head. I just didn't want to see ... because it hurt so much and completely changed the idea of my perfect child. I feel the tears collecting at the rims of my eyes. I reach into the pocket of my cardigan and retrieve a tissue, dabbing them away. It had simply been too painful to try and truly imagine his point of view ...until now.

Growing up

Seven different schools, and fifteen years later, Lucas was sprawled out on his bed. He could hear his mother talking on the phone, imagine her sitting on the bed next door, kept upright by a pile of cushions so that her sore back was well positioned. She should just stop eating all those cakes and do some exercise, just like she tells him, he thought. It was incredible, how parents were quick in offering their advice but unable to set the example themselves. He knew her weaknesses. Dad was too pathetic to interfere or maybe he was being a bit unfair to him. He'd probably simply given up.

With two clearly indecisive parents, he concluded that he deserved to get what he wanted. It wasn't his fault that he felt devastated about leaving London to move to a boring place. He kept telling his mum that it had been a stupid idea. Her sad and worried face had been priceless. He knew that she'd do anything to make it right – absolutely anything.

He could always hear his mother talking next door, mostly about him. He knew what he was like and what he was definitely not like. He could count on his mother to interfere in any conversation or comment that centred around his behaviour, to set things right, because she'd be able to interpret his every move … favourably, of course. He had never had to work out himself what was right or wrong. Why bother if you had a mother with super-natural powers, breathing down your neck at every opportunity, someone who even to this day laid out a freshly ironed school uniform on his chair every night? He was fifteen, for crying out loud, not a baby any more. But then, who had to know? He knew full well that she'd never admit to mothering him like this to anyone. Oh no, she was too proud for that. He was sure that she told herself he was simply a late developer when it came to independence. There was always, always a way to explain anything and everything to someone's advantage. He knew better than anyone.

At times, on very rare occasions when she got angry and frustrated and aimed feelings of exasperation at him, he told her he was confused and then fell back on his irresistible charms, most of all his capacity to appear innocent and deeply hurt. Criticism genuinely felt like a strange, sudden sting that left no physical mark on his skin, yet his tangled thoughts and a lingering sense of being lost were very real. He was a person who could not lie, he was kind, very handsome and supposedly part of the group of people who could be said to be hyper-sensitive. She had repeatedly said so herself. So, in the end, she'd always caved in - much to others' annoyance, he could tell that much. But who he was had been ingrained into his psyche for what felt like a very long time. He had learned to keep a firm grip on the vocabulary that described him in such flattering terms and he never wanted to let that go.

And yet, there had been other voices over the years, different comments overheard here and there that had disgruntled him and, worse still, his mother. They'd caused the heavy weeping he was able to exhibit almost on command – usually by sobbing into the sleeve of his T-Shirt or running off into the garden, howling like an animal. He knew that she hardly managed to endure it. His dad would just shrug his resigned shoulders and roll his eyes in a 'please, not this again', type of manner. His mother had always managed to avoid the fact that maybe, just maybe in some cases, he should have been told that his behaviour was completely unacceptable. She'd seen another parent's struggle and knew that confronting one's child was uncomfortable at the best of times, yet still necessary in order to set healthy boundaries.

He was maybe a little bit lazy, she would concede – as she just did again on the phone next-door, tediously loud enough for him to hear - but he had great potential, was very clever and one day, voilà, his many talents would shine through and guide him. You could teach someone to study but you could not teach cleverness, she continued. That would always be there.

'Quite right it will. I'll make sure of that,' he said under his breath. She sounded so sure of herself that he could not help adding a private snort and a comment. All he really ever needed was a good teacher to do his or her magic, she said. It was not his fault that his school reports were abysmal. He then knew what would come next. He'd heard it so often that his ears sometimes rang upon hearing the words pronounced to whomever was prepared to listen. He'd been the victim of bullies ever since he could remember overhearing his mother talk to other parents or new friends. And there she was again, fuming, probably to another mother, about the appalling service at the school, the lack of attention which allowed bullies to cause harm to her son. Couldn't they get rid of the pupil who was causing him to come home frustrated, causing his work to suffer due to the snide remarks of fellow students? Who could blame him? The teachers hardly seemed to care, either. Her husband had also said that much. He had briefly taught in a private school after graduating from university and hence knew what constituted good teaching. She was at her wits end, he heard her say next. She saw no other solution than having to stomp into the headmaster's office and speak up against the harmful conditions that were allowed to fester in the school's classrooms.

When the endless passionate tirade was over, there was silence for a while, then he heard her answer to what must have been a very direct and unsettling comment. But no, of course she knew that he was often late and that there was very little motivation for him to take in homework. Wasn't it just typical for kids, boys in particular? Who, really, could blame him? she repeated again, words that made him shake his head with exasperation. School wasn't the be all and end all, she said. To which he was privately adding a sarcastic, *No*, rounding his lips into a perfect circle. They had a life, many friends to entertain. He was used to the comings and goings of guests to their house, the late nights. It had done him no harm. On the contrary, children needed to learn how to behave in company. The sound of her voice suddenly changed, she appeared uncomfortable, and it had dropped in volume so that he needed to concentrate in order to hear her words.

He thought of Alice, his babysitter of many years, like a second, much stricter and more tiresome mum. Then again, his mother was tiresome, so very tiresome, too. His feeble attempts to stop her from shouting at the umpteenth incompetent teacher, and barging into a headmistress's or headmaster's office, had led to the very same scenario again and again. She had tried to make him work and, to put it bluntly, he hated work, so invented every illness, bully, discomfort and sore foot in the long list of excuses one could come up with in order to avoid doing any of it. And he knew that his mother hated seeing him in pain, any sort of pain for that matter. He didn't see the need for school because why tire yourself out with writing when you could lie in bed playing video games or watching movies? What was the point of learning to spell when all you needed to do with your essay was put it through a spell check?

He gasped when he next heard his mum's raised voice. 'What? Are you trying to tell me that he actually insults fellow students? Of course, I know he's got to defend himself, he is a normal kid, you know.' There was a moment of silence and then she seemed to jump into the conversation with renewed passion. 'That's just typical. People distort events all the time. I know he doesn't mean any harm. Look, you just don't understand him like I do. He is *my* son, after all.' There was another pause before he heard her answer. He knew that the lady at the other end of the line was right. He did swear and insulted other pupils whenever he could. He felt real enjoyment doing so and that was something he had concealed from his mother very well so far. It had become a game of hide and seek, mouse and cat. He felt sudden apprehension, one of his veins pulsating at the temple. After all, she could of course find out the truth and then about much worse … so, he had to quickly find a way to divert her attention if she were about to confront him later.

For some strange reason she had always been obsessed with bad language. He had heard her use it as well though, so really, where was the harm? A severe cramp would do, he thought, and should the question of his swearing rear its head during a conversation, he'd just look at her with his big green eyes, widened innocently, and simply say that the other person must have misheard. It worked every time. It was like popping a balloon. When the air was out it was out. She never had a word to add other than utter, 'of course, of course'. He sniggered, just picturing the scene.

Shortly after, he heard his mother say something that he had heard so often before...that he had suffered from the years, when only a toddler, he'd had to attend a local Belgian kindergarten. Allan's job had taken them to Brussels for a contract and, come to think of it, she thought of it with dread as well as nostalgia. She couldn't quite put a finger on it other than a feeling that it had been a missed opportunity. They had lived in a lovely bungalow villa with a generous surround of garden and a cosy balcony overlooking a field with horses. She remembered the two ladies and their children that they had befriended one afternoon. There had been the potential for normality. It was the reason why they were discussing taking Lucas out of school and moving to a more rural area, somewhere they could all get back to basics.

Back to basics? He jumped at the words, the small hairs at the back of his neck raised like a dog's, ready for defence.

His mother didn't expand further on her words but, instead, she continued talking about her time in rural Brussels, where she said she'd hoped for more simplicity. He'd only been five years old, his potential limitless in her eyes. It had been the first change of scene for them. He switched off by focusing on a new computer game because the event recounted was a story he was tired of hearing chewed over once again.

I remember my brief encounter with two Belgian women and their children, whilst living abroad with Allan and a very young Lucas. I've heard people say that specific events might remain vivid in your memory, whilst others get discarded, forgotten or only partly remembered. Yet, every time I set foot in a forest in autumn after that meeting, it was as if I was transported back to that playground where Lucas had hurt his foot, an event we both subsequently used to claim had permanently injured a joint. I laugh out loud, remembering my gullibility and, still, I cannot help but think back to the day when the air had smelled of fallen leaves, humid earth and a lasting, strong feeling of missed opportunities.

Little Emperor

Lisa had seen them before whilst exploring her new neighbourhood. She had stumbled upon the two mothers and, what seemed, their two young children in tow at the local playground. What had caught her attention was the fact that for some reason the children spoke English to each other while the women conversed in French. In her mind, she pictured them as ideal play mates for Lucas and, with any luck, she'd make new friends, too. From the very first day, Lisa had been astonished about the Belgians' remarkable language skills. So far, her attempts to speak either Dutch or French had failed miserably.

One of the mothers had jumped over a tree stump, accompanied by the sound of a happy squeak which was coming from a small person with light-blond curls, skipping past her. Two bikes lay discarded by a wooden bench where a bulky rucksack sat on a table. Directing her eyes up to the crown, Lisa could make out an array of orange, brown, yellow and green colours. It didn't only look like autumn, it smelled like autumn and the crisp air felt like autumn. As a girl she'd loved to look up to the top of the trees covered in autumn dress, then she would start turning on herself, the colours becoming a long streak of warmth until her head would spin, eyes blurring. Eventually, her knees would buckle and cause her to fall to the ground, gasping for air.

Barely a week lay between first seeing the two women and their children and her returning with Lucas. She had plotted about a forest adventure with him, coaxing him out of the house. He'd been complaining about a very sore tummy and Lisa had decided to keep him off pre-school as a precaution. A breath of fresh air would do him good, she'd thought. She knew that some kindergarten schools were closed for teachers' conferences, so hoped Lucas would meet a few new friends. When they eventually arrived at the gate, Lucas pouted, refusing to take any further steps.

'What is it darling?' she asked patiently, alarmed by his angry face.

'Don't wanna play.'

'Why, sweetie?'

'Them.' He pointed to a girl and a boy in the distance, jumping and laughing with delight.

'Come on, Lucas. They could be your new friends. It'll be fun, trust me.'

The smell of damp grass and leaves was overwhelming. Lisa watched as one of the mothers laughed, visibly out of breath after chasing the little girl and nearly slipping on a dark patch of moss. She turned to another lady, smiling and shaking her head as they watched the girl skip away and climb nimbly to the top of a slide, beckoning her friend to follow. Lisa yearned to be a part of this little group. Some people aspire to become an astronaut or a doctor; she simply aspired to be a loving mother and to be a part of this picture of normality.

'Lucas, I'll get you an ice cream if you come along. You'll see it'll be fun,' she eventually whispered into his ear. Here it was again, she thought with dismay. She had to offer something in return for him to go and play with other kids on a playground, something she thought, surely, should come naturally.

'Greta, Mummy, watch me,' the girl exclaimed in French, sliding down the shoot.

'Me, too. Look at me. Look!' the boy said, imitating his confident little friend.

'Marie! Anton! Take your time when you climb the

ladder, please,' Greta called over to the children, watching them race each other to the steps. The girl's cheeks were pinked with the effort of climbing and sliding and her eyes shone brightly. She responded by nodding her head energetically, her curls bouncing in the process. Despite the cool air, she was in the process of taking off her thick coat and just throwing it over the wooden railing, carefully watching her mother's reaction while smiling mischievously at the other woman standing next to her. Her mother, as if connected to her daughter's every move and thought, frowned from the distance.

'The joys and fears of being a mum,' Lisa heard one of the mothers say.

'How could you be annoyed with them?' the other responded.

They laughed and settled on one of the benches where the sunlight was not obstructed by the high trees around. Brussels was surrounded by one of the greenest forest belts in Europe where cyclists and hikers delighted in daily exercises and experienced the splendour of the changing seasons. At this time of year, the falling leaves offered a splendid soft carpet for people to walk on.

That's when they looked up and watched Lisa and Lucas edge closer to the seating area, acknowledging them with a friendly smile. So far, they may have secretly hoped to have the space to themselves, Lisa thought. If they had, they didn't let on because within a short time, they introduced themselves. She established that both women had an English speaking partner and they were excited that Lucas would add to their bi-lingual skills.

'Here comes a new playmate, make sure you share with him,' Greta called to the children, who stopped building a big hill of sand and observed the newcomer from the corners of their eyes. They seemed to have learnt already that watching others for a while could give them vital clues to how they thought they might get on with them.

'Be careful, guys. I don't want Lucas to get hurt.' As soon as Lisa called out her warning she knew that her wording must have seemed a bit awkward. The women didn't know just how nervous she was about Lucas. He was still so small.

'Don't worry,' Anna said to her, diffusing a short silence. 'I'm a paediatric nurse. I'll come to the rescue if anything happens, okay?' The reply did the trick. She felt a bit better about letting Lucas climb the frames.

'He's such a sweetie,' Lisa told Anna and Greta, 'and so sensitive. I'm sure at school they don't supervise them enough. He always comes home with bruises or bumps.'

I cringe at remembering my criticism of the Belgian school system for minor bruises, and I walk back into the house to fetch a jacket. The clouds have covered the warming sun but I'm determined to stay on the terrace for as long as I can.

'Oh, I'm sure children need to *feel* their experimenting as well. The teachers can't constantly protect them,' Anna said.

Lisa nodded.

'Lucas, go and introduce yourself.' She clapped her hands together with delight and gave her son an encouraging wink. 'Oh, silly me, I just did that.' She burst out laughing. 'Oh well, he's only five …'

Lisa felt chirpy and delighted when the two women invited her onto their bench. They quickly ascertained that she was English while Lisa was intrigued by the fact that Anna was a French-speaker and Greta Flemish. She'd stood in front of the mirror for ages that morning, wondering what to wear, and was pleased then that she'd chosen simple delicate jewellery, her washed out tight jeans and a simple blue and white striped top underneath a long thick woolly cardigan. She had swept up her hair in a loosely set bun, revealing two white pearl earrings and a delicate necklace holding a small sparkly heart-shaped pendant. She wanted to convey an image of elegant simplicity. Lisa noticed Anna's unkempt hair and the slightly scruffy trousers Greta was wearing. She couldn't quite put her finger on why she took such care and importance in her own looks. She yearned to see Lucas wear a school uniform with its crisp white shirt and tie. Somehow tidiness calmed her nerves and pacified her nagging doubts.

I'm startled out of my recollection by the thought that maybe my relentless need for orderliness was a way to hide the chaos that lay beneath. I must have thought that looking prim and proper would convey the idea of a woman in control of her life. I look up and see myself reflected in one of the living room windows. I look like someone who's aged before her time, my cheeks slightly sunken, eyelids drooping and my hair a short, scraggly mess. My wardrobe is full of beautiful clothes, yet these days I seem to always dress in the same few pairs of trousers and especially the warm cardigan I'm wearing now. It's like a child's one and only teddy bear that, no matter what a parent may offer in order to replace it with a new one, she'll hold on to it even more vigorously. I bought this one just prior to my pregnancy thirty-two years ago; it's a reminder of a happy, carefree woman. I've kept it all this time, wearing it sparingly until now. I rub my hands together and cuddle back into it, my thoughts drifting back into the past.

'Do you come here a lot?' Anna asked her.

'It's the first time with Lucas, actually. We moved to Belgium six months ago and I'm still discovering so many places.'

'Are you enjoying living here?'

'Yes, I am, but as you can hear, my French is *comme ci comme ça.*' She chuckled an infectious, hearty laugh again. 'My son goes to one of the local kindergartens,' Lisa added.

'Oh, ours as well. So is he off today because of the teachers' meetings, too?' Anna looked over to Greta, smiling. Just as Lisa wanted to answer the question, they heard the children's sudden shouts. They got up and walked over to Marie and Anton, who were glaring intensely at Lucas.

'What's going on?' Greta asked calmly.

'He's destroyed our sand house.' Tears collected in Marie's eyes as she told her mother about Lucas's onslaught on their creation.

'Oh darling, I'm sorry. He doesn't mean to annoy you. He just wants to play,' Lisa instantly intercepted. 'He was not one hundred percent this morning. He had a sore tummy. I can tell that he's not himself. Are you okay Lucas?' She turned solicitously to her son.

'But … he's still destroyed the kids' sand castle,' Anna said, frowning. Lisa knew that Lucas was unable to say sorry yet, much to her dismay.

'Oh sweeties, I'm so sorry, really sorry,' Lisa quickly said, emphasising her remorseful tone of voice while looking at Marie and Anton, who saw that she was genuinely apologetic. 'OH, maybe Lucas is coming down with something after all. There's an awful bug going round at the school at the moment. But, having said that, don't worry, I don't think he's contagious. I just kept him off in case. I believe you can't be too careful when your kid goes to a state school. The things he could catch or get told. Lucas has never ever said a nasty or rude word to anyone and now I know for sure that he hears it daily.' She was shaking her head, almost as if to herself, oblivious to the idea that the other two women could be offended by her criticism.

'Well, I think children should not be over protected but, you're right, I keep telling the teachers that washing hands is the best and simplest way to teach them how to stay safe from most bugs. As for swearing, again, it is up to the parents to tell them that some people don't speak nicely and that they do need to learn not to imitate,' Anna answered amicably, yet Lisa could tell she was annoyed that Lucas had not been put on the spot at all. Her lips were pressed together and she gave her son a quick, stern sideways glance. Lisa had tried to diffuse the situation but, still, she could tell that she'd probably lost a bit of the other women's respect.

They walked back to the bench, Anna pulling out a thermos and offering each of them a cup of coffee. They had barely taken one sip when they heard Lucas screaming for help. Marie and Anton had rounded up on him and before they could start pushing him, Lisa appeared by their side.

'What do you think you're doing?' she scolded them, her voice a pitch too high. Lucas smiled at the other children smugly and left them standing, skipping towards the climbing frame.

'Lucas, what happened? Stay here please.'

'He called us names,' Marie answered, her lips quivering, as she told her mum, now standing next to her.

'Yes, he's nasty, nasty,' fumed Anton, and his mum wrapped him in a comforting hug.

'You can't round up on him though, Marie. I think you should all apologise and make up,' Anna said.

'I agree, let's all be friends, yes?' Lisa added, relieved.

It took her at least ten minutes to convince Lucas that he had to say sorry. He stomped the ground, started to cry and repeatedly said he'd been called names, too, and that it wasn't fair.

Meanwhile, Anna and Greta diverted their children's attention and set up a picnic, laid-out on the wooden table. The children watched as some of the lovely food appeared in front of their eyes, then raced back and forth between the table and the bags to help bring everything else into the open. Anna had her wet wipes at the ready to prevent the little sandy hands diving straight into the neat piles of sandwiches displayed on paper plates, a big bowl of crisps and plastic dishes containing chunks of raw vegetables.

'Did you bring the biscuits we made, Mummy?' Marie shouted, fixing her eyes on her mother while chewing her first bite of cheese and tomato sandwich.

'Of course love, would I forget our amazing biscuits? Please don't talk while you're eating. You may choke, remember?' her mother said with a wink.

'See, Lucas? All's well. No one is upset anymore, so please calm down,' Lisa cajoled her son. They'd been walking towards a climbing frame, Lucas sulking and glancing over to the other children, envy written all over his face.

'Would you like to join us, Lucas?' Greta called to the boy, who instantly pretended he was imitating Tarzan and ignored her. Marie shook her head intensely from side to side, shocked. Anton just stared at his mum.

'Look, we are nice people and yes, he was rude but maybe he's …' she was at a loss for words. 'Maybe he's jealous because we've got each other,' she suggested, just loud enough for Lisa to hear. She called Lucas over again, raising her voice a bit higher this time. There was no answer but Lisa decided to respond in his place.

'I don't think he's hungry yet... his sore tummy, you know. But thank you so much. We'll see you guys in a bit. I think it would be good if we stayed out of your way for a little while,' she said, and smiled.

The two children sighed with relief and continued eating, engrossed in their food, munching on juicy cucumber sticks and tucking into a bowl of crisps.

'I finished, Mummy. Can I have a biscuit now?' Marie chirped.

'What do you say?' Anna asked.

'Pleeease,' Marie replied.

As she opened the tin box containing their freshly baked chocolate biscuits, she inhaled the delicious aroma of chocolate and vanilla through her nostrils.

'Mmm, that does smell yummy.' Next, she looked startled to see Lucas standing right by the table. 'Oh, hello Lucas. I didn't see you coming.'

'Can I have one?' he asked, pointing his finger towards the box.

'I'll have to ask your Mummy first, and there is a magic word that you need to add to your question! Anyway, I remember your mum saying that you have a sore tummy, so a chocolate biscuit is probably not a good idea. You can eat a little sandwich first, then see how you feel.' She looked up to Lisa and widened her eyes with surprise as she just gestured approvingly.

'Are you sure?' Anna asked, frowning.

'Oh, one biscuit should be okay,' Lisa said.

Anna turned her attention back to Lucas. 'Well, what do you say then, Lucas?'

'Please,' he said after a long pause and with visibly great reluctance. He walked off with a biscuit in hand, skipping and kicking a few stones lying on the path.

'Well done,' Lisa whispered, as he walked passed her.

Marie and Anton wanted to follow suit but their mothers stopped them.

'Oh no, you eat your food at the table. You could choke.'

'But what about Lucas?' Anton asked, pouting.

'Well, he's not our child, is he? Sorry guys. I know this seems unfair but different mums allow different things. It's how it is, I'm afraid,' Greta answered. The words stung and although Lisa knew the women were right, she was just relieved that the previous, awkward situation seemed to have been ironed out.

All of their movements stopped in mid-air, their jaws frozen, when they all heard a sudden piercing scream echoing through the small wood that surrounded the playground. They shot their heads towards the noise then looked at each other with querying eyes. Lisa was the first to make a move and by the time the others reached the scene, she was already frantic. She headed over to where her boy was now crouching on the floor, howling in what appeared to be excruciating pain.

There was always a feeling of uncontrollable distress and panic taking over my body whenever I witnessed my son in any kind of pain or anguish. I wanted to be there at every step he took, to protect him, keep him safe from disappointment or sadness. I remember my own loneliness all too well as a child.

I get up from the chair and wander around the garden for a while. A light breeze has come up and the smell of roses waft over to me. I briefly close my eyes, inhaling the sweet scent. I know now that my behaviour had been disproportionate.

Lucas had fallen and hurt himself and was screaming in the same measure as Lisa's hysterical cries - panicking about doctors, broken bones or torn muscles. Anna rushed over, kneeled next to the boy and managed to quickly ascertain that there was no blood flowing and hence tried, in turn, to calm her. Upon hearing Anna's comforting tone, she had temporarily felt reassured and so was Lucas, whose screams had quickly turned into heaving sobs.

'Do you think you can get up, Lucas?' Anna asked,

once both mother and son had completely composed themselves.

Lucas took a few feeble attempts in getting up, yet as soon as the sole of his foot touched the ground, he groaned with apprehension. Lisa inhaled with fresh fear, sharing her son's pain, flapping her hands in distress.

'Oh, these playgrounds here are so dangerous. Back in England, this would never have happened,' she mumbled under her breath.

'Would you like me to have a look at Lucas's foot? I could tell you at least if he's broken anything or if there's any serious damage,' Anna offered.

'Oh, oh please do. Just be really careful, okay? I fear that he has seriously hurt himself.'

'Of course I will be,' Anna said reassuringly, and looked at the boy gently, smiling. 'Are you ok if I have a quick look at your foot and then we can see what's up?'

Lucas gave a little nod. Apart from sniffing loudly he had completely calmed down, no longer wailing or crying. Anna kneeled next to him and, with a practiced gesture, lifted the boy's injured foot off the ground. She checked his face for any sign of reaction but he was now calmly observing her as she prodded his ankle gently and pressed the toes up towards his knee to check the flexion. Lucas made no sound, only the odd little grunt of worry when she gently stretched his leg full length, then she swiftly cupped her hands under his arms and lifted him so that he could place his feet slowly on the ground by himself.

'There you go, little chap. You're fine. Your foot was probably twisted a bit when you fell but there is nothing broken or torn, thank goodness.' She gave out a happy laugh and added, 'Yay.' Lucas imitated her expression and was off in a flash with the other children, who gestured for him to follow them.

'Oh, thank goodness, all seems well after all. What a terrible fright. Thank you so much for checking on my little angel. The local council can count itself lucky that I don't need to pay them yet another visit for a complaint.' Lisa beamed with pride and relief and trotted off after the three children who had now run towards the slides, screaming and laughing.

'Oh, I don't know. Children do need to explore and test their own strength. That sometimes ends in tears but, believe me, I've seen much, much worse during my job.'

'I guess you're right but Lucas is my angel, my everything. I cannot bear him getting hurt or suffering,' Lisa retorted.

I clearly remember Anna's emphasis that she'd seen much, much worse. I understand now that I must have ridiculed myself. And not only then but many times thereafter. I look up, noticing heavy rain clouds darkening the sky. I trudge back towards the terrace and pick up my empty coffee cup, carrying it to the kitchen sink. Then I wander into the living room, passing by the many framed photographs standing on the sideboard. There he is, my little angel, I think mockingly. From tempestuous toddler, he became a fully-fledged disgruntled teenager, yet nothing in the pictures reveal any of it. On the contrary, they seem to reflect images of a normal, happy family. But when I try to recall moments of affection and love between us, I can only remember one specific time when Lucas was unusually attentive and kind to me. I had put it down to the fact that, despite his obvious reluctance to leave London, moving to the countryside had finally brought out the best in him. How mistaken I'd been. I slump into the sofa. He's never been my perfect child. No, a little emperor more like, intent on getting what he wanted irrespective of what others felt or thought. As hard as I try now, I can't even conjure up one single time he asked me for my opinion or thoughts or cared about my feelings.

Lisa walked back with the two women, joining them for a nibble and another cup of coffee, mortified that she'd not brought a single item of drink or food herself. For the next ten minutes all was fine, besides the odd shriek from the children.

The attack came unexpectedly and took everyone by surprise. The whack Lucas gave Anna over the head was vicious, delivered from behind with a long stick. He laughed, running off, oblivious of the intensity of the blow. Marie lunged at him, watching her mother wincing with pain, and shook the boy. Lisa was there in a flash, pulling her off.

'How dare you jump on Lucas like that!'

That's when the bubble burst. Anna spun round and faced Lisa with an angry stare.

'Excuse me? What did you just say? How dare your son attack me. This wasn't a funny little tickle but a very painful whip he gave me. Unacceptable. So, Marie doesn't deserve being told off. It's your son who does.' She rubbed her sore head while Marie was burying her weeping head into her lap.

'I'm sorry. I'm sure he was just playing,' Lisa retorted, more feebly now.

'I've had enough and I'm sure Greta thinks the same. From the moment you and Lucas turned up, there's been one incident after another. Our children played peacefully until Lucas destroyed their sand castle without an apology. Then he called them names and you defended him. The tip of the iceberg is the fact that, supposedly, your son has got a sore tummy, yet he gets a chocolate biscuit – without any proper food. You must be joking! And now he whacks me over the head, then my daughter who, may I remind you, is only four, defends me, and you dare to tell her off instead of your son. Let's go, Greta. Sorry children, it's time to go.' They disappeared and, mortified, she never set foot on the playground again.

I cringe just thinking about their sudden, angry departure and Lucas reminding me at that moment, as if nothing out of the ordinary had happened, that I'd promised him an ice cream. I know I should have been angry with Lucas, made him apologise and not given in to his sweet tooth ...

I cup my face with both hands, shaking my head, then groan with regret. Lucas never learnt to respect boundaries, not at home and not at school, either. What he'd learnt was how to avoid having to make an effort. Taking him out of a school or changing the environment by moving to Romsey had hardly been enough to turn his behaviour round and to say otherwise would only prolong the delusion unnecessarily. I now know better than anyone how to decipher his mind.

Country Life

He felt irritation most days but especially when it came to having to follow teachers' orders. What had at times still seemed awkward, now had become his aim in life: to get what he wanted no matter what, with the least possible effort and, ideally, the greatest support imaginable from … well, anyone really.

What had he just heard though? His mother's voice had become more secretive and muted during her conversation but he was sure that he had heard every single word. They just did not seem to want to enter his head in the correct fashion. They somehow bounced around before they finally did come together and make sense to his fifteen-year-old self. Hearing was not always understanding, he knew that. His blood quickened and he sat bolt upright, repeating the sentences slowly and clearly to himself in his head again. *We've decided to move to the countryside, start afresh. He'll go to the local secondary school and the change of air will do him good,* she had said, but the rest of the speech was lost on him. He knew exactly what this meant. In a big state secondary school out in the country, there was no chance for someone like his mum. There was no way she could rub shoulders with the teachers or let them taste a drop of her poison if they underperformed according to her demands. He tried to picture his mother, who always wore elegant but simple dresses, perfectly combined with matching nail varnish and jewellery even for a walk in the woods. He imagined her wearing wellington boots and, what did he just hear? *Walking a dog*. She wanted to get them a dog, try and live a simpler life, she'd said. He wanted to laugh out loud but thought better of it. He sniggered. *We've already found a nice house in a village and Lucas will take the bus to school*, he then heard her tell the person at the end of the line. These last words were the tip of the iceberg. He got up and punched the air angrily.

'You'll pay for this,' he whispered. 'I'll give you hell.'

And his parents did pull off doing what *they* wanted for once, irrespective of his opinion. How dare they?

He had tried his usual - normally effective - sad sulk but, even so, they'd moved to the countryside, signed him up at the local school and insisted that he had to start pulling his weight at last. Reality sunk in then. He'd felt as if someone had literally pulled a carpet from under his feet and left him to fester, sprawled on the floor. Despite his mother's encouragements and unfailing conviction that it would all work out, he'd felt betrayed. No matter how much his parents tried, he couldn't but feel he was entitled to get what he wanted, especially because he'd complied with their whims to join the country bumpkins. He was determined to never let them forget that he'd come with them against his will.

It took him one week to work out how to turn the girls' heads and find a small group of willing 'friends'. It took him one month to create a rock solid reputation amongst the students and teachers that he was charming and clever. He'd never, ever admit it to his parents, but he actually enjoyed the novelty of living somewhere new, the fuss many girls were making about him, and he quickly adopted the idea that a big school had many advantages he could explore. He was not the tallest of teenagers, not the quickest in lessons nor the strongest or fastest, but he was driven like no one else at his school by the desire to enjoy himself to the fullest. Anyone uncovering his techniques to avoid studying would either receive the silent treatment, a threat, or he'd do what he had learnt to perfection: talk them to the ground until they'd cave in with exasperation.

'Lucas, it has come to my attention that you are using a few girls in your class to do your homework, help you with research and even bring you print outs to school. I have also been told that you are selling drugs, all kind of stuff on school premises. If there is any truth in this? May I warn you that we will take serious action against it,' a teacher had told him during a meeting six months after he'd arrived in Romsey.

'Excuse me? I need help from other girls in my class? That's a sick joke, isn't it?'

'Look, this is a warning ...'

'With no proof. I will sue you for falsely accusing me.'

'Calm down, Lucas. I have not accused you but I've simply stated that these issues have come to my attention.'

'Do you always believe what anyone tells you?'

'No, but this is not *anyone* who's told me this but a teacher's observation.'

'How dare you treat me like a thug.'

'I am not treating you like a thug, I'm simply ...'

'I will talk to my parents about this and you will be sorry for accusing me of something I haven't done.'

'I'm just telling you to be careful and ...'

'I agree I have to be careful. People are just jealous and like to see me sink. I'm sure of this, Miss. Oh, let me guess, it's Mr Regner who's come up with this idea,' Lucas interrupted her again.

'Nobody has come up with this idea. It is based on observation and students …'

'I'm telling you it's all lies,' he huffed, then looked downcast.

'Okay then, Lucas, I take in what you're saying. Just take it as what it is – a warning.'

It worked every single time. His good looks and expensive taste for clothes quickly led him into many bedrooms and helped to pass time during the dreary last years of school. There was more than one boy who'd happily see him squirm in the head master's office. He knew he had to act tactically. After the chat with his teacher, he decided to lay low for a while, enjoy some time off from dealing, then make another move during the upcoming school trip. It was all his parents' fault anyway. Country life was so boring, he told them repeatedly. What soothed his nerves every time he felt annoyed by someone's criticism was the fact that he knew he was safe. His father's health was declining already and surely, when his mother would pass, he'd inherit a nice heap – properties and jewellery he could sell. He sighed and told himself to relax.

There was just one thing that niggled him immensely and he didn't quite know why. His mother had gotten herself a dog and for the first few weeks it was as if she'd given birth and had another baby to cherish and coo over. It was disgusting to watch. He couldn't believe her selfishness and decided that he had to get rid of the little bastard. She was *his* mum and he had to set things back to normal. If he'd been led astray by girls and drugs, she was entirely to blame.

After all these years, it dawns on me that my own son had been the one to open the gate after I'd safely parked the car in the garage then closed the front gate at the bottom of the lane. I remember it so vividly – my tender care and attention for the pup had been without reproach. I can still hear Lucas's question – should he let the dog out? Had I closed the gate? 'Of course,' I'd said in response, and 'how kind of you to remember asking.' It had been odd. But I could not think he'd be able to devise a plan so cunning and cold blooded anyway. My son could not do such a wicked thing to a pup. Yet, the little one was found dead later that evening, despite our frantic searches. Someone would have lifted him onto the pavement and there he lay, lifeless. Lucas had cried when he heard the news. He'd cried ... then hugged me when I was shaking with grief and guilt. Lucas had shown his soft side, telling me that he felt awful for letting the dog out, blaming himself. Of course, it wasn't long before I'd taken all the blame instead. Worse, I declared that maybe it had been a sign, that I was probably only able to look after one baby. Pathetic is the word that enters my mind now.

The awakening

It all began with a phone call on a Saturday morning. Lisa remembered waking up content, realising that she was fretting less and less about living by herself. She missed her husband dreadfully and the painful pull at the centre of her stomach had at times gotten so intense that she could not eat for days. Over time, the ache had dulled, it was weaker and more bearable. On that Saturday, she'd taken her coffee and a buttered slice of toast out onto the terrace, adjusting a light jacket around her soft waist before sinking into the chair, sighing with nonchalance. The morning sun had just been strong enough to warm her, and she remembered taking a lungful of air, that had smelled of the nearby roses and freshly cut grass, when the phone rang. She had contemplated not answering but had thought better of it, walking into the kitchen and lifting the receiver.

'Mum?'

'Lucas, good morning. That is …'

He had not let her finish the sentence but the flood of his words had rolled over her like a steam train. Come to think of it now, she admitted to noticing that he must have perfected that skill for years. She knew that for a long time she'd lost track or had simply given up on deluding herself in believing that somehow or sometime in the future, he'd magically come to his senses. She had read somewhere that what died last before a person drew their last breath was hope. It had certainly been the case for her … until that phone call. It would take weeks and months to sink in properly but, in the end, the result was the same: there was no hope left.

After the flood of her son's elaborate account had subsided, she'd felt numb and exhausted as she eventually put the phone back on the base. A jolt had torn through her chest when the words started to sink in properly later that morning. *Debts with the in-laws. He lost his job a year ago. Loans he could not re-pay at the bank. His wife wanted a divorce. When did all this happen? How had she not seen it coming?* The questions were flying through her head like a colony of bats that could not see their way out, incessantly bumping into the inner walls of her skull. Then the veil she had held in front of her eyes for so long had lifted, revealing the ugly truth. With the devastating news came a massive migraine.

She'd had no choice but to take him in for a few months. What she did not do however, for the first time since the day her son was born, was comfort him, reassure him or even talk much to him. Ever since she'd first set eyes on him in the hospital room, her senses had been scattered and had cruelly and successfully pulled apart what should have been her common good sense. She'd built a dream son in her imagination. And on that momentous day when that bubble had burst completely, her common sense somehow came back together as well and all those numerous past comments, warnings and premonitions reared their heads with bitter, merciless revenge. For weeks, she'd been unable to do anything mundane without her thoughts reaching back to the past, mistakes that she could never atone for now. Strange memories rose to the surface of her consciousness. The day she'd taken Lucas to the playground and he'd hurt his foot. She'd been an hysterical silly woman in front of complete strangers. And she'd done it again, again and again thereafter. The shame of her exaggeration made her hands shake, cheeks burn, and cold sweat trickle down her back. Why did she ever think that his behaviour had been acceptable and that she could blame it all on others? And the realisation had, of course, come much too late.

Maybe her doubts regarding a molesting complaint during a school trip in the Lake District had, after all, been founded, she thought. He'd been such a lovely caring son after the little dog died, when her mind had been in a constant guilty fog. She thought that there was no way the allegations had any foundation whatsoever. Then there were those three perfectly sweet girls covering for him, reassuring the teachers that they'd been with him all along. The realisation that he'd somehow made them do what he'd wanted had been the last straw, sealing the newly formed picture she had to accept of her own son. Until then, she'd miraculously managed to brush the incident under the carpet. Why exactly did the three girls cover for him though? She never really found out.

It was one of only a few important puzzle pieces that I seemed unable to find. Then again, had someone not mentioned that one of the girls had spoken to her mother about a dare during the school trip and that a boy had rescued her from drowning...?

Parts of the conversation come back now. There'd been a challenge to jump into a lake. I'd dismissed the

254

rumour at the time because I'd felt by then that, if I – of all people – attempted to investigate further, I'd only open another can of worms. But now I suppose that it must have been Lucas going to the rescue. Rhoda had been the name of the girl, one of the three stating that he'd been with them all the while. I know that he would normally have relished looking like a hero, saving someone's life, unless he'd done it to cover up another bad deed. It sounds exactly like him, I think.

Reaping rotten fruit

From the sheltered area where he stood, he could just make out Rhoda closing her eyes during a few seconds of concentration, standing at the top of the crag of Ullswater lake. The secondary school were on a three-day camping trip to the Lake District and there were a few students determined to prove that they were dare-devil enough to take the plunge from the crag into the crystal clear water of the lake below. He admitted that the peaceful, almost glass-like surface of the water looked enticing and scary all at once. He could just make out the gentle ripples at the outer edges where the water leapt up to the shore. The sun had not yet set when he stood by a row of bushes, looking up to the top where he saw Rhoda, goaded on by her two friends who were already swimming in the lake. He'd stumbled upon the intriguing scene by coincidence. He'd been wandering along the path alone after a disastrous rendezvous with the most gorgeous girl from secondary. She just wouldn't do what he wanted, so he'd forced the game a bit. Now she'd run off in a flurry, threatening to expose him. Their teachers had strictly forbidden any swimming during the trip, considering that the water was still too cold, despite an unusually warm spring. So, watching the three girls had been a welcome diversion until he'd be able to come up with a plan for himself. He agreed that a camping trip was not complete without a jump into one of England's most beautiful lakes, so he started taking off his clothes as well. He shivered briefly, then jumped on the spot to warm up his muscles prior to taking a leap. What these girls could do, he surely could as well. He was tired of trudging around National Trust houses and listening to overly enthusiastic adults trying to inculcate the students with some culture. What they wanted was a thrill that they'd be talking about for weeks, months even, not some boring dusty old house, no matter how pretty the setting and clever its former owner. He stopped in his tracks as he heard one of the girls call up to Rhoda.

'Come on, Rhoda', she shouted. 'Stop pro … pro … procrastinating or whatever it's called.' It wasn't clear whether the girl had difficulties saying the fancy word or was simply too cold to speak clearly.

Rhoda stepped from one foot to the other. He conceded that the warmth from earlier in the day was fast being replaced with cool evening air. They all had to be quick.

'Yes, yes, it's just I'm freezing even watching you,' she called.

'You're not going to chicken out now. Quick – just do it! You don't want to feel like an epic fail, do ya?' Kelly replied, splashing around to keep her body warm.

'Come on. You know we have to get back to the camp in time for dinner preps. Come on, go, go, go,' Joyce added encouragingly.

Next, he watched her jump. She disappeared in the lake but when she resurfaced, a strange gurgle echoed over the water. Next she gasped, dove under again and rose with another desperate intake of breath. He knew then that something was wrong. Maybe she'd jumped awkwardly because of the lack of light and had injured a muscle. If she had a muscle cramp, she was toast, he thought matter-offactly.

'Help!' she gasped, as soon as her head broke again through the water.

'Hey, Rhoda. Are you ok?' Kelly's eyes narrowed, hearing Rhoda's gasp for air. Daylight was vanishing fast and a few thick clouds had appeared overhead, promising some evening rain.

Kelly and Joyce shouted her name, they all watched as her flailing arms surfaced.

He quickly made up his mind to get involved, picked up a nearby thick stick and waded into the water as fast as he could. The air was momentarily sucked out of his lungs as he realised just how cold it was. He felt sharp pain in his calves but ventured on, calling towards the girls, who were now screaming in a panicked frenzy, trying to heave their friend above the water. It was literally like wading through a big bucket full of ice cubes.

'Lucas?' Joyce called, squinting her eyes to see who was approaching them.

'Yes, I'm coming.'

'She's drowning, quick Lucas, quick.'

'Hey, I'm here. Where is she?'

'Oh, quick, she's further to your right now. She was moving too much; we were all sinking …. there, I can just make out some bubbles.'

'Here, hold on to the stick. I must get her up first, then make her grip onto it so we can drag her back to safety,' he said, swimming over to the area in a few strokes.

Kelly and Joyce were holding on to the wood firmly.

'My toes are going numb,' Joyce chattered through her teeth.

'Mine, too.'

When he first managed to get hold of Rhoda's body, he was startled by the intense chill she emanated. He heaved her up with a sudden pull. It was like looking through a fog and trying to keep hold of a moving person. Then they emerged together, her mouth instantly opening with a desperate gasp for oxygen. Joyce and Kelly had been quick to help manoeuvre Rhoda onto the floating stick and pull her shaking body to the shore. They slumped onto a soft bit of grass, heaving, shivering and groaning. Kelly ran up to where their clothes lay, pulling hers on as fast as she could, then ran back with the remainder of the pile. He used his jumper to rub some life back into Rhoda, then the other girls helped her into her socks, jeans, T-Shirt and jumper. She had not said a word and it wasn't clear how alert she was. The answer came with a sudden thump as she slid onto her side, unresponsive. Panic broke out again and Lucas was the one calling out instructions.

'Lie her on her back, lift her chin up so she can breathe better.' He then pinched her earlobe and gave her a shake. She came round again, groaning and spluttering.

'Are you with us, Rhoda?'

'Yes ...' she answered in a whisper. 'Just so cold.'

He rubbed her back and limbs again for what seemed an eternity and eventually she was able to sit and talk calmly.

'What happened out there, Rhoda?' Joyce asked.

'I had a cramp, a stupid cramp in my thigh. I couldn't move with the pain of it. I'm so sorrrry guys,' Rhoda stammered through clattering teeth, fear and shock written all over her face.

'Can you stand? Maybe you tore a muscle or something?' Joyce suggested, once they were all dressed, had rubbed each other's backs and kneaded life back into their hands and feet.

'Thank you so much for saving my life,' Rhoda whispered, when they eventually got to their feet again to walk back to base. She was looking pale but stable enough to walk, albeit with a limp.

'How do you know about all this first aid stuff, Lucas?' Kelly asked him as they hurried back as fast as they could.

'I did a course once. Just wanted to kiss a girl who'd signed up to it as well,' he replied with a wink. 'To avoid all problems with our beloved teachers and all - let's just all agree that I was with you all this time, okay? I was your guide, showing you interesting paths. In exchange, I won't tell anyone what you were really up to.' He smiled mischievously and walked off with a swagger, the three girls rushing to keep up with him.

'Okay,' Rhoda replied, her lips blue. 'Sure, okay. If my parents found out that I nearly drowned … and oh my gosh, thanks Lucas, really. How stupid was I?'

Her next steps were shaky but she did manage to hop to the camp in time for dinner, her wet hair concealed under the damp hoodie. The girls had not exchanged many words, but as they stood close to the camp fires and their bodies had started warming up again, Lucas couldn't help but beam inwardly as he noticed that three girls were looking up at him as if he was God himself.

She owes him her life, I'm sure of it. Does that make Lucas a better person? Does that not count as some kind of atonement for what he had really been up to before he strode into the ice cold water for her? Can you combine these two attributes – life saver and ruthless, selfish manipulator? Of course, I think. Just as any cunning person can be helpful and kind to someone, so could Lucas have saved Rhoda's life and found a way to either look good by telling the world about his good deed or to simply use it to ask for a favour. Either way, he came out as a winner.

The phone rings just as I hear some movement coming from the upstairs bedroom. Lucas has been back home for a month now, after his latest escapade has ended in a true disaster.

I pick up the phone.

'Hello?' I say tentatively. These days I'm not sure whether it's any good to answer the phone. 'Oh hello Georgina,' I say. 'Thank you, yes he's stable. The doctors say that he's been lucky – considering. The stroke was severe but he'll probably walk again and his speech is a little better already.'

Georgina carries on commenting.

'Yes, I know. I've been going through a rollercoaster. I blame myself really. How could I have been so blind?' I say, without expecting an answer really. 'You know, his ex-partner told me that he was always laughing at her concern about his high blood pressure. She called him an idiot and you know what? I completely agree with her. I told him to get it checked, too – many times. His own Dad died of a heart attack, for crying out loud. How stupid can you be? Well, at least that makes two,' I say in dismay.

Georgina then attempts to comfort me, one of the very few friends I have left and who has not given up on me.

'No, I'm not beating myself up over this. I'm just so upset that I'm lumbered with him again. His last girlfriend disappeared swiftly into thin air,' I tell her. 'I've created a useless leech! You know that he found this new girlfriend

while all the nasty divorce proceedings were going on? He wasn't even divorced yet and off he went with the next. Unbelievable, but true.'

I gasp and a desperate sob rises in my throat, but Georgina finds the right words to say.

'I know, and thank you for being there for me, Georgina.' I say, after wiping my eyes on my sleeve. 'You know what the worst thing is about this whole story? He's turned into a lamb, a sweet, kind lamb. I've been told that it's quite common for stroke victims to become very emotional and all, but what's the point of that now?'

Georgina adds a few facts she's read about stroke patients and their change of behaviour.

'Yes, they did tell me that, too - so I've been warned. But don't worry, I will do everything to get rid of him now. I know that doesn't sound like me. It's harsh but you see, I'm through with him after all he's done. Don't get me started because the list is long ...you really don't want to hear. If I keep him under my roof it will kill me ...not instantly, but like an unbearably slow suicide. It will, I can't put it any other way. It's one thing to suffer the whims and demands of a toddler, another if they are the needs of an ill grown man.'

My voice rises an octave too high so I take a deep breath before resuming.

'Of course, I missed the boat a long time ago and couldn't row back. As a parent you only have a few chances to get it right.'

I'm pleased that I feel composed and able to speak normally again.

'I've raised a son who was good at making fiction. I admit I believed and fully encouraged it. Now - for the first time in my life as a mother - I hear him speak with empathy

and genuine interest in me. The very first time. He actually asks me how I feel ...isn't that something?'

I pause and, when I rally and raise my voice again, my next sentence comes out laboured and croaky.

'It's just, I'm not at all interested in how he feels anymore.'

ABOUT THE AUTHOR

Helene Andrea Leuschel was born and raised in Belgium to German parents. She gained a Licentiate in Journalism, which led to a career in radio and television in Brussels, London and Edinburgh. Helene moved to the Algarve in 2009 with her husband and two children, working as a freelance TV producer and teaching yoga. She recently acquired a Master of Philosophy with the OU, deepening her passion for the study of the mind. *Manipulated Lives* is Helene's first work of fiction.

Printed in Great Britain
by Amazon